BEYOND THE MOUNTAIN

By the same author

ISLAND SOJOURN

BEYOND
THE
MOUNTAIN

Elizabeth Arthur

HARPER & ROW, PUBLISHERS, New York
Cambridge, Philadelphia, San Francisco, London
1817 *Mexico City, São Paulo, Sydney*

FIRST EDITION
Designer: Sidney Feinberg

Library of Congress Cataloging in Publication Data

Arthur, Elizabeth, 1953–
  Beyond the mountain.

  I. Title.
PS3551.R76B4   1983   813'.54   83–47551
ISBN 0–06–015189–7

83 84 85 86 87 10 9 8 7 6 5 4 3 2 1

For Steven, more than words

Acknowledgments

I am thankful for a grant from the Vermont Council on the Arts which gave me the time to complete the first draft of this novel.

I am deeply grateful to Corona Machemer, an editor whose dedication, compassion and intelligence are rare in any profession and whose work on this book was herculean.

Finally, I am indebted to all those mountaineers, both living and dead, whose deeds I studied and whose books I plundered to learn what I could about climbing. If there are technical errors in this novel, I apologize to them and to their calling.

All the peaks around it are bare. Why is this one covered with snow?

Zen koan

APPROACH

One

At home I have a picture of the mountain. I picked it up in Jasper one year, at the bookstore, in back of the great wooden bear. He stands on his hind legs, seeming in pose to fend off a threat, though his expression is placid, almost happy; the tip of his nose points to Mount Edith Cavell. Nicholas and I were trying to do the Kaine Face on Mount Robson, but it snowed on the mountain for almost two weeks straight and we spent a lot of time in town between attempts, bickering with one another and watching the dogsled races.

I never buy posters of mountains; they all look alike to me somehow, voiceless and flat, as empty of meaning as plates. But this one was different. The photo was old, taken in the days before color, by one of the early wanderers—Newton, perhaps, or Mallory or Shipton—and the shadows of the black-and-white images are as clear and solid as stones. I was bored and restless and the whole valley around us was in fog, so I bought it—dreaming, of course, with one part of my mind, of someday going to climb it, but having no real faith that this would ever come to pass. The Himalayas were too far from anywhere and I was too young then to realize that the only places that are truly far away are those that are under your nose. Those you can never see for what they are. Distance brings perspective.

And besides, Nicholas didn't think we'd ever get there. "We're never going to have the money to go to Nepal," he said. "It's as simple as that." Which was a favorite phrase of his at all times —"It's as simple as that"—and when he would say it, implying that even the simplest things were inaccessible to someone of my limited perspicacity, and, more, that the parameters he operated within were always those of reason, when in fact he was one of the most utterly irrational people I had ever known, it used to stop me dead, because in my universe nothing is ever simple—or at least I try not to make up a set of rubber-stamp phrases that will deal with every situation and erase with their inky rigidity all the subtle chiaroscuro of life itself. So even before the accident occurred, I was getting ready to leave him. And when the letter from Margaret arrived in the autumn, inviting me on the climb, I actually burst into tears. It was like suddenly having a storm stop, to know I was going away.

Nicholas—I don't know what he thought. He thought perhaps I was crying with joy in the mysterious way women do when they get an award they haven't expected and don't feel, truly, they deserve. But I was not. I was crying with sorrow at the enormity of my own relief that I would not have to leave Nicholas myself, would not be called upon to act. I could just let the wave of my life carry me away, I could go to Nepal for a climb and simply never return. That relief made me ashamed and somehow aghast at my cowardice and at the fact I suddenly felt to be true—that I had been using Nicholas for months, ever since my affair with our friend Beckett, clinging to him only because no better raft had yet appeared. When he picked me up and whirled me around his head in congratulation, I cried even harder. "No men allowed?" he said. "Well, it's your funeral. Though I hear the Sherpas will carry women to the top, if you pay them an extra ten rupees." We closed our climbing shop for the day and went to the Wort Hotel to eat deep-dish cherry pie, and Nicholas did his best to conceal from me his jealousy of my chance to climb the mountain. He tried. He really tried. But when I left at last for India he wasn't there to say goodbye.

▲

My plane landed in Bombay at 10 P.M. local time and the temperature then was ninety-four degrees, according to the rather malicious disembodied voice of the captain. The Air India flight was absolutely jammed; they have a rule, apparently, that Indian citizens have to give preference to their national airlines, so even the 747's are always full. I was sitting toward the back of the plane, my boots mashed under the seat in front of me, along with my rucksack and—I suddenly realized—an *empty* water bottle. My seatmate, an enormous Indian woman who had sat in silence for fifteen hours and steadfastly refused any of the six meals which flashed by us like sunrises in a time machine, sat stoically while I clambered over her, water bottle in hand. The steward was very polite when he told me that they did not carry cold water on the plane. "We have hot water, madame," he said, "which we can put frozen ice in to help it remain cooler."

"That'll be fine," I said, and took the hot water back to my seat. I was ready for a fight by that time and would have started one except that even more than fighting I wanted to stretch my legs and breathe some uncanned air. When I got my boots on at last —my feet seemed to have swollen after fifteen hours in the stratosphere—the plane had almost emptied and the patch of a smile which the steward, now stationed at the back door, strove to hold on his mouth was wearing pretty thin.

The air outside the plane—God! It was so wet I could hardly breathe it and it smelled something like a mixture of cooked lamb, raw sewage, incense and rotting corpses. That's just an approximation, of course. I had never smelled anything like it before, and the one thing I was certain of by the time I got to the ground was that I never wanted to smell it again. The passengers ahead of me were climbing onto a bus which stood uncertainly near the plane like a horse ready to dash away at the slightest excuse. I followed them. My clothes were already pinned to me and my face was covered with moisture. I would have followed anyone, done anything that was suggested to me. My arms hung at my sides like optional accessories, detachable, unlikely to be needed. With the first smell of the Indian night, my will had been removed from me.

You'll say it was just the heat. Well, it wasn't just the heat. I mean, I've always hated heat and loved the cold; but it wasn't just the heat. It was the East.

When I was in junior high school in Wyoming and we read about the British Empire, they talked a lot about the bad effect of the Indian climate on the Victorian ladies who went to live in it. The ladies seemed to sicken and die with startling rapidity, and cynic that I was, to the extent that I believed this information at all—and even then I somehow felt that most history is just a construct of lies and fabrications and that historians have got to be the most self-deluded people on earth—I thought it was a reflection on the Victorian ladies themselves and their bizarre fondness for tight corsets.

Inside the transit lounge the smell persisted. They had large wooden fans turning slowly overhead, stirring up the moisture as laboriously as butter churns, and everyone, but everyone, sat on the black wooden chairs in absolute resignation. There were rows and rows of empty pop bottles standing on a counter in resignation, Indian women in saris looking at their feet in resignation. The only things that weren't resigned were the rats, which scurried along the corners of the tubular metal ceiling trusses, above a bright-yellow sign which read "No Exit." I looked around, vaguely, for Naomi. Margaret had written that I might meet her here.

I'd seen pictures of Naomi, of course, though we had never climbed together. I wasn't sure I'd know her in the flesh. But she came around the corner from the bathroom suddenly, her hair, almost blue-black, curly around her face; there was very little doubt that it was she. She had, if you can believe it, white frangipani flowers tucked behind her ears. She was calling over her shoulder to someone out of sight behind her and carrying a jhola flung over her arm. Her fingers, lean and clever, still looked capable of action—hell, of more than action. She looked ready and able to climb the enormous drainpipes which ran down from the roof to the floor, just where you were most likely to trip over them.

Had I met her under any other circumstances, I might have disapproved of her from the start. I mean, anyone who climbs in bright-purple gaiters and has a matching purple rucksack . . . and in the first five minutes we were together she managed to let me know that she had led Cenotaph Corner in Wales at the age of nineteen, not that *that* was any surprise to me. One fall when Nicholas and I were living in Jackson Hole, not long after my brother Orion had lent us the money to open our climbing shop, everyone who came through the store was talking about this black-haired woman who was leading every major free climb in Yosemite. Plus the way she concocts the most ridiculously far-fetched schemes—hang gliding off El Capitan, rafting up the Ganges—and then actually manages to pull them off; but that night she was a gift from God. She certainly isn't stupid, after all. Her intelligence is just the nonlateral kind. She doesn't see things straight on; she looks at them out of the corner of her eye and gets a different view from everyone else. In some respects she reminds me of Nicholas. The way she figured out the ladder extensions in the lower icefall: it really blew me away. Of course, I didn't let it show. I find it hard to praise, more than twice a year or so, people who are better than I am. Besides, at that point I could hardly stand the sight of her.

So anyway, there she was. She came around the corner suddenly, wearing this bright-orange skirt which somehow swirled around her knees, an old lace blouse cut to the navel, and small gray klettershoes with short gray socks. None of it was sticking to her. None of it. My face felt as pale as a Kleenex and the other white faces in the room were pasted to the backs of the chairs like the wings of dying moths. But her face was dark with the Indian sun and she skirted the two ragged untouchable women who sat by the door of the bathroom with little twig brooms, ready to scurry ahead of you when you went in and whisk out the toilet so abjectly and furiously you'd rather burst than pee in it—she skirted them with the absolute nonrecognition of a princess. Or so I thought. Actually, she probably felt just as bad as I did; she just wasn't letting it show. And at that moment, sitting in a miasma of heat and resignation, I admired what I thought was her coolness. But I ignored her until she came up and spoke to me. That was the beginning of our acquaintance.

It's funny, now that I think about it, but beginnings often hurt more than endings. Endings you anticipate; no matter how bad they may be in reality, your imagination has always made them worse. Much longer, much more painful, much bigger altogether. Because when the endings are over—endings of loves, endings of lives, of hopes, of climbs, of summers—there you are still, if you're there at all, relatively unchanged. But beginnings are different. In our culture, at least, they're always supposed to be good, so you don't think of preparing for them. They're supposed to be something that you jump into, like puddles: Go on, get your feet wet! But when you get right down to it, they're more like something you fall into. Crevasses. You're halfway down them before you know it; all you can do is hope your belay will hold. Of course, you don't scream. You don't want to make a fool of yourself, after all. You've been in crevasses before.

So I'd thought, if I thought at all, that what I had to do was get myself on the plane to India and things would be easy from there on out. I'd spent months doing the equipment, packaging the food, working in the back of the shop as if it were no longer in Jackson at all, and nowhere near the Tetons. I'd done it by myself, as a kind of expiation, as a way to forget. I could do it by fierce concentration, but it was totally abstract. An imaginary expedition to an imaginary mountain might or might not take place someday in the mythical kingdom of Nepal. Margaret offered to find someone else to do the equipment after she heard about the accident. She should have known better than that. She's a doctor, after all. It was all I had to cling to, all that was holding me back from the edge of that deep crevasse. That and my dharma study group. I thought I'd be a budding Buddhist. But now I was in Bombay and I was falling, and suddenly there was Naomi, apparently unaffected by a country where the jewelry the women wear looks like something you'd rig a corpse out in and where, as I sat looking at a little girl's crossed brown legs, I could see, latent in the flesh, the legs from birth to death: plump and smooth with babyhood, sensual with womanhood, emaciated with age, all revealed in the skin like a series of time exposures, a bizarre, nightmarish vision of a kind I'd never had before that night.

Of course, I grabbed the hand Naomi held out. I greeted her as a long-lost friend, hoping that she in turn would thus greet me. And though one of the first things she said to me was "You know, this is going to be the first expedition I've ever been on where I won't sleep with one of the other climbers," and then proceeded to tell me that her record for lovemaking was eighteen thousand feet, on Pumori, I didn't care at all, not then anyway. She was a woman and she was a climber and maybe she'd be my new partner. What I didn't realize, not for weeks, was that she has room in her life for only one real relationship, and that's her relationship to her medium. Black rock or white snow, it's all the same to her; she applies herself to it the way a painter applies his brush to canvas. The only embrace she truly would miss is the kiss of the rock on her fingers.

Nothing is ever what you expect, though. When I got to India . . . I guess in a way I thought I wanted to stop *desiring*. Enough of that, that longing. Look where it gets you in the end. The longing for something beyond oneself, the craving to possess—a man, a summit, the world, the truth. I'd always wanted it all. And after the accident I wanted something else—oblivion, I guess, temporary but complete. A black night, no stars at all, or else maybe only one, enough to see the unmarked snow, running straight to the edge of a cliff. When I sat in meditation, I tried to see that star.

But nothing is ever what you expect. India, so full of resignation—not desire but acceptance, and more, dullness, hopelessness, ennui—the shock was so great, the transformation in me so instantaneous and complete, it suddenly occurred to me that I didn't want to be passive at all. And the irony, of course, is that going on an expedition to climb one of the highest mountains in the world is a hell of a way to try and escape from desire. I guess, in fact, I wasn't trying to escape from it. Just to make it simple, manageable once again; no falling in love again, no convolutions of human relations, but the simplicity of a mountain, gold and silver in the first light of morning, a promise of completion carved hard against the sky.

Two

In a way, I think, I hated Nicholas from the first. Or "hated" is not the right word for it; I resented his expertise and his arrogance and the way he pulled his hat brim down over his forehead so that only his eyes were in shadow. Why is it that when somebody makes you feel inadequate—just by being, really, just by being—you feel it's a personal challenge? But I didn't have the slightest idea how to meet it, didn't even recognize that that was what it was, so I just went out of my way to ignore him and wrote vituperation in my journal in the evenings when I was so exhausted from climbing all day that I could hardly hold the pen. But I was driven. We both were.

The other climbers called him Cowboy Nick. Because of his hat and because he was a native of Wyoming and because he had climbed the Grand Teton in cowboy boots once—and because they were friendly. I didn't call him anything. Sometimes I hissed things at him when I couldn't avoid it, when he told me to trust my boots more, or demanded that I explain the theory behind a complicated anchor setup. The thing is, I was a good climber already. My brother Orion and I had been climbing together for years and we were at the Jackson school mostly to ease my mother's mind about it. She had the faith of her generation in formal education and certificates, and though Orion had already finished his junior year at the Colorado School of Mining and I was planning to start college at Laramie in the fall, all that wasn't quite enough for her. Since she never had the time—or so she said —to see us climb herself, she wanted some assurance that we were capable of doing it. Which was ridiculous because Ryan had already written up several of our climbs for the magazine *Off Belay* and we were getting almost famous. Still, we wanted to meet some other climbers and the school seemed a good way to do it. But I thought Nicholas thought I was despicable and I didn't understand why. Maybe because I'd never climbed the Grand in cowboy boots. I was a native of Wyoming too, though, and I wasn't about to take any shit from him.

I varied between demonstrating my loathing outright and being elaborately polite.

"Pardon me," I would say. "Pardon me, but would you mind terribly if I went ahead with my rappel now?" This at the top of a two-hundred-foot free descent, the first one I had ever done over quite so much blank air. I had been very hot on the ascent and had led the last and hardest stretch of rock and my second had fallen in the last ten feet and he was good. I was young enough and stupid enough to be pleased by that. Birds were wheeling below me, abruptly stopping and changing direction, riding the updrafts like butterflies, hanging poised, motionless as leaves. I stacked the rope twice to make sure it wouldn't tangle, then clipped it through the anchor and tossed it over the cliff. I watched it falling, whistling, looping downward, and suddenly I was so scared I could hardly breathe. I felt that *I* was falling downward, giddy with terror and chilled to the bone. My hands were stiff as I set up the brake bar which would slow my descent on the rope, and I managed to cut my left one on a sharp edge of metal. Then Nicholas came along, very officious, and asked me if I was quite sure I had set up the brake bar correctly, because a good friend of his had been killed when he hadn't managed to do that.

"He bought the farm," he said. "Make sure you never do the same."

"I don't even intend to make an offer," I said. "Pardon me," I said, and went over the edge.

Fear is a funny thing anyway. It helps you do things you'd never do otherwise. You ride it like a horse, leaning with it, squeezing it with your knees, reining it in or kicking it on. You just have to make sure it doesn't squeeze you back, or roll over you. And with Nicholas—long after I met him, it seems to me now, but still very long ago—I started finally to let him know when I was scared, to share it with him as a gift of love; and then my fear stopped serving me. Maybe that's what love always does for you in the end —keeps you from reaching for your limits. Or maybe it's not so simple. We always had each other close by in the hills, and two people who love each other can manufacture together almost any logical excuse for action or its converse—it's really a kind of madness sometimes, a folie à deux; whether or not you share your doubts, they rule you. But then, being with Nicholas gave me a different kind of strength.

Jesus, he was impossible then. He had a watch, a cheap Timex watch, maybe not even a Timex, worse than that, a dime-store model with plastic straps and probably plastic insides. The face was cracked and the pins that held the strap to the watch kept popping out and almost getting lost. But that was our timepiece at the school, that watch, because it was on his wrist. His arms were very brown; he tanned so easily, you could practically see him getting darker in the sun. He set the times for the classes with that watch, times for the climbs, times for departures. And it gained at least ten minutes a day, maybe more. In his view, everyone was always late.

That was my first introduction to his inner clock. Actually, it was very simple, as simple as the dime-store model that reflected it. Nothing ever happened soon enough for Nicholas. He wanted so much; he wanted everything. And because he wanted everything, and wanted it now, he lived in the future, which made the present hard. He was always halfway to South America, halfway to the moon. He grudged the present moment for surrounding him with importunate demands. Sometimes I thought that was childish, babyish. But babies do not grudge the moment. They make demands, then rest. They know what it is to have desire fulfilled. But Nicholas never did.

I was eighteen when I met him, and he was twenty-five. Sometimes when one of the students asked a silly question he would say, "What do *you* think?" and sometimes he would say, "Do what you like." And he was supposed to be the head instructor, he *was* the head instructor; his skill was in his feet.

But I hated idiots too and when someone asked what the lightening holes in the biggest pitons were for, and he frowned, thought deeply, and said, "I suppose they're to reduce the risk of the chrome alloy attracting lightning in a storm. They couldn't be just to make the thing lighter to carry, I don't suppose," I suddenly liked him so much that it astonished me and I purposely started to talk with my brother, muttering rudely and plucking pieces of grass to chew. He had such self-confidence then. He seemed to think he could fly.

Ryan liked him from the first. Although he was four years younger than Nicholas, even then he seemed almost older—just wiser and generally *growing*, which Nicholas often was not—and besides, he liked strays and eccentrics, and he rarely made up any rules. Then too, they were both of them men and in that particular club everyone knows what it is to be taught you should be invulnerable, so they have some sympathy for literal interpretations of John Wayne–style independence. Or anyway Orion did. He laughed at me for letting Nicholas get to me. And he had never laughed at me before. He'd read to me and tested me and taught me what he knew. In the days before Nicholas, things were simple. My brother was all my world.

▲

I was born on the desert in Wyoming. Literally born there, that is to say, with my brother and my father standing by, and though of course I don't remember it, I've seen the place where it happened. The time was early autumn and my parents had been hunting. It was a beautiful morning; mist was rising up out of the Lander valley, the alfalfa fields were still bright green and a dusting of snow lay across them. Behind the valley the mountains thrust up, red earth, white crowns, earth rivers running to the sea. My parents were on horseback, with Ryan riding in front of my father and the rifles slung across the saddlebags behind. Though my mother was very pregnant and my father had tried halfheart-edly to persuade her to remain behind, she was more stubborn than he was, and it was Orion's first hunt.

All three of them told me the story, but I like Orion's version the best. Maybe I just liked Orion the best, or maybe I heard his more times; my mother early got tired of transmuting her life into myth and my father—though he loved to set me puzzles to solve—never quite trusted me, I think, with secret forms of knowledge. He worked as an engineer for one of the oil companies near Lander, and liked to solve things or to name them. He always had great faith in words. But though my mother was a teacher, it wasn't words which moved her, and more than anything else in life she loved to go on hunts. One of my earliest memories, in fact, is of watching her, her fingers stiff with cold and blood, quartering an antelope and cutting out its heart.

I was born on Orion's half birthday, so it's really his story, not mine. My mother, for all her apparent pragmatism, loved the formality of celebrations and had as many in our lives as she could possibly arrange. So we celebrated saints' days, although we were-n't Catholics, and we celebrated the equinox, and days on which ancestors had died. She liked to dress up on all these days, so when they rose that morning in the early dawn to follow after a deer, she wore a long green dress over loose wool pants and on her red hair a blue cap. She looked, Ryan said, quite lovely. And she promised she wouldn't shoot.

But when the deer jumped she broke her promise. A little dried-up riverbed concealed a five-point buck and she aimed and fired in one smooth thrust, then slid at once to the ground. The deer just looked at her, surprised, as if she had hurt his feelings, not his flesh, and then he fell, all in a rush, his head twisted back toward the sky. My mother fell too; they fell together, he forward and she back against a snow-slick rock, and she went into labor when she landed. My mother swore a lot, said Ryan, but when I was born she laughed and threw a snowball at my father, and she insisted he gut out the deer before he went off to get help. Then, "Orion," she called out, "here's Artemis. She's a birthday present for you."

Orion. That's a wonderful name, don't you think? Of course, everyone knows about the constellation, the hunter and his belt of Rigel and Betelgeuse, the supergiant stars, the gaseous nebulae. But not so many people know that in the Greek myth Orion was a hunter and a giant, who pursued the Pleiades and was finally killed and became part of the sky. The Pleiades were the seven daughters of Atlas, the demigod condemned to hold the heavens on his shoulders. When I was a child they seemed to me like snowflakes, or a little girl with a mantle around her back. Ryan and I would sneak out of the house at night—climbing from the window of my room to the clump of sage below it—then sit wrapped in an Indian blanket, just staring at the stars.

My brother and I read a lot of myths when we were children. I think from the start we sought in myth an explication of our nature; he was Orion, yes, but what after all did that mean? A brilliant set of stars, gas and energy, striding across a sky that another man held aloft. A motionless, faceless figure, a loose arrangement of points which was given shape only by other people's wild imaginings. And out of it all—well, Orion was the closest thing to a woman I've ever seen in a man.

Not that I've known any women who are like him. But he was like women as you think they *should* be, when you're reading a good book or feeling a bit of hope about the future of civilization —women in velvet, in the fantasy mode. I mean, the female principle has been, historically, basically anarchic, honoring order without pressure, rule by custom rather than law, while the male principle is to enforce order. One person gives commands and the others do as they are told—first in command, second in command, third in command—and even if the ship is running up onto the rocks because the first in command has gone out of his mind, woe betide the second who gets out of line. Well, Orion was never like that. He got beyond the lust for power to simply letting things be. The earth itself was god enough for him and it was he and no one else who allowed me to become the climber that I am. Or the climber, I guess, that I was.

He was relatively short, Ryan was, five feet eight inches tall in his stocking feet, but he stood quite proudly; he never seemed embarrassed about his size, not even when he was a teenager. People always said we looked a lot alike, though I could never see the resemblance myself; I'm small and wiry too, but dark, not blond, as he was. And Ryan's head was quite large for his body, the head of a taller man; Nicholas told me once, when he was mad at Ryan, that my brother carried his head as if he had found it somewhere, then placed it on his shoulders as a test. But Nicholas was jealous of Ryan from the first—or not of Ryan but of my love for him, and really only *at* the first, since once we started climbing together that jealousy was replaced by need and by a tolerance he never showed toward me. But at the beginning, before we three made our first climb, his jealousy overlay everything like a shroud; and it was foolish—more than foolish, mad—because although I loved Orion, loved him as I loved the desert sky, he could never be a man to me, except as shadows can be men at times, the part of you you never lose and never make more real.

The house we lived in had a tower, a tower my father built on. It was supposed, I think, to be his study, but my mother used the ground floor for her trophies, and Ryan and I made the upper story ours. On special nights we asked to sleep there, where we could make a bedroll on the floor, and one special night we learned to climb there. That night the moon was a huntress riding across the sky and we couldn't sleep for watching her. So we got out Father's fire rope, tied it to the mullion of the window and slid to the ground with it wrapped around our backs. Once down, of course, we had no way back up, and were afraid that if we knocked on the door my mother wouldn't let us sleep in the tower again. His voice a careful whisper, Ryan asked if I thought I could climb, and since his presence always made me feel safe, I said that I knew I could. And climbing, I found, was no harder than breathing; there was air below me, but above me was the sky.

By the time I was eight and he was eleven we were climbing everything we could find. We'd climb the chimney on the house and then rappel back down it; we had routes on the tower we could have climbed blindfolded, and a place on the desert where the shadows fell like velvet and where we lost ourselves in red and burnished stone. Then, we did everything together; except when we were at school, we hardly left each other's sight for years, and after my father was killed on an oil rig Ryan seemed all that I had, and enough.

He made me feel so safe? Well, kind of. But he loved to scare me also, not in the physical world but in the world of the imagination—finding, for example, the most frightening of all the fairy tales and then relating it to me with deep relish. In fairy tales, of course, everything is always about to go wrong; everything hangs from a single chance, all happiness from one thread. Remember Bluebeard's wife, the last one in that hopeful, brainless parade? She was allowed to open all the multitudinous doors of the castle —all of them except one. Or the king who held a great christening feast for his daughter and invited everyone he could think of to partake of it, including each of the fairies—and then forgot to ask just one, the nastiest one of all. Or how there was still time to get away before midnight, but then, bang, the clock struck twelve, the coach turned into a pumpkin and no one was going anywhere anymore. When frightful things could happen, they always did. Everything hung from a thread. And it broke. That used to scare the hell out of me. But Orion reassured me. And I imagine that I looked forward to being afraid because then— afterward—I would feel so warm, cozy, tucked in, safe in the circle of his arms. He made the shadows come. And then he made them go away.

With Orion, I explored the world. We read books together and ate watercress and stonecrop; we picked wild plums and poked at wasp nests with a stick. We hiked through the desert, disturbing flocks of sheep, and we watched the ducks fly north and south in long and cranking lines. And when we could, we camped on the ground, and dreamed of our first real climb.

By then we had a rope. An old-fashioned manila rope, it was heavy and scratchy and frayed at both ends, hardly more than a clothesline. We had pots too, and long johns and a tent—but very little else except ambition. I don't know where Orion got *that,* maybe from tales of Olympus, but the rope was a gift from my father, just a week before he died. And after he died my mother never recovered. Although she did not exactly wear black, she stopped dressing in interesting clothes, and more and more she let Ryan decide things, and was glad when he learned how to cook. We were pretty young to be off by ourselves, but one weekend we went to the hills.

It was early dawn when we woke up. The ground was covered with a white like powdered sugar and the first leaves of autumn had frost on their undersides that brought out all their veins in stark relief. I'd been so excited the night before and probably so cold that I hardly got an hour's unbroken sleep; at sunset, the mountain had lit up with alpenglow and we had put our bedrolls with the heads facing the door, so we could watch the redness till the last ray faded and the dark awning of clouds had come up to cover the stars. Orion told me stories while we lay there, and in the morning tickled me awake.

So eager were we to get on the climb, we didn't bother with breakfast. At first the path we were following, which was little more than a game trail, rose slowly, running underneath the south face of the mountain. There were flowers everywhere, peeking up through the tiny layer of snow—harebells and dwarf forget-me-nots, and higher up moss campion and sky pilot and everywhere violet asters. As the ground got steeper, I kept close to Ryan's heels, where the scent of snowy, crushed bushes was almost over-powering. Just as the sun came up over the mountain we reached the lower snowfield.

We knew nothing about route finding and very little about snowfields. Orion just picked out what seemed like the easiest way to get to the summit and I—tied into our rope a hundred feet behind him—just followed in his footsteps. The snow got softer and softer and in its viselike grip one of my boots, too big, kept coming off and sitting, empty, in its nest, and I would call "Ryan" while I kept on walking bootless in the wake of the moving rope, until he heard me and stopped and came back and put on my boot, saying, "Temis, try and keep it on; we'll never get up at this rate," very patiently and kindly, and then making me wait to move until the rope was stretched between us once again. By midafternoon, when we still hadn't reached the top and when every deceptive crest revealed another one beyond it, I was in a daze of hunger, thirst and sun, and sometimes was almost in tears, but by then Orion had tied my boot on with a length of twine and he kept saying from in front, "A little farther, Temis," or "Artemis, come on."

We made the summit about four in the afternoon. My heart was beating very fast and my wrists were chapped from sweating into my mittens. When I showed them to Orion, he rubbed them with some snow, then set me down on a lump of rock and said:

"Is it worth it? Are you glad?"

A sheep was bleating somewhere. Below us, an eagle wheeled and circled, and on the ridge opposite ours the snowfield, high in its hanging cornice, assumed, as I watched it, strange forms—an elephant, a duck, the head of a hungry lion. I felt as if I had no clothes on, or as if I were an animal myself. I nodded. It was worth it. The world was shining below. And off in the distance, in a spot where I hadn't once looked before, there was a clearing on a far, far ridge, and where the trees parted like fingers to reveal the sky behind them, a mountain grew, ethereal, transitory, vulnerable to the touch of a finger. I started to cry when I saw it. I felt as if someone had hit me in the chest right above the heart, knocking the wind from my lungs and most of myself from my body; as if I had been lifted out of myself and was floating freely, somewhere in the air above my head, untethered, waiting to be pulled back down. There was a luminosity about the world, a transparent, diaphanous clarity, white snow and great space and forms below that space that lay across its slopes like slabs of time, complete; one of those forms, as long as I lived, one of those forms was me. I was me, and the world was wide, with space not just below my feet but more, beyond the farthest reaches of my eyes, its luminosity something I was to see again and again, each time I climbed—when, after deep effort, there is a relaxation of the body and the spirit so complete that even the face relaxes, the eyes widen and the fingers dangle, used like all the notes of an instrument in a clarion explosion after which great silence seems to hide great laughter, just like the act of love.

"We'll get there," said Ryan, not moving. "Don't worry, Temis, it's ours." But what he knew and I knew, even then, was that we already *were* there, that there *is* no there more here than that overwhelming physical effort which throws you into space itself. And like a duck emerging from its egg, which fixes its heart on the first set of moving feet it sees, I bonded then that love of life itself to the sight of Ryan's boots ahead of me in the snow, and always after that my love for him and for the mountains were just two halves of one great love, the palm and knuckles of all I longed to hold. The one love was, I already sensed, forbidden; the other, so great was the sorrow it brought me, for all I know may be forbidden too.

We got back to camp in the darkness. "Hey, Phillips. Good climb, hey?" was all my brother said.

So from that day on we called ourselves Phillips and Phillips, and thought of ourselves as that as well. Not that we didn't like our first names, odd as they were; we loved them. But it was like being in disguise to be Phillips and Phillips—no one would know us for who we were. When we started to do first ascents together, we were listed as Phillips and Phillips in all the guidebooks and it seemed to us as intimate as if they were our nicknames. But when Nicholas joined us, or we joined him, we were Phillips, Phillips and Rhodes. And had it not been for my brother, I never could have stayed with Nicholas. Ryan certainly saw from the first what I did not, that I only hated Nicholas as long as I couldn't have him; and when I could, I felt as if I was standing in the center of a clearing in the middle of a deep pine forest, with sunlight streaming onto the needles and drenching me in warmth. Half the time we were together we were struggling for power, but the other half, that warmth held me like a cushion or a rug: I was mainlining Nicholas, plugged in to him, and we drained each other and filled each other with desire. Desire was what we lived on anyway. Desire was why we climbed. In the end, it was why I went to Nepal, where I thought I could leave it behind.

Three

Naomi and I waited three hours in Bombay for our flight to Delhi to be announced. Although this was two hours longer than we should have waited, the guards were totally unresponsive to our pleas for information and spoke English only disdainfully, "as if," Naomi told me, "it was something nasty they'd tasted." So catatonic and lethargic did I feel that I simply put myself in Naomi's hands for all this time, following where she led. She explored the tiny bookstore at the end of the room, discovering with great delight several books on Tantric sex, and she bought a bottle of Kama Sutra oil, specially packaged for tourists. When I discovered that I had left my water bottle on the plane, hot liquid, frozen ice cubes and all, she urged me to stay calm—as if I could have been anything else—and tried out her iodine pellets. From time to time she went over to speak to the guards, who wore Sam Browne belts and faded purple-blue cotton uniforms with three gold braids on their sleeves. They seemed straight out of the nineteenth century, as did the entire scene. All this inspired in Naomi an urge to discuss the British Empire; in me, it inspired nothing but dread. Dread that we would never leave Bombay. Dread that we were stuck with death for life.

Finally, we joined the sticky line to pass through security clearance into the main waiting lounge. The guards stood behind a wooden table and allowed us to place our carry-on luggage in front of them like offerings. With a flick of his palm, my guard indicated that I was now permitted to open my rucksack, and he poked through it condescendingly before, with another flick, he allowed me to close it. In a small curtained alcove, a woman in a sari frisked me slowly and carefully, her hands patting my body uninterestedly, but with the attention to detail that a prostitute might give a customer, and then—after asking me for a cigarette —she too flicked her hand, disgustedly, and let me go.

But the overriding lethargy of the scene was suddenly transformed into high excitement when I laid my passport on the desk. One guard, who had a little more gold braid than the rest of them, told me courteously that he would have to detain me for a moment. I wasn't surprised—by that time I had no real hope of ever leaving Bombay and nothing could have surprised me, nothing— so I sat carefully on the edge of a chair while two guards, who were whisked in from the wings for the big occasion, started to question me. My catatonia started to change to fury, and I'm sure I would have spent the night in an Indian jail if not for Naomi, who was just behind me, and came up to join me then. Though the guards tried to wave her away when she approached, she smiled brightly as if she knew that *could* not be what they meant, and proceeded to demonstrate some of the Hindustani she had acquired a bit of on the way to the Taj Mahal. Clearly, she was asking what was going on, and why her good friend, her dear friend from America, the woman in charge of outfitting and supplying a large expedition, as well as a famous and respected climber, was being so rudely detained in the middle of the night. After a minute or two of studying my passport again and asking me questions about my birthplace for the sake of saving face, they let me go, smiling and nodding at Naomi. Anyone who wonders at the surprising successes she corners in mountains should take a look at her technique with men. So she got me out of Bombay.

Delhi wasn't much better, though. It was cooler, less humid at least, which was nice, and the fans in the transit lounge seemed to be working more effectively. But I wanted to check into the

progress of the expedition gear, which was scheduled to be trans-
ferred to a Royal Nepal Airlines freight plane, and at three o'clock
in the morning there were no officials in the Delhi transit lounge
except for a morose-looking baggage handler who kept sticking
out his hand, furtively, every time I looked at him. Even after I
put a dollar bill in it, he wouldn't let me through to the main
terminal, where there might have been someone I could talk with.
But Naomi, with an act that I thought bordered on genius, went
up to him with her hand between her breasts, and after sugges-
tively plucking at the lace of her bodice, got us both neatly
through the gate. We couldn't find the gear, but just as our
baggage handler was starting to get tough, an announcer trum-
peted out the information that our flight to Nepal was boarding.
The first light of dawn was in the sky, the horizon red with haze
and sunshine. At last, after a detour through the first circle of hell,
we were on our way to the mountain.

Margaret and Laurie were waiting for us at the airport in
Katmandu, and by a miracle, our gear was waiting with them. It
was piled in huge, generous heaps along the walls, on the counter
tops, everywhere I looked, and a smiling crew of Nepalese officials
stood by it. More than civil, they were friendly, joyous, welcom-
ing. A cool breeze blew across the landing strip and only one small
plane stood in the center of it, insouciant and bold. There was an
air of delighted conspiracy in the airport terminal, as if it were the
vestibule to an enchanted place, a place which luckily very few
people had been able to find. The mood that morning was very
much the same mood I found again when we got to Manang,
where the high-hill Buddhists, in contrast to the lower-living
Hindus, were gay and bawdy and raucous, singing out the saluta-
tion "Namaste" long before they got close to you on the trail,
prolonging the word with the unfettered delight of a child licking
an all-day sucker.

Basically, I'd been awake for forty-one hours when we got
there. I had all the shipping invoices carefully lined up in my
clipboard and the contents of each box written out in triplicate,

but I was feeling more like having someone scoop me up with a spoon and tuck me into a feather bed than like negotiating my way through customs. I looked around for Naomi, but she had disappeared to greet an old Sherpa friend of hers, and was plastered to him in an embrace which could not have been easily broken. And Margaret, a Scottish doctor who was famous for always getting *someone* to the summit of every climb she'd led, stood at attention in the middle of the floor, her shoulders straight, her face very brown and wrinkled, her hair cropped short to her head, then strode forward with her hand outstretched, so there was nothing to do but take it.

"Miss Phillips," she said, taking my hand firmly in her own— I could even feel the calluses on her palm, one below each finger. "Margaret McKelvey. So glad you could make it"—as if I had arrived for tea on notice that was, perhaps, just a little bit short for polite society.

I was in awe of her reputation already and this was almost too much. But, "How do you do?" I said, all my childhood training coming back to me, visions of tweed coats with little fur collars and matching round fur caps (the proper outfit for going to town in Lander, Wyoming, in the fifties, according, at least, to my mother, who usually wore jeans) coming to my aid like a special lip stiffener. "I've been looking forward to it." Not too gushy, not too brusque.

We showered Nepal with papers. Then she drove us to her house outside Katmandu, where, though I went to bed, I could rest only in fits and starts, so blown away was I by Nepal: the mountains and the people within them.

▲

Perhaps it was lack of sleep that made the next few days so strange. The team arrived slowly. Robin Harrington, a computer programmer from Denver, arrived feeling pretty outclassed and talking about all the times she'd soloed the Flatirons, but she soon proved an accomplished ectomorph with more energy than any three people should have. Tall and thin, with thick blond hair that she wore in a single braid at the neck, she would shimmer around our temporary house playing the flute and talking about her children with a kind of clinical pride. Dervla was delivered to Nepal by her coal-black husband, Nati, an anthropologist whom she had met while she was on field study in East Africa, and she quickly made it clear that her real interest was not in climbing at all, but in the character of the Nepalese people. We got a telegram from Tina saying that she would be late, and that, or something else, seemed to sour Naomi's temper rather markedly; although she didn't mind working, she didn't like doing more than her share, and she let everyone know it. Laurie was at least nominally my friend, since we had climbed together in the Canadian Rockies, but in Nepal she seemed more homely and reserved than ever and her eyes—which appear to be *made* for looking at things from great heights and through dark-tinted goggles—were always looking through me and out the other side. And Margaret was upset because not only Tina, but Sibyl and Taffy, were also going to be late. Everyone, in fact, was suffering from some kind of vertigo, and I was no exception. Except for Naomi, all the other climbers seemed either married or professionals, and I felt both jealous and awkward, and startlingly insecure.

At first, I spent a lot of time at the windows. In the distance I could just catch sight of terraces of dried dun earth and golden wheat, with piles of bright-orange brick around them. One morning in the street below my room a tiny barefoot old woman carried a battered tin teapot, its surface as dim as light through thick plastic; bent forward as if she carried great weight, she nestled it in her arms as they linked behind her back. A younger woman, scrawny and tall, carried a baby on her back in just the same way, her hands linked under its buttocks. Finally, the third in the procession, a crippled dog, dragged himself along the street. His two back legs were shriveled, useless, but his two front legs still strong, and though his stomach was covered with mud and dung, his expression was quite determined, even hopeful, as if he knew where he was going. As if he had a destination in mind. And I was in this totally spaced-out state of amazement, to find that there really were places in the world where people didn't have infinite desire and didn't go the way of India either, embracing death like a lover. I tried meditating, but I felt like a fool with so many hard-assed climbers looking on.

So I finally started to move. The whole time we were working, before the last three climbers arrived, every chance I got I went off to the bazaar or walked in the hills outside the city, with the sense that there was something there I had to find—a doorstop, a temple, a clue—a sense that now I had arrived in this delirious place I couldn't just sit by and let its sensations bombard me; I had an active responsibility to try and sort things out, to try and find my own path to the mountain that was contained, surrounded by this land. And this was hard, because I couldn't remember now why I had come.

Getting there, being there, it was not that I had no past. The past was with me as I walked, sweat dripping from the tip of my nose, my black cotton umbrella hiding me from the sun and the rain. But the past, though it was with me, continually broke up beneath the rays of the sun, a diamond fragmented by a laser, and the chips fell about me like hailstones off my umbrella, cascading to the ground. I tried to gather them in again—to remember Jackson Hole and Nicholas and Ryan, consummations that I understood—but I could not. All I could do was look and smell and touch, as if I'd had a stroke and was trying to regain the neuron paths of my own brain.

All I remember of those days is images—impressions, disjointed and intense, in color as vivid as a Disney movie and with something of the same sense of unreality, the sense that what I saw was only cardboard thick and that just out of sight in the streets beyond were cameramen wheeling their machines along on trolleys, scriptmen carefully studying pages clipped together at the corners, crews of workmen spreading mounds of dung and refuse, carrying bundles of vegetables in carts, aging the awnings over the bicycle rickshas. One woman sat behind two wilted bundles of lettuce spread thoughtfully on a plastic cloth; she stared down at them, puzzled, as if trying to read in them the secrets of life itself. In the darkness of a storefront, a minuscule, low-roofed cubbyhole in the wall, a dwarfish woman sat calmly, one bare leg thrust right into an enormous pile of crabbed potatoes. A tiny child held an even tinier one in her arms, carefully rooting around in its small pink ear with her finger.

And I walked through this stunned. Not unhappy; not passive; but as bright and hopeful and active as anyone can be who has been hit in the head with a baseball bat and gotten to her feet minutes later, the unwitting victim of a serious concussion. I had thought that I was coming here to climb a mountain. I hadn't thought that I would first have to make my way through an obstacle course, a maze of stimulation as unsought as mescaline in my punch, as complicated as the bazaar which was its objective correlative.

It was humanity itself that bewildered me. I thought I had, through eight long years with Nicholas, learned to know what ruled it. But here, in the Katmandu valley, although I saw just people—two eyes, two arms, usually two legs—I couldn't see their lusts, couldn't understand their motivations, couldn't imagine the direction of their desires. Yet they seemed to live such public lives —no hiding behind picket fences, no riding off into the sunset, but draping their underwear on bushes to dry, pissing and shitting in the streets, tossing dead rats out their windows. What made it a Disney production was not the colors, not the tinny, keening music, not the incense or the dung, but the impression this somehow all added up to that the people here were simple, happy, that they weren't ruled by the lust to have more, know more, be more—that they lived thoughtlessly. Nothing could mar this impression for me. I remember one little child trying to sell me some stamps. He followed me for blocks, holding up his booklets, brandishing his wares. He was dirty, smelly, ragged—an unnecessary child who nevertheless seemed to me amazing, unique, an incarnate human soul who lived in a kind of perpetual present and this even as he followed me, wheedling, a budding businessman, a survivor-in-training at the age of eight or so. At last I stopped and told him I didn't want any stamps.

"Not today," I said.

"When, then?"

"Maybe tomorrow."

"Today is tomorrow," he replied without pausing.

"Never, then."

"Oh, never!" He shrugged and went away.

So perhaps it isn't lack of desire. Perhaps they simply use desire differently than we; they let it work for *them*. On the approach march, at lunch or dinner, when the children gathered around our camp, I used to take off my alarm watch and dangle it from the strap, setting it to go off after a moment with a thin burring noise. The kids, who would actually have been quite contented just to watch the hands go round, would listen to the burring, quite still until it stopped. When Tina wrote in her notebook, they watched the pen on the paper, crowding close, not touching the notebook, not touching the pen, but soaking up the smooth curves of the ink as they revealed themselves, until I wondered there was any left for the paper to absorb. There was one girl, in red trousers and a red blouse, who stood longer than all the rest, never coming close. Her milk pail dangled as if it were a painted pot. Only her eyes moved. If only Nicholas could have seen her. We might have learned a lot from the people of Nepal.

Four

I'd been asked on the expedition on Laurie's recommendation, since Margaret knew Laurie well. Of course, she had heard of me through other people too—Phillips, Phillips and Rhodes: it sounds like a law firm, doesn't it?—but I think she was a little uncertain about whether I was capable of climbing with other women. I was a little uncertain myself, even when I first was invited, since I hadn't had that much to do with women in my life and had often thought that I understood them even less than I did men. The only team I'd climbed with, after all, was the team of my husband and brother, and they always made me feel very special, more like a freak than the norm. So maybe I'd been afraid to let myself understand, afraid that on close examination women would turn out to be everything men have sometimes claimed them to be—devious, perhaps, or manipulative, cowardly or un-disciplined—and that would be a bad piece of news to acquire. Obviously, it would mean that my own conception of myself was nothing but a chimera. Or perhaps there was the even worse fear that men's judgments would turn out to be nonsense and that actually women were just men in disguise. Even worse because, whatever the difficulties of being a woman in a man's world, I certainly didn't want to be a man.

But actually, considering my one past experience with a women's expedition, it's amazing I agreed to go to Nepal at all.

In the summer of 1974, the Russians put on a mountaineering extravaganza, and Nicholas and Ryan and I were part of the American team. We had been promised the chance at some spectacular first ascents and except for the fact that our radios didn't make it through customs and the fact that when we arrived at base camp there were fifty-nine weird-looking Austrians already in residence there, a motley crew who turned out to be a kind of tour group of hill walkers, possessed of potbellies, lederhosen and sprightly wool caps, things started off well enough. But they ended very badly, and it was mostly because of the Soviet women who froze on Lenin Peak.

The Russian women were uniformly gorgeous. Healthy and young, with a remarkable solidarity, they went everywhere in a group and burst out of base camp for training climbs across the river as if they were bursting out of a starting gate. They didn't mix with the other teams, but they didn't seem to need to, and an air not just of eagerness but of mission exuded from them like a deadly gas. As if the fate of the German Eiger climbers in the thirties had not proved that climbing for the Fatherland or any other grand conception was a surefire way to get killed. And in the case of the Soviet women, they seemed intent on climbing not just for Mother Russia but for the honor of all women everywhere.

This women's team was scheduled to traverse Lenin Peak. The fact that it was Lenin Peak was hardly surprising, as the main concern of the Russian organizers of the convocation seemed to be to get as many climbers as possible to the top of that one mountain, where they could—presumably—rub the great man's electroplated bust and affirm the imperative of history. But the traverse that the women were scheduled to do is very demanding; you have to carry full packs up from the east on the Lipkin ridge to the summit and then down the Razdelny on the west. And it couldn't have helped them much to realize that they were the focus of a big internecine squabble in Russia about the wisdom of letting women do anything at all without male leadership. A couple of times I saw them doing calisthenics outside their tents. Calisthenics. Can you imagine?

What a summer that was! No one could possibly have predicted the series of catastrophes that dogged the Russian mountains that July. Earthquakes kept shaking the slopes we sat on. There seemed to be nothing that didn't avalanche, cornices toppled like leaves, and it actually poured rain for days on end at twenty thousand feet and higher. With conditions like that, it's amazing that anyone survived. But despite the wrath of the gods, some good climbs got carried out. A strong French team took Peak Sixteen, and Nicholas and Ryan and I managed to climb Peak Twenty-four. We were already back in base camp when the Russian women set out on their traverse. They carried enormous and oddly balanced packs, loaded, as rumor had it, with some of the worst-designed equipment the climbing world had yet produced, all of it Russian made.

I guess it was four days later that the major storm warnings went out. The unending stream of rain and snow had already turned base camp into a sea of mud, and it was hard for any of us to believe that a storm could be more major than the one we found around us. But climbers were peeling off Lenin Peak in a wet and dismal procession and it seemed hardly necessary to warn anyone in his right mind that conditions in the mountains were anything but good. There were over forty people at twenty thousand feet and higher, and the Soviet Meteorological Survey was predicting winds of hurricane force.

Well, the women went for the summit. No one knows why they did so, as they themselves never said, but they probably had some very good reasons that they passed back and forth like crackers, satisfying, though inadequately, the hunger of their hopes. Whatever the logic they used to support this, it was a crazy thing to do. They camped just below the summit and by morning the first of their lousy tents had blown apart. The wind slab was too tough for snow caves and the youngest woman was hypothermic. As each woman fell sick, the others felt compelled to stay with her until she died, and all of us down below were treated to the excruciating ordeal of staying with them too, since they remained in radio contact throughout the next five days while the storm raged on and one by one they died. They had no food. They had no water. And finally, they had no tents, no life.

If they hadn't been warned of a major storm approaching; if they hadn't reported in with such pitiful regularity; if they hadn't been so obviously obsessed with their honor . . . anything would have made it better than it was. But it was a nightmare, a full-blown nightmare, and Nicholas, somehow, made it into his own. He wanted so much to save them, as did we all; he wanted to stage a rescue in that storm. But it was impossible, more than impossible, crazy, and half of our energy went into calming him down. He sat in the radio tent each night, listening to their transmissions, withdrawn into a world of unmitigated pain. He tormented himself with their anguish; he wandered around like a ghost. One of their last transmissions was an apology for dying, and if there was one thing I was glad about in our position on the mountain, those eight days I lived through with Tina in that tent, it was the fact that our radios had fallen in the river with Changpa when he drowned, and if we had died on the mountain it would have been ours alone to know about. And though, on the eighth day, Naomi climbed the wall, and though, on the ninth day, somehow she got us down, I don't think we'd have lasted to see that time if we'd been in touch with the world down below. The women asked when they would smell the flowers, and who would care for their children when they were gone. Later, when the storm stopped, we went to recover their bodies. They lay like felled trees upon the snow, and Nicholas, when he saw them, started to cry like a child. He hadn't been able to help them, though he held them tenderly, dead.

Did I say I wouldn't like to find myself a man? Did I say that distance brings perspective? Well, both, it seems, are nonsense, since I've wanted to be a man since I was born, and since I still see those women's bodies in my dreams. My dreams, in any case, are long these days. I dreamed last night that I was back on the mountain with Tina. The camp looked as if a hurricane had hit it, and the storm was driving snow in through the back seams of the tent. But the air was sweet, and Tina's arms were warm, and both of us were whole.

▲

Before Tina arrived in Nepal—God, it seemed an endless time in the city. She didn't get there until the last minute because she was finishing up editing a film before she came and going over the proofs of her latest book. Her father runs a small publishing house in Anchorage, Alaska—one of those tiny artsy presses that publish thin books with woodcuts on their covers, woodcuts of women with sharp features, standing over woodstoves in long aprons, holding bread pans, looking like futuristic impressions of themselves—and he published her first book, *Freelance Adventuring*, all about how to do what you want to do in the adventure business and get paid for it. She arrived laden with cameras and lenses and notebooks, her pencils sharpened, and started commenting about the madness of a country where they have hand blow dryers in the bathrooms even though the electricity is off half the time, and taking pictures of the team—The Team Packing Boxes, The Team Discussing Strategy, The Team Sitting on Their Asses— half of the pictures staged, all of them, really, except the sitting on our asses ones. But though normally all this would have driven me quite mad, Tina made it seem all right—more than all right, funny—because although her pencils were sharpened she seemed to keep dropping them and although she'd written three books she claimed she'd never read them, and she staggered through doorways and bumped into lintels, then laughed like a baboon. She had a faded black-and-white snapshot of a bull moose pulling a plow, which she extracted from her pocket and thrust at people at odd moments, explaining that she'd raised it from calfhood and that its name was Ben.

I had first met Tina in Santa Fe, more than five years before. She was living with another woman at the time, as a kind of permanent houseguest, but she spent a lot of time with Ryan, doing climbs in the Sangre de Cristos. Ryan had put an ad in the local paper: "Climbing Partner Wanted, I Can Lead 5.11," and Tina had answered it by phone with a long-winded account of her experience on rock—which at the time didn't amount to much —and more important, an endless and complicated tale about the fact that she didn't have a car just now, which was a great frustration particularly because the woman with whom she was living had gotten involved in some litigation over the shape of the roof of her house. The roof was not, like most roofs in Santa Fe, flat, but was more the shape of a Quonset hut, half of a barrel, high and vaulted and with tiny skylights sprinkled across it like glitter. The neighbor who was suing Tina's housemate, Elanor, for having such a roof was not just litigious but actually quite a rat fink (Tina's term), and would come over to the house in the middle of the night and make loud noises on the lawn with an ancient noisemaker, a wooden contraption of paddles and brass which had, in the nineteenth century, been used to summon police. But *actually*, Tina told Ryan on the phone, *she* thought the reason he was so nasty was not because of the roof at all, but because he suspected that Elanor and Tina were lesbians—which you would think in a place like Santa Fe would go quite unnoticed even if it were true, which it wasn't. At the end of which explanation, Tina got back to the car she didn't possess, and said that she wanted to get out of town more, and would be happy to climb with Orion. He had graduated that spring and had gotten a job as a mining engineer, and when I went to see him that winter, I was half intending to stay. But Tina was already quite a fixture.

She came over to dinner the first night I was there. She arrived wearing pink and black—black pants, black shirt and short pink jacket—and around her neck a small silver ice ax and an equally small silver climbing shoe. Not only was she six feet two, with legs like a horse and shoulders to match the rest of her, but she had the shortest blond hair, harshly whitened by the sun, that I had ever seen on a woman, and bangs which fell across her forehead like a curtain. She seemed to explode into the house, her eyes within her face as bright as sudden birds, and she threw her arms around Ryan and hugged him till he gasped. Then she shook my hand and shook her earrings also, four-inch-long hawk feathers which were hanging beside three-inch-long beaded strings and which later on in the evening got mixed up with the spaghetti sauce and had to be thrown away.

At dinner, Tina talked. She was full of the latest excitement, which was that Elanor, who was in the midst of countersuing her neighbor for being a malicious nuisance, and who was also at the crucial stage of her own barrel-roof defense, had just that day discovered that her neighbor had nonconforming windows! If nothing else, he would certainly be reprimanded by the Historical Styles Committee and the Planning Commission of the town. Orion kept trying to get Tina to pipe down, but Tina was irrepressible and finally he just leaned back in his chair and gave in. Usually, he was as crazy as she was, though, and even that night at one point he smeared spaghetti sauce on his cheeks in two neat blobs of color, then blew them out as if he were a chipmunk. I wasn't at all convinced that Tina was really straight; she kept flirting with me, as she flirted with Ryan and seemingly with her whole world. She flirted with the silver on the table, the flowers in the vase, she flirted with the wine and the spaghetti and the hot garlicky bread. Nibbling this, devouring that, she dominated the conversation just exactly as long as it would bear it, then effortlessly shifted over to questions, staring with her gray-blue eyes. Irresistibly puppyish, she carried all before her, and I could see that Ryan was more than half in love.

I hadn't seen Tina since that visit and hadn't thought I'd be glad to. She and Ryan had broken up not long afterward, and she hadn't come to Ryan's funeral but had sent me a long and disjointed letter explaining that she hated funerals, that she had seen enough dead bodies in the mountains and that she wanted to remember Ryan as he had been, calling down to her, "Tina! On belay!" Furthermore, she wrote, she would be seeing me in Nepal;

at least, she hoped so, if I didn't change my mind and decide not to come. She thought that would be a bad idea, since you had to pick up and get on with your life. But when she arrived, I was truly glad to see her. Though I was, of course, still jealous then of her relationship with Ryan, it was clear enough that *she* didn't know it, so why should I make a big fuss? She felt, in fact, that they'd had only a friendship, and in that she was probably right. Because when we were grown, I think Ryan felt about me much the same way that I felt about Nicholas when first I got to know him. He was not as passionate as I, as Nicholas, if by passionate you mean reckless; he never cared to risk the things he loved the best. Nor did he seem to need, in general, those intervals of stark intensity which were to Nicholas and me the stuff of life. When he and I were together, though, just the two of us, he came closer to being gripped by longing than most people would have thought wise, and when we were apart his life was governed still by that and by his knowledge—which neither of us talked about—that in another world, another time, we might have been sufficient to each other.

Well, Tina and I, if nothing else, could at least share a common remembrance. And with her arrival in Nepal, I felt suddenly that yes, I *could* remember my past, could gather in all those pieces of the diamond and then put them back together again, that there *was* a real world, and it was the world of the camera itself, the seeing eye rather than the scene the eye sees. All those beautiful sights that had enthralled me—the purple-flowering ginkgo trees, the piles of bright-orange brick, the terraces of dried dun earth and golden wheat—were either real or not real, but it didn't matter anyway, because it was what you did with them that counted, how you used them to interpret your own past and future.

So in that mood, the mood, I suppose, of a professional tourist, I made the mistake of going on a tour of the Katmandu valley the day before we left for the mountain. I'd been feeling a little sick, as if I were on the edge of contracting the Katmandu Krud, but instead of staying in bed like a sensible woman, I took some aspirin, don't ask me why, and climbed into the tiny tour bus with the rest of the team.

We went to temples and chortens and more temples and spun prayer wheels and listened to our tour guide—Banni, a dark Nepalese, impeccably dressed in white linen trousers and a fine-combed cotton shirt—tell seemingly endless stories about the way a particular temple came to be built, which usually involved a father sacrificing his son, or vice versa, in the dead of night, without knowing who he was, only that he was the single man in the kingdom virtuous enough so that his death would release the rains and free the land from drought. I'm not saying they weren't interesting stories: the king who set a brass bird on top of his stone statue and said as he went off to war that as long as the bird was there he was alive and if he were killed it would fly away in the wars—no, no, if he was killed in the wars it would fly away.

I was a little giddy with suppressed hysterics by the time we got to a temple with ten enormous steps leading up to it and on each step a pair of animals, and it turned out that each consecutive set of animals had three times the strength of the set before and instead of just indicating this fact and letting us figure out the arithmetic, our guide took us up step by excruciating step, from the monkeys to the cows to the lions to the elephants, finally ending, I think, with the griffins, which had, not surprisingly, three times the strength of the elephants. Then Naomi, delightfully malicious, asked Banni to repeat the last three animals' herculean statistics.

Well, that would have been quite enough. But there was one final temple to do, and our guide had saved it for last because it was by far the most important and sat on a river that had the same significance for the Nepalese that the Ganges has for the Indians. We bumped through a hundred back streets to get there, so that my stomach, which had been only potentially queasy when we started, was definitely queasy when we stopped. When we stepped off the bus we nearly landed in a pile of sacred cow dung and then almost ran into the sacred cow, not a cow at all but a great black bull with horns painted blue, that sat in the middle of the road regarding us with superb self-possession. With my stomach feeling the way it did then, I wanted to be anywhere but there and I didn't exactly approach the Rammadir temple with an open mind.

There was a series of concrete platforms spaced along the edge of the river, at intervals of perhaps fifty feet. On the one that was nearest to us when we arrived, a great fire of logs was burning and on top of the logs a corpse. A man stood by the ghat, desultorily poking at the fire with a pole. It wasn't so much the corpse, or the smell, that disturbed me. It was the river which was the focus of the scene. It wasn't a river at all, it was a sluggish sea of brown mud, with stagnant pools of water filled with the debris of burning —half-charred logs and scraps of clothing, bits of bone and piles of ashes, none of them traveling anywhere, simply rotting in a sea of putrefaction. Just below the ghat where the corpse was burning, three women in aqua and red saris were doing their washing, and three or four children, unclothed, were playing in one of the puddles. One man crouched on his haunches, washing out a brass teakettle, and one very old man was taking a spiritual bath. He was white and bony and his legs looked like two sticks. He had to be helped into and out of the water. That anyone could go near that river, much less bathe in it, play in it, wash in it—I simply couldn't believe it. I focused my eyes on the ground and kept them there while Banni, in a bright professional tone, told us that the huts we saw were dying huts.

"To the truly religious," he said, "it is best of all to come here to die. A special privilege. Everyone wants to die here. Not all do so, of course. If they think they are dying they may come and then not die. Some stay for a day, some for three days, some for months, three months or four. Maybe at the end of that time they still haven't died and they go home. That is too bad. But they cannot know, of course. And if they do die here, their souls are especially blessed, it is a great blessing. I think there is someone dying now."

We moved on up the hill. On the bottom set of steps sat a leper, a young girl of fourteen or fifteen, dressed in a sari, her hand outstretched so that it almost touched my leg. She had only half a nose and the skin on her face was horribly disfigured with red and white blotches. A Hindu holy man, his face decorated with vivid colored paste, his hair drawn up into a topknot, crouched on his heels and keened, an endless, mournful, shrill whining, like the hum of mosquitoes at night. A monkey, excrement hanging from its bare pink ass, ran by us, then leaped onto a woman's chest and grabbed a bag of food from her jhola before he ran away. Western hippies, their languid faces empty, sat on the steps smoking dope. When a sudden furious barking erupted on the hillside below and a mass of ten or twenty moiling dogs rushed into view, seemingly hysterical with anger, Banni looked down at them benevolently and said, "Ahh. Mad dog." Even Naomi was taken aback. In an effort, perhaps, to avoid a response, she went over to one of the dying huts and peered through the door. Her voice was fairly subdued, for Naomi, when she said, "My God. There's a corpse in here."

I didn't look. If I had had the power—truly, awful as it sounds —if I had had the power I would have gotten the biggest bulldozer you've ever seen and razed that place, leveled it as flat as a football field, the river and the corpses and the temple monkeys, the lepers and the shit and the dogs. I would have pushed it all into nothingness and maybe even set up a concession stand promoting balloons and pure air and soap. I had thought that I believed in freedom, or at least in letting things be. But I did not. I wanted things to be nice, I wanted the earth unsullied, and above all I wanted death to be sudden and putrefaction sweet. I wanted no body bags, no sphincter muscles and no pain. Just roses and an odor of sanctity. Some Buddhist, eh? Some Buddhist. Or if not roses, even better, a moment in a blue crevasse, a sudden fall through windy space, a perfect, gentle instant in the snow, when what has been becomes what is not and the sun, golden yellow, shines down to waft you upward to the sky. I wanted to check out in the mountains and nowhere else, my feet on rock, my hands reaching for the silver clouds above. We all wanted that, I guess. Maybe that's part of why we were there. But for me, perhaps it was something more. That I didn't die with Nicholas and Ryan. That I didn't die with the men I loved. After the avalanche, in the months that followed it like boulders, sluggish in the wake of a glacier that has passed on, I wanted nothing myself but to die. Not because I wanted to die, not really. Oh, God, how I wanted to live! But that they could die like that, so suddenly: it ripped the bottom out of my world. I missed them desperately and was full of guilt and longing; but it wasn't that, you know. It was that if they could die I could die and if I was going to die anyway I wanted to do it and get it over and have that much less to fear. When the first spring thaw came and the sagebrush poked up through the snow and smelled as sweet as birthdays, as weddings, I didn't want to smell it, I didn't want to know. The world was full of celebrations, but the more I loved it, the more I would have to lose. I didn't want to lose even one thing more—the leaf of a sagebrush, a crunch in the snow.

Five

People always thought it was romantic, a team of a woman and two men. Romance is not what I would call it, when Nicholas was at his worst. And they always thought, of course, that Nicholas and I were the Phillips and Phillips and Ryan was the Rhodes. It used to annoy Nicholas unspeakably. Not that I never took his name, but that people couldn't keep his straight. He was Nicholas Rhodes the mountaineer. There was only one of him. But if that sounds arrogant, it shouldn't. Nicholas—he was an idealist, under all his macho. To succeed wasn't what he wanted. He wanted to live in a world where failure was impossible. And the mountains —the mountains were the one place where he was not afraid of success.

That sounds quite crazy, I know. But Nicholas, from the day he was born, knew he was special. He didn't have to *prove* that —God, no. All he had to prove was that the world was worthy of him. Which is quite a task, when you think about it. And also, if you look at it right, it's a very humble, self-effacing trait. It made him delicate, so easily hurt, so scared of succeeding out in the other world. He was scared that if he once succeeded there he would be forced to try it again, he would get the taste for it, the taste for competition, and then he would have no peace. He would be compelled to try it over and over again until finally he ran up against something that demanded more than he had, and he would know at last that the world was a place where you could be Nicholas and still fail, a loathsome place, a chasm in a storm.

I never saw it when he was alive, but I know now that it's true. Nicholas was so damn arrogant he was brimming with humility —and that made people uneasy around him. People are sometimes such cowards. They don't know what to do with anyone capable of absolute contrition. They always think in terms of dichotomies and they equate contrition with the aggressive verbs that sometimes bring it about—to conquer, to subdue, to humiliate. People can't stand saints, really. They just can't understand them. Not that Nicholas was a saint. But that side of him was the side I loved, from the moment he first touched me with his hand.

We were standing at the top of a boulder. There were only two days left, or three, before the climbing school was over. It had rained for the last few days and turned icy cold and we'd all sat around in our parkas and shivered and eaten tons of chocolate and nuts and listened to the instructors give theoretical classes on the physics of lightning and high-altitude physiology and other dulling subjects until we were quite insane with ennui and nonspecific desperation. When the weather finally broke, none of us wanted to have anything to do with one another and at the same time we were all so eager to get climbing that the whole group was simply greasy with friendliness. We could have picked our own climbing partners quite adequately by then, without any help from Nicholas. But he stood up there and parceled people out like packages of food. And he picked me for his rope team.

I was almost sick with fury. During the whole ten days of the climbing school I'd never climbed with Nicholas, and I didn't intend to now if I could help it. I thought his selecting me was a special burst of venom, accumulated from two long days of frustration. He knew how much I detested him and surely he must detest me just as much. What other reason could he have for picking me than a peculiar brand of sadism? He was wearing his Annapurnas and they shielded his eyes like the hood of a cobra, but I went up to him anyway, tingling with defensiveness, and told him I'd really rather do some other climb. He was doing something on Teepee's Pillar, something fairly hard—5.9 or 5.10, and they hadn't yet invented 5.13.

"What's the matter?" he said nastily. "Don't think you can hack it?"

I felt like hitting him with a rock. We were camped quite high, on a nice big moraine, and there were these beautiful smooth flat rocks lying around everywhere and I stared at one and thought what a pleasure it would be to bring it smashing down on his head. I actually bent down and picked one up and held it in my hand, clutching tightly.

"I'm just afraid it will bore me," I said. "But if *you* want to do it, hell, why not. I've been bored enough since I got here; I guess I can take a little more."

I'd never talked like that, never. I dropped the rock and turned away, trembling, aware as I did so that something had happened to Nicholas's face. He looked shocked, as if I had actually hit him with the rock, as if his mother had scolded him for something he hadn't done. I went to get my gear, and to find Orion and complain, but I kept thinking about the look on Nicholas's face, the way you think about a beautiful moment, a moment when the air is still and all you can hear beneath the early sun is the crunch of your crampons on the snow.

I suppose it really began then; but I didn't know it, any more than you know the first time you hear that crunch on a morning ridge that you'll never be able to live without it again, that you'll come back over and over to find that moment, that sound, that journey upward across the snow. Nicholas's look then just became a part of me, instantly and without words, and I didn't even have to admit that I treasured it. There was no admitting, no consciousness involved. If I thought anything in words, it was "Well, it served him right," which certainly is typical—not just that my feelings and thoughts were often utterly at odds, not just that I was on the defensive from the start, but that my love for him was always touched with power, that I loved him because he was vulnerable to me and also because I felt that in probing that vulnerability, in letting him reveal his helplessness to me, I was giving him the greatest gift I could give him and that more—soft words, caresses, help or adoration—was unnecessary, because what he needed more than anything was someone who could perceive his helplessness and administer pain like an antidote to his search for invulnerability. Not that the soft words didn't come.

▲

There were supposed to be two of us climbing with Nicholas that morning, but at the last minute Beckett decided not to go. It really is rather ironic that Beckett was at the school that summer, Beckett who later almost tore us both apart. Not that *he* had anything to do with it—a delightful man, funny and half unhinged. Ryan and I had known him first in high school, had met him through the Outing Club the only year that we were all at school together; we found ourselves walking alongside Beckett one day as we approached a climb. Though he wasn't as good a climber as we were, it never bothered him in the least, and we all hit it off from the start. On an Outing Club trip one morning, when we woke up very wet, having slept without a tent and gotten hit with an early, soggy snowfall, I lay in a half sleep for hours, having to pee desperately but too immobilized by the little cocoon I had managed to make out of my damp Dacron sleeping bag to do anything but clutch the muscles of my abdomen to me like a football, until I had terrible cramps and could hardly move with the pain. I finally rolled over and muttered to Beckett that I felt dreadful, I had pains in my stomach and couldn't relax. He came instantly awake and said to me, sympathetic as hell, "Lady pains?" I had to giggle, even though that hurt worse. He got up and made a big pot of tea and filled a water bottle with hot water for me to hold until the knot in my muscles released and I could get up and pee and enjoy the damp sweet smell of morning. By the time Ryan got back from wood gathering, Beckett had me laughing like crazy.

Beckett loved to play games. Once we came back from a climb near Union Pass—me and Ryan and Beckett and two other guys from our high school—and we were eating some junk food in a sleazy hamburger place, where they had picnic tables put together out of what looked like condemned barn siding, on which endless generations of young locals had carved their initials and their remarks. Beckett had stayed out in the car for a moment and we were already sitting down when he came in, all of us grubby and smelly, and Beckett the wildest-looking one of all, in torn knickers and with a four-day growth of beard which looked like nothing so much as pubic hair. He had on a bright-orange balaclava and we were all sitting around dazed and exhausted when he came up to our table still carrying his ice ax, and rammed the tip of it into the boards with a tremendous crunch, his face contorted by anger.

"So," he said, his fake French accent cracking with the strain of expressing himself in such a foreign tongue as English. "You thought to leave me on the mountain, hey? No one does that to old Pierre—and lives!" If you could have bottled the silence that suddenly fell on that greasy spoon, it would have been as good as suddenly halving the population of the world.

After Ryan went off to college, Beckett became my friend— a Ryan substitute, maybe. He had a great susceptibility to things that are not real—to stories of medieval courtesie, to tales of trolls and elves and goblins, to lovers who love for life and die in each other's arms—and in that he seemed a lot like Ryan. We hung around together at school and studied together for our exams and often in the evenings we took a rope out to Sinks Canyon to climb. I was really very fond of him— though never as a *boy*— and had suggested to him that he try the Jackson school. He had been nursing a sprained ankle, though, during the days we sat in the rain, and the ankle was still badly swollen the morning we were able to climb. Wrapped in an Ace bandage, it could not be stuffed into his boot. By the time he discovered this, most of the others had already left for their climbs, so (although Nicholas as head instructor should certainly have taken more than one of us

that day) there were just the two of us together when we set off
for the cliff. Later, of course, it occurred to me to wonder whether
Nicholas hadn't picked Beckett specially, knowing he would likely
turn back; but at the time as we made our way across the big
moraine, all I was aware of was Nicholas's presence.

It pressed against me like a jet of water, powerful and intense.
It was as if I were trying to cross a river and the sudden force of
the current was riveting, so there was nothing I could do but lean
into it and work with it, hoping the stream wouldn't knock me
off balance, hoping I wouldn't be swept away. I *had* to lean
toward it; leaning away would have meant that I'd drown in it.
But we were perfectly balanced, the river and I, and in the
boundaries of our balance we moved, not conversing. There was
really nothing to say. Though I had known Nicholas for almost
two weeks by then, it was as if I had never seen him before in my
life, except once perhaps, long years before, when he had been a
sudden face on a subway, a pair of eyes across a countertop. He
didn't speak to me either, all the way across the broad moraine,
and though he carried the rope as arrogantly, as competently, as
ever, I knew that he, too, was feeling what I felt, a dim sense of
recognition, no more significant than a flash of déjà vu, perhaps,
but longer, enduring as we picked our way between the rocks. And
when we got to a narrow spot between two boulders and we had
to climb one boulder as big as a house to get beyond it, he leaped
up, then turned, resting lightly on his boots like a dancer, and gave
me his hand in silence, lifting me beyond the crux.

That was it, then. His hand. He proffered it and I took it and
when I reached the top of the boulder he stood looking down on
the moraine we had crossed and I stood beside him looking down
on it too, a maze of jumbled rock suddenly transformed from our
new vantage point into a long smooth plain of stone. He seemed
in no hurry to move on; his piton hammer hung at his belt in an
old leather holster and he linked one hand around it as he stood.
There was a breeze gusting at times, quite warm, and from somewhere below us in the rocks solid currents of air were flowing. In

that gray-brown country, the colors of Nicholas's equipment were as brilliant as desert flowers after a rain. The safety sling of his harness was crimson and the rope a royal blue. When we turned to go on, I knew that he wanted to give me his hand again, but he did not—and it didn't matter because I knew now that whenever I wanted to reach out and take it, that hand would be there, and because I was so full of wonder that he could risk himself that way; he had courage far greater than any courage of mine, one which was concealed well by the armor of his skill on the rock and his hat brim pulled low across his eyes.

I can remember every move of that climb. Usually, climbs up long exposed towers are so repetitive that you can recall few details after they are over; perhaps just the sweetness of the air, the gentle tapping of a hammer in the stillness, the red of a sweater against the sky. But even now I think I could write a guidebook on it, the endless jam crack, the tenuous traverse across the face. The rock was cold in the shadow and hot in the sun. Once a bat came squeaking out of a crevice as I drove in a piton, and looked at me malevolently before he flew away. Every time I leaned forward to trace a bit of mica in the rock with my finger, the clinking of the hardware racked across my chest was like the tinkling of bells, the rustle of aspen leaves in the forest. When we got to the base of the cliff, Nicholas stacked the rope and tied into the bottom of the stack, and what I might have seen before as a subtle test, a dare to me to prove myself, I now saw as natural politeness giving me the first lead. When I drove in a piton for the first belay, the steel rang neatly with an ever-ascending pitch, and the crack didn't bottom out but held the piton as sweetly as if it had grown there.

▲

We started living together that fall. I gave up my plans to go to college, with few if any regrets, and we rented a tiny metal trailer on a weed-filled lot in Jackson Hole. In those days it was almost impossibly hard to find a place to rent in the Hole. We were grateful when we found our little tin box. My mother didn't much approve of it, but she didn't much approve of Nicholas either, and at least we weren't jammed right up against someone else's little tin box and actually had a view of sorts of Snow King and the ridge beyond it. But the place was so small that when we had stored our climbing gear and skis and junk in the bedroom, there was no room left for a bed. So we slept on a bed in the other room, the one with the stove and the icebox and the table in it.

I didn't care. If Nicholas left his running shoes or his helmet on the floor, right where you couldn't fail to trip over them, I didn't care. They looked like him, they smelled like him, they were his objects: I would as soon have been annoyed at tripping over him as at running into his possessions. Every time he went out alone, the presence of his clothes, his books, his old guitar—and all these, in a space as small as ours, loomed very large indeed—gave me a sense of security and pride; really, I suppose, of possessiveness. The helmet was not mine but it was better than mine. I owned the man who owned it. And that loop, that bypass, made them even more thoroughly mine than my own things, since my own quickly became strange through familiarity, while his I continued for a long time to see for what they were. Each hole in a sneaker, each scratch in a helmet—they were his birthmarks, and my talismans.

That fall we ate a lot of bacon. Nicholas couldn't cook anything but macaroni and cheese, bacon and toast, though he had some wild ideas about things like fondue, which we would periodically try and which would periodically end in near disaster, as when the hot oil almost tipped into his lap because I bumped the shaky table with my knee. So we ate a lot of bacon. It was not that I couldn't cook or didn't have some idea at least of the variety of things you could prepare and then put into your mouth, but off the rock I tended—then—to be very reticent about suggestions. Nicholas was seven years older than I was, after all, and he'd started off as my instructor. I assumed that he must have picked up some of the secret knowledge that you gather with age like lint,

and since I didn't know how to recognize secret knowledge—
which would after all, to a novice, seem to be disguised—I settled
for his ideas on shopping trips and we came home with bacon and
toast. The toast would be broiled in the oven or fried in a pan full
of butter; the bacon ditto, though not at the same time. We
would take to the table a platter of toast and a platter of bacon,
sometimes leavened by a platter of sliced tomatoes. It was fine
with me. I loved it. The diet bound us together as surely as sex
did. I felt that we must both emanate the odor of pork grease and
semen when we walked together down the street.

We were really madly in love. He didn't know it, couldn't know
it, since his experience gave him no real basis for comparison and
since his thoughts did not run to that kind of analysis. But I knew
it, as surely as I knew my own history, as surely as I knew that
my brother had taught me to climb—although I had no basis for
comparison either. And the irony was that only when I started to
feel less sure of my need for him—though he had filled an empty
space inside me, filled it forever, nothing could change that, and
though he had, like a Universal weight machine, given me
strength I never would have had without him to push and pull on,
fifty leg presses and the ecstasy of rest—when the time came that,
like someone in training, I began to wonder whether I should not
just go ahead with the real competition, the battle of self-awaken-
ing, self-knowledge, leaving him behind, then and only then did
he begin to see his need for me for what it was. A need not for
a climbing partner but for someone he could care for, someone
whose soul he could nurture and protect.

In the beginning, though, every time he kissed me, thanked
me, wrote me a letter, I felt that he was doing me a favor to love
me, giving me a present like a helium balloon. I didn't see that
the real favor he was doing was much larger than that one, the
biggest favor you can ever do another person; he was accepting
the love I offered him, as if he were a bottomless pit, an infinite
strip of blotting paper, absorbing all I could give. Poor man. He
was addicted to me before he knew it. He used to joke about the

hippies too, with the careless scorn he reserved for the stupid. "Come on," he'd say, mocking drug dealers. "The first one's free."

But that autumn was a hard one. We had no money, we had no decent jobs, and I was on the phone with Orion thirty times a week, moaning about how horrid Nicholas was. We fought a lot and almost broke up fifty times and more, even packing our things and striding to the door, while Nicholas told me I was in love with my brother and I told him he was totally self-obsessed. The weather was rotten for weeks on end and no one was doing any good climbs. We tried to go to Yosemite, but the truck—the best three-hundred-dollar special in the state of Wyoming—broke down before we got out of the state. I refused to hitchhike all the way to California and we struggled back to Jackson with our incredibly heavy packs, cursing at each other all the way.

Six

Well, naturally we got married. That winter, in Jackson Hole. It was Christmastime and things were very festive; red bells were hung on wires over the streets, and streetlamps were swathed in tinsel. All the houses were lit with fire, and chimney smoke wound up to the sky. Everything was crisp, if you know what I mean—people's comments when they met on the sidewalk, the sounds of grocery bags and doors. And we felt crisp too, we felt like *doing* something, so when Ryan came up from Santa Fe we went to a justice of the peace. We didn't know we were going to get married. All we knew was that we'd quit our jobs. The weekend before, on the way back from skiing in Driggs, the truck had broken down in a blizzard—again—and Nicholas, after futilely trying to start the engine for almost thirty minutes, had bunched his fist together and smashed the dashboard, smashed the instrument panel, smashed the windshield itself, until the glass was all broken and the vinyl a maze of cracks, and his hand was bleeding from a hundred tiny cuts. I was feeling close to crazy, since I couldn't help him at all, and glad, I think, when something gave, as long as it was our jobs. I called Orion and begged him to come for Christmas. He got to the airport still dressed in a three-piece suit.

We decided that night to go into the Gros Ventres. We had heard there was a cabin there, below the bowl of the mountains, and though the snow was unusually deep that winter, it sounded easy to find. We'd have a long ski in to Bootjack, but better a cabin than a tent, so we got out our double boots and greased them, then packed up a great deal of gear. Ryan, who fit better than we did into our diminutive trailer, kept hugging me and then hugging Nicholas who acted extremely annoyed, and then reading ridiculous directions from the insides of military surplus hats and pants. The pants and hats had come from the climbers' school where we'd all met; because they lacked storage space they kept their extra equipment in an old automobile in an empty lot and one night when Nicholas and I were sleeping in the lot—that fall, before we found our little trailer—we had discovered that the "green car" was open, and stocked up on khaki clothes. "Place right leg in right trouser. Be sure to button fly," read Ryan. Though Nicholas hadn't wanted Ryan to come and had said all sorts of nasty things about him before he arrived, most of them had come from a fear of rejection, since he really liked Ryan a lot, and he wanted a male compatriot, actually, as much as he wanted me. So with that sudden grace he had, he impetuously gave in. Laughing, he still acted slightly gruff, but now rather more pleased. Outside, down the street, people were caroling and at some point in a fit of giggles we decided to sing along. Ryan had brought us matching socks for a present. They had little Christmas trees sewn into their borders and we put them on our hands and pretended they were puppets, giving us directions on what to take and what to leave behind.

"One tent," I said, quite firmly, "in case this cabin is a myth."

"One rope," said Ryan after me, "in case we find a wild horse."

"One wife," said Nicholas. "How about it? You want to get married tonight?" And though we couldn't find a JP's open that evening, we found one the following day. Nicholas held my hand all through it. And *then* we took our trip.

▲

Our packs were incredibly heavy and we decided to go in on skis. A recent snow had dumped a foot or two of powder all over the lower Gros Ventres, so we had to break trail for almost ten miles and were still skiing when the sun went down. We were in deep forest then and the temperature, which had been hovering at just above zero, dropped suddenly to ten below with the exit of the sun. My double woolen mittens, wet from several epic falls, froze almost solid on my hands.

"Let's put up the tent," I said. "How about it? I'm ready to eat some food."

Nicholas seemed to be willing, but Ryan wanted to go on. That in itself was such a strange reversal that I hardly protested at all, so we kept on skiing through the forest, the two men in the lead. I fell behind, to a place where sounds were indistinct, and my hands, in just minutes, were numb and wooden as the trees. The moon began to rise and as it came above the outline of a treetop —like an ornament set at the top of a fine old broom—it threw a light across the snow that was almost as pure as dream light. The shadows of the branches were decals pasted neatly in place, and each trunk as it thrust down into the whiteness had a two-dimensionality as purposeful as art. In fact, the trees seemed to me to be full of intention, and in the great silence of interlaced shadows they mediated between me and my growing coldness like gentle guardians, more numinous than real. I lost sight of Ryan and Nicholas, slowed to a walk, and stopped.

Who knows how much later the men skied back. They took one look at me, and then looked at each other, and without exchanging more than a few terse words, they set to work to warm me up and reverse the slow process of freezing. Nicholas whipped off his pack and set it upright in the snow, and unzipping a bright-blue pocket, took out a spare set of mitts. Ryan took my pack off my shoulders, then knelt down and unfastened my skis, and by the time he had them off me, Nicholas was tucking mittens on my hands. In very little time, they had a sleeping bag stretched across the snow, and a stove roaring gruff reassurance, and Nicholas was taking my boots from my feet and then holding my feet on his bare stomach. Ryan thrust some tea into my hands, and dumped about a pound of sugar in it, and together they urged me into the bag and then took some time to consult. I was still very placid, and very unconcerned, and they decided that they'd better find the cabin, if they wanted to be sure I'd live through the night. As if from a great distance, I heard Nicholas saying matter-of-factly that since he was the stronger on skis, he would go find the cabin, while Ryan remained with me, and whatever jealousy he might ever have had, he certainly lost it then, since he watched while Ryan climbed in the bag and held me tight in his arms.

I fell asleep. When I woke up, the moon had risen high into the sky. Ryan was gone, but my pack was still there, my skis set upright in a drift beside me. My boots, two tiny boats, were at their feet. Motionless, warm, I lay where I had woken. The luminous woods stretched all around me and the frozen stars had been hung. I have no idea how long I lay there, but certainly two hours had gone by while I slept. Finally, for something to do, I shouted a great hello, and from just behind me in the trees, Nicholas spoke softly.

"We found the cabin. There's a fire going. Come on, I'll help you dress."

So he helped me dress, and I let him help me dress, and then he strapped my pack to his, and led the way through the woods. Smoke was curling like lace from the chimney and the moonlight poured down from the mountain, and when Nicholas kicked open the door to the cabin, he picked me up to carry me through it. Ryan was standing at the woodstove melting cheese, which all of us drank like a liquid, and when a container of snow had been melted, we all drank gallons of that. And there was a line there for me, a line on one side of which was perfect bliss, the moment when all your mind and body comes together in the stillness and on the other side of which was sadness. Watching the cheese bubbling in the pot, and the soft kerosene glow on Nicholas's hair,

I found it odd, somehow, that axes should hang on log walls, just so, and that cold should so easily kill. Odd, too, that men should know such love and three people be as one.

Just before we went to bed that night, when Nicholas was already in his bag and I had yet to climb the ladder to the loft, he called down to me to bring him a pot—"What kind of a pot?" "Any pot, Temis. A big pot"—and when I had located a pot, and handed it up the ladder, he bent his head over it and threw up into it, again and again and again, all of the water and all of the cheese and all of who knows what else, and then, without saying a word, took the pot to a wood-shuttered window and threw its contents out into the night. That night, before I managed to sleep again, I thought for the first time in many years of my father and the way in which he'd been killed. Out inspecting an oil rig, he'd been high on a scaffold when a girder had fallen, and the cable that was carrying it had snapped. In its backlash, it had swept him off the ladder and shoved him a hundred feet to rocky ground. No wonder my mother hated our climbs. But there it was and here we were. "Be sure to button fly."

The next day was utterly blue. We got up just before the sun and huddled around the stove, melting some snow. Nicholas was in very high spirits; he'd seen a snowshoe hare bounding away from the cabin when he emerged, and picking up a piton, had thrown it at the hare's great legs. In one of those miraculous coincidences of thought and action, the piton had hit the rabbit squarely on the head, so we ate roast rabbit for breakfast. Nicholas cleaned it neatly and fried it like a gift. When the snow had melted, we all drank hot chocolate, and at one point Nicholas took my hand and held it tightly, then whipped out a kerchief to cover the link and tucked it under our thumbs. When Ryan, sitting with his knees up, fastening his gaiters, looked over at this, amused, Nicholas said quite gravely, "More sanitary like this. It helps to settle the germs."

We climbed the mountain by the ridge. We weren't out for a record, not then, just for a beautiful day. Ryan was best on rock, but Nicholas was good on anything, and he started off in the lead, picking a pace that was perfect for all of us, and keeping it up with great ease. As he cut each step, his ice ax swinging easily in his hand, he was already halfway onto that step, his legs gliding over the air. His feet spread wide, he would stand relaxed for moments at a time, reading the ridge above him until I thought he would never move again, and then all of a sudden would move so swiftly that he made the slope seem quite flat. In the mountains in winter I never saw him look cold. On crackling mornings, when the dawn was as black as night, he'd turn over in his bag to light the stove, his bare fingers holding the metal as he pumped until the gas ignited with a roar. And that day, when a wind came out of the north so that the rope stretched out on the ridge between us was blown southward in great looping whorls, Nicholas simply pulled down his hat and kept on, quite undisturbed.

Halfway up the first hard slope, Ryan's crampon came loose. We stopped and stamped out a platform and ate lunch while he worked on the steel. With the same old-fashioned courtesy with which, the first night we ever slept together, Nicholas had asked if he could "put his arm around" me, he asked Ryan if he could help him with the crampon, and when Ryan said, "Of course," the two of them bent over it, their heads almost touching, their four hands working as two. While they worked they told stupid jokes, which I heard with only one ear. Gradually the jokes got bawdier—"Why did the snowman pull down his pants? He was waiting for the snow blower"—and though usually such jokes do not appeal to me, that day everything seemed fine.

When we left the platform, I took over the lead. The wind was blowing so hard on the ridge that I traversed into a gully on the left, but no sooner had I reached it than I realized there was ice about a hundred feet up into it. The sun was shining straight down the gully, and so dazzling was its glitter that I couldn't really see if it came from snow crust or ice, but whichever it was, I was up for it, and I kept on cutting steps. I was cutting them deep and close together; two or three blows of the ax, and the steps were big enough to walk. Never had I felt so graceful. Never had I been so sure. I was only a small parenthesis in time, but I felt I was climbing toward eternity, and the blue of the sky that arched above was the blue of a monarch's robes. A cerulean blue. A cobalt blue. The blue of a sapphire in silk.

How can you describe the feel of the mountains? You proffer what they demand. And the more you give them, the more they will give you, so that—as in a martial art, where resistance simply increases the strength of surprise and you undo your partner by the simple act of succumbing—to climb is to know the way to submit, and by submitting, to win. The sun is so sharp on the snow when it shines and the blue so dark in the sky, and your boots have only one place to be, and that place is just where they are. And as I cut steps, and then more steps, I knew I could cut them forever. I stopped at last. Nicholas kissed me. Ryan took over the lead.

Because of the wind, and the detour through the gully, it was late when we got to the top. The final stretch of ridge was rough, and we were all quite tired. When at last we sat at the summit, the sun was a molten pear, but we didn't hurry to get back to the cabin, we simply sat and stared. Nicholas crouched with his arms around his knees, and Ryan had his feet stretched out and crossed, and I lay back in the snow and watched while the sky turned black. To say I was happy would be lying. I was beyond happiness, in a moment out of time and space, when everything I loved seemed to erase me, and there was nothing that stood between me and the stuff that wove the world. At last both Nicholas and Ryan rose, and each held out a hand to help me up. Though each of them alone could hurt me, scare me, fail me, the two of them together—they never let me down, until they died.

Seven

We drove to Dumre in a caravan of old buses which belched diesel smoke and roared like jets; we were held up for an hour at a gas station because the driver couldn't get the engine started after he turned it off, until, with a wonderful, phlegmatic calm, he discovered that by rolling the bus backward and kicking it hard in the side, he could coax it once more to action and we could leave. I spread out all over two of the seats, opened the window wide and watched the sights. There was a tiny triple-arched brick house set beside a lone tree in a field, a soft blue shirt draped over a bush in the breeze. Three small orange fires burned under the shelter of a spreading banyan tree. The green of the grass was intense and commanding and above the terraced paddies the erosion was like a netted hammock, spread carefully on the hill to dry.

Tina kept giving us facts, which she dug out of a little book she had bought at a fruit seller's stand. "Nepal is eroding away more quickly than any other country in the *world*," she said, reading from page 23. "I can believe it. Look at that hillside. My *God.*" She was silent for a while, then reported, "The infant mortality rate for children under five is *over sixty percent.*" When we pulled off to the side of the road to allow a canvas-covered truck to pass us—coming up, it seemed, from India—"Indian salt is crushed," she said, "but Tibetan salt comes in lumps." Her voice, though rather loud, seemed very soothing, and I listened to her as I fell asleep, to awake and find that it was raining, pouring down in great blinding sheets which turned the road into a river and drenched the little children who stood forlornly on the embankments, holding tins of bright-orange berries in their small brown hands. By then we were above the Trysali River, and when we got to Dumre, if the weather cleared we'd be able to see the mountain. Tina led us in rowdy songs and I moved up and sat beside her, and a crack in the rain clouds showed ribbons of blue and everything fell away.

▲

We slept in a muddy field that night, with the smell of dung all around us, and the next day started walking at last, just walking toward the snows. We were so low at Dumre it was as though we were in the tropics, with banana trees and grass-thatched huts and children naked on tatami mats. The heat was all but overpowering and the endless stone staircases a sort of endless joke. I started sweating that morning and didn't stop for a week and mostly I looked at my feet and not at the astonishing country around me. But I was walking again and nothing else mattered. We moved like a circus through the countryside, traveling jesters for all to see and enjoy. "Expedition or trek?" a tiny porter asked as he passed me. He carried a crate of Coca-Cola and his tumpline was made of reeds. "Expedition," I said. "All memsahibs?" Delighted, he stared and stared.

People always ask you when you started climbing, why you started climbing, how you started climbing, as if there were an answer, as if you could point to a particular piece of rock, argillaceous schist perhaps, something soft and boring, and say, "Oh, I just wanted to go on up." You'd think they'd never perambulated from one place to another without a set of wheels beneath them, you'd think they'd never felt the splendor of motion or the sense that somewhere up ahead there lies an answer. There was one little house that we passed, a house without walls, and in the courtyard a rooster strutted, his comb as red as raspberries. A little boy stood beside him, wearing a short red shirt, and when I saw them—the same size, the same colors—against the hard-packed dirt, hope exploded inside me like a detonation, it started burning slowly at the end of a long string fuse and then began to sizzle and splutter, rushing across the ground, until at last it hit a pile of dynamite and pow, I was alive again and walking, with a million stars dancing me along.

The whole first week was like that. It was like—the only thing I can compare it to is suddenly being in love. Three days into the hills, I picked up an Indian newspaper from a table in a teahouse and almost every report was of a catastrophe—a disaster in which numerical equivalents tried somehow to capture the essence of mortality. You know. "Fifty-one people killed when roof collapses in Delhi" or "Twenty-three dead in train collision" and so on. All of which seemed so absurd, so distant, that I tossed it back on the table with a laugh—who could believe that news had any importance?—and ordered another cup of lemon tea.

Everywhere I turned there were people I *wanted* to look at, people with smiles as open as the sun; no crying children, no wailing, no beating of wives or husbands. And when one night, after an incredibly hot and grubby day during which the monsoon rains had gathered on the horizon like the chorus of a Greek tragedy but never managed to release their water, Tina and I went for a swim in the river, walking across five or six rice paddies to get to a spot where we could be alone and taking off our clothes, seven men appeared from nowhere and stood in a silent, respectful line, waiting for us to emerge. What could we do? We got out of the river as dignified as people on a pilgrimage and the men watched us as we got dressed. Tina was holding back the giggles, and finally she could contain herself no longer and said, to one man—who had been circling around in an effort to get all the best views—the only word she knew in Nepali then, "Ramro," meaning "good."

"Ramro?" She smiled, a foot taller than the man she spoke to, and half again as wide.

"Ramro, ramro," he said reverently, and we climbed back up to the paddy fields, then turned around and waved. They all waved back.

Could I ever have dreaded the smell of the sagebrush? Everything was detail, but detail which revealed itself bit by bit and about which there was consequently no doubt. A baby hung in a square wicker basket from the gable end of a porch. Its kicking rocked the basket, endlessly soothing it. A child clutched a baby owl, nearly strangling it with pride, and offered it to us for five rupees, then four rupees, and finally for just one. In the soft mud outside a village a myriad of animal tracks had been impressed— water buffalo tracks, goat tracks, chicken tracks, pig tracks, and the stamp of bare human feet. The female Sherpas, the Sherpanis, held each other's hands on the path ahead of us, singing in high tinny voices. Three tiny goats, small and gray, with floppy white ears, climbed on a boulder as if they were front-pointing. Except for Tina, I hardly even talked to the members of the team. There would be time enough for that, I thought; for everything. Once when we sat at lunch, high on a bluff above the Marsyandi River, an old man, a Brahman in rags, came, leaning on a stick, to stare regretfully at our spread tablecloth. For twenty or thirty minutes he stood there, not envious, just saddened—old and still puzzled by the mysterious working of life. Once he had had much. Now he had nothing. The packs were so bright, so ingenious, so new. He took up his stick and tiny cloth bundle and walked on. After a time he raised his umbrella and held his bundle behind his back.

It was as if I were back in the sixties again, before I met Nicholas, before I became a well-known climber. Everyone was a flower child here. The wedding processions were marked by the sounds of flutes and drums; women in gold-shot saris washed their clothes on flat wooden benches or bent each other over copper basins, searching hair for lice. The porters bounced up and down as they crossed suspension bridges, making them into roller-coasters or the floor of a fun house. One of the porters—Ram, an ebullient, dashing young kid—wore a T-shirt that read "Never

Trust Anyone Under 8,000 Feet." The grass ran wild on the hillsides.

One night that week, a few days after we reached the hills, Tina and I got into camp much earlier than the rest. We had taken by then to walking together, talking together, being together with unself-conscious ease. Although we aren't really anything alike, the Sherpas thought we were sisters and so did the kids we passed on the trail, and whenever people mistook us like that, we both were as pleased as children. Most of the team had lingered over lunch that day and stopped for some chang in a teahouse, and a lot of the porters had stopped as well. Only the Sherpas had gotten to camp before us. In Ghoropani, Hakpa, our lean and kindly cook, had purchased some chickens for our dinner and they were standing in the field, the rooster's right leg tied to the hen's right leg with a piece of dirty string. They were otherwise untethered. The rooster faced east and the hen faced west and both of them were disgruntled, peeved, especially the rooster. He kept picking up his free leg and putting it back in place, a tiny stomp of disgust. A tree was framed against the small bit of blue sky that still remained in the rapidly clouding canopy, and tendrils of blue smoke were light against the green. None of the tents had arrived yet, so we took a bath in the river, then sat beside the three cook fires, poking the flames with a stick.

Very silent it was, very peaceful. Khanche, one of the porters, sat next to us, smoking a cigarette laced with hash. From somewhere came the smell of wild mint. I felt clean from my bath, tired from my day, and I was thinking—quite remotely, in a way —of my marriage and other things. Scraps of memory came to me, then ripped away and blew off. Being with Tina was like being with a friend from high school; maybe that was it.

You remember how in high school you used to talk endlessly about the most absurdly abstract things? Like would you ever die for a cause, and the wisdom of polyandry? Well, I was recollecting sitting with my best friend in tenth grade, a friend I had totally lost track of in the years that I spent with Nicholas. Not that it was his fault he consumed me; it was mine, my choice, and by then I had little in common with Wendy. But there we were, sitting on the concrete steps of the school building watching the wind blow an ice cream wrapper across the walk. Wendy had gone to California for the summer and met lots of boys, sophisticated boys, that is, not the kind you met in Lander, Wyoming, and we were talking about whether or not we would ever marry someone who wasn't our intellectual equal.

At least, those were the terms I insisted on discussing it in. Wendy, who was very bosomy and had soft red hair that curled under in a pageboy, wanted to discuss whether or not we would marry someone who wasn't our intellectual *superior*, but I wouldn't do that. That was too ridiculous for me to even waste my breath on. After I had made it clear that of course, number one, I was never going to marry anyone at all, I maintained quite stoutly that there was no need for this nonexistent man to be my intellectual equal. He could be as stupid as the day was long and I would marry him anyway if I loved him. That's what women's rights was all *about*. Wendy was doubtful. But I got quite irate, stamping my foot on the pavement with all the fervor of confusion: Did I want to marry anyone quite that stupid? I never had the least patience with even the semi-brights in my high school classes. Finally, we decided that he would have to be better than we were in something, otherwise it would be just too dull. Then we went downtown, I think, and drank root beer floats while Wendy told me about making out on the beach to the sound of the surf with someone who wanted to go "all the way" and told her she had beautiful eyes. I was fascinated, the more so since I had never made out with anyone myself. Anyone, that is, except my brother Ryan.

Not that we ever slept together. Or rather we slept together many times, in beds, in fields, on walls, and slung in hammocks. We watched a lot of dawns and sunsets and smelled the first clean snows of many winters, and often, when it was very cold, we zipped our bags together and slept in each other's arms. We touched each other too, with hands that looked remarkably alike; we studied each other's skin and eyes and infused into our contacts an understanding so complete that it erased the line between all pain and pleasure of the flesh. I don't know when that started; I just know that whatever guilt we felt was merely at our difference from the normal run of men—at our sense that we inhabited a place so special that anyone who knew of it might envy us and wonder what the two of us had done to earn such grace. I got to know my brother's body better than I knew my own and my sensitivity to the slightest touch of his fingers was a sea I floated in, a moon that bathed me in light. Yet the kind of sadness that so often follows unfulfilled desire never overtook us and we could move from such immersion to the clarity of full sun and start off on a climb full of that directed strength which can heal even darker, harder unions. No wonder I'd never made out. Though I was theoretically eager for love, I despaired of ever finding someone other than my brother who liked me and didn't also bore me. Already I was spending all my spare time in the mountains.

Anyway, I was thinking about that—about the fact that when I was young and convinced I was never going to marry, it was, I thought, because I was convinced that I would never meet a stranger I wanted to spend more than two hours at a time with, a man who would not after that become a burden. And in Jackson the year before, just about the time I got the invitation to the expedition, I had had my first affair in seven years of marriage and Beckett and Nicholas were both willing to do almost anything to hold me. All these groupies were hanging around the shop too, wanting my body, I gathered, mainly because they wanted to put another notch in their piton hammer, and I had begun to have again that incredulous, disgusted sense I had had in high school, the sense that I was never going to meet a man who didn't, finally, bore me.

Only now it was more complicated. Because now I was starting to blame myself for it. I felt that I had been continually growing stronger, tougher, more able to cope, and that with every bit of growth I achieved—as a climber, as a seeker of truth—I was making it more and more difficult to stay interested in Nicholas. Not to put too fine a point on it, there were a lot of things that I couldn't respect in him, and I could admit then, though I had been unable to do so in high school, that in the end that was what I wanted—someone I could, if not exactly look up to, at least respect profoundly. I couldn't stop myself from wanting to grow until I almost floated away, yet I felt that really I was cutting the branch I sat on. Because God, how I wanted to love him.

Tina was still sitting beside me, drying her hair and not saying much, and the pressure cooker with the rice in it was letting off periodic bursts of steam. Bundles of wood purchased at a nearby farmhouse were stacked around the embankment we sat on. Hakpa sat beside us and kept hitting my knee with his as he peered across the valley to try and spot the porters with the tents. The pressure of his knee, brown and tight as a drum, was very friendly and reassuring and I tried to bring myself back to the present. I wanted to tell Tina something of what I'd been thinking, but just as I was about to, the first few drops of rain fell. Tina got to her feet then and stretched her arms above her head, and as she stretched, her breasts came tight against her shirt—a lemon-colored shirt with the logo "Climbing is hard, but not as hard as growing up" sketched on it, front and back—and then she sat down with a smile and leaned over and gave me a hug.

When some porters arrived with the tents, the Sherpas all converged on them, eager to get them up before the deluge struck, and then it started to rain, to pour, the skies unloosed and rushing to the ground. The Sherpas got the cook tent up, holding its sides, which flapped wildly in the sudden wind, and before the cook fires could go out—hissing in rage at the great drops which landed among their flames—stretched a tarpaulin over the triple conflagration. Everyone was rushing about and suddenly porters were starting to arrive, pieces of plastic spread over their heads and across the tops of their loads. So I had no chance to speak to Tina, but I didn't think, then, it would matter. I ran for my parka, thinking of all that once had ruled me; no loss if I was done with it for good.

▲

That night it thundered, and lightning reached down to the hills with a hundred forked fingers. In twenty minutes the expedition tents were up, the duffel distributed inside them, the rain flies zipped taut. One of the Sherpas stood by the trail into camp, making sure no one missed it in the deep storm dusk, holding a tall pole in one hand and pointing to the pines with the other, for all the world like a knight guarding the gates to the city or the door of his mistress's chamber. We were now in big country, space so big it swallowed us up, and the Sherpas seemed to feel they had gotten home. A porter, after he dumped his load, did a manic dance in the rain. The Sherpanis were singing from the shelter of their tent and our Sirdar, Tensing, looking very jaunty in his new Gore-Tex parka and his little short-brimmed hat, personally dug the trenches around the tents, staying as clean while he did it as Teflon. No mud would dare attach itself to him.

The storm stopped later in the evening, just as we sat down to dinner on our wicker stools. Hakpa had somehow managed in the torrent of rain to prepare fried chicken, fried potatoes, chicken soup, cauliflower, tomato sauce, dalbhat (a kind of lentil slush), and, if you can believe it, cake, and six Sherpas carried the food in, giggling, while Hakpa hovered behind them, his expression serious and intent until we burst into applause and everyone went off to eat, happy as so many kings.

What with the long day and the rain, there was little talk for a while. We addressed ourselves to our food. Some cups bobbed on the guy lines of the tent and we watched them as if they were the evening's entertainment. Then some Manangi traders arrived on ponies and they rode by the dining tent, showing off their horsemanship and good looks. They were all wearing Western-style clothing—blue jeans and baseball caps—and some of them had radios hanging on straps around their shoulders. Their ponies were dressed as if for a circus, heavy with bells, glittering with mirrors, fringed with purple and pink plumes. We watched them —they were better than cups—and after dinner Naomi and Tina got rides, Tina from sheer giggles, Naomi partly to show off her ass. Some of the traders spread out tarpaulins at the edge of the field, next to the last of the climbers' tents. Margaret, who had been in Nepal for three months now, long enough to know exactly what is worth paying for, dickered for an hour over the purchase of a whole set of old brass horse bells set on a worn leather collar. Robin, though she didn't buy anything, looked over a couple of prayer wheels and some small wooden rice bowls with ill-fitting lids.

In the middle of the night we were awakened. A piercing scream brought me bolt upright—and then a couple of shouts, running feet and tent flaps being unzipped kept me there. Robin had requested a single tent that night and apparently had sat in the doorway combing her hair before she went to bed. So naturally one of the traders had got ideas and came back and stuck his hand inside her sleeping bag and squeezed one of her breasts. She woke the whole camp with her scream.

The next morning she was quite embarrassed. After all, she's a married woman, with two children at home; she's had her breast squeezed before. She didn't talk much at breakfast; she seemed to think that screaming bloody murder the night before had proved to us all without hope or mistake that she would never become a great climber. Of course, later that proved to be true, but everyone went out of her way that morning to cheer Robin up, to say that they would have done exactly the same thing in her place. Naomi joked good-humoredly that if she were Robin, she'd sue, that was all, she'd take the trader to small-claims court —Robin has very small breasts—and at least come out ahead by a prayer wheel, a pack of cigarettes, a rug. The pun set us to laughing, and even Robin managed to smile. We set off that morning with more fellow feeling than we'd had before, thinking we were over the hump. Everyone was happy, hopeful, eager; and the next day, we saw the mountain at last.

The tropical climate of the lowlands had given way to a colder, leaner air. But we were still ten days away from base camp, a straggling, slow crusade, and we had not yet had a really clear morning greet us from the north, where the morning sky normally looked like the anatomy of a storm, laid out as in a child's primer. So I was unprepared when Pasang, waking us with hot wash water, added to his perennial cheerful "Good *morning*, memsahib"— the good morning not of a nurse to a difficult patient but of one incarnate soul to another, as if the morning that we shared must inevitably make us one—the news that the sky was clear and the mountain could be seen. I bolted out of the tent in nothing but my long johns.

At first I could see only the thin blue sky, the distant hills, the great green bowl around us. Then, in the far distance, form emerged, like an image coming up from silver-treated paper, a line of white like a wave rising from the sea, ethereal, transitory, vulnerable to the touch of a finger—the mountain, our mountain, the mountain I had come to find. Beyond the mountain a cloud hovered, a long lenticular cloud that didn't touch the summit but stood above the stillness of its upper reaches, a ghost cloud waiting, like me, to be sucked back in to the spell of the mountain, by the incantation of dreams. And though Nicholas entered my thoughts, and Ryan, and I remembered a hundred climbs when I had roped with them, racking the hardware as neatly as a palette of colors, the memory was as vaporous as the cloud beyond the mountain and I felt—if I felt anything at all—that I was glad to be alive, fiercely glad, triumphantly glad, even if they were dead. If I had ever told myself that I would climb the mountain only because they would have wanted me to, only, in fact, in memory of them, I could retract that tale

now as nothing but the treachery of guilt and admit that I was
climbing the mountain for no one but myself, because one
morning long ago I had risen in the Tetons before dawn when
the sun was a golden censer over a sharp horizon, and the ridge
lay just below it, a white place waiting to be marked.

THE GLACIER

Eight

The autumn we bought the shop, it rained a lot. Somehow we had managed to survive our first two years. Mainly because we'd started climbing with Orion, and Ryan always healed us, like a wash of herbal balm. He'd been promoted twice already, and had gotten a job in design, and he was making lots of money, which he wanted to lend to us. I think he thought that buying the shop would root us; but right from the start, the shop was a big mistake. After we finally opened for business, Nicholas used to come home from working tight as a fist, smiling and outlining some incredibly trivial detail of planning that had assumed magnificent proportions in his mind while he served a customer or went through the stock lists. Suddenly his whole life would fall into place like the sections of an orange around this central, ragged point of reality —which was, say, advertising the shop in the Casper paper, or getting the brake drums on the van reground before the week was out. If these things were not done instantly—faster than instantly —all other plans we had made were worthless, might as well be scrapped. But he had no time, no time, that was always the problem—and so he expected *me* to produce instant action on this thing, whatever it was, which was important only to him and only because it represented the potential for a real completion in a world where no completion satisfied him ever. Except a well-driven piton. Except a graceful move. When I declined to act—

when I put it off—when I showed anything but instant and wholehearted agreement—he would take out his frustrations on me, threatening that since this too would have to be done by him, this too, in addition to all the other details of his life, my own cherished dreams would never come to pass. We wouldn't be able to try a new route on Mount Owen that weekend; he'd be too busy fixing the brake drum. He claimed that I wanted to keep him from climbing. He controlled me by his disdain.

Well, it wasn't really disdain. It was, I think, a kind of world-weary ennui, an ability to negate our relationship totally by a word. After a fight, an argument, even a disagreement, when I would be in the process of repairing the rent, examining the cause of the explosion, I might say, "You tend to put words in my mouth, Nicholas," or some equally universal lament, and he would say, "Well, you won't have to worry about that anymore," in his mind already halfway to the airport, and it transformed me in an instant from someone trying once again to analyze the nature of a relationship she was not in her heart convinced was a good one, to someone determined at all costs to hold on to that relationship. He was always so damned ready to take off; it made me determined to prevent him. To discount our relationship that easily—to say, at every possible opportunity, "So long"—every ounce of stubbornness I possessed would be marshaled against his casual dismissal. He talked about "picking up his own life once more," as if it were something he had dropped along the trail somewhere and had now to go back and get, something that was by its very nature invisible to me, a piece of equipment too specialized for me to understand, which, had he had it with him all along, would have made it impossible for us ever to be together at all, his own life being unarguably male, a backpack that, once he shrugged into it, held him incommunicado, a mystery behind a lead-lined fence. His favorite phrase at such moments: "It's as simple as that—you're comparing me to your brother . . . it's as simple as that—we just can't get along," used to stop me dead, as if I had in fact come up against that lead-lined wall, smack, so hard my nose grew white. Perhaps I *was* comparing him to my brother. My brother, at least, believed in choice. After my father's death, one night when my mother was sobbing, he took out a frying pan and started to cook, though he'd never cooked before; and if it wasn't the best meal I'd ever eaten, at least it wasn't watered by tears. But Nicholas believed in destiny, and most of what made him impossible stemmed from that simple fact.

I see now, of course, that Nicholas's blunt hammer of sudden judgment was simply a powerful tool, and that without realizing what he was doing, he pitted his contempt against my obdurateness and held me that way by the bonds of my own personality. It's a good technique, when you think about it, a technique that bears a marked resemblance to giving someone a rope long enough to hang himself. How long a rope does that take, after all? Not one hundred and fifty feet of kernmantel, that's for sure. One rather threadbare six-foot length of clothesline will do the job quite nicely. And he had it—"I'm leaving, it's as simple as that" —and would hand it to me regularly, returning with one toss the sum total of that insignificant, contemptible affair which was, it seemed, our partnership. Until I fell at his feet in tears once more. And we went on.

Still. I don't know if this makes sense, but I continue to think of a lot of the fights Nicholas and I had as nothing but pure release. Not our earliest fights, of course; but later, after I had started to learn the subtle rules of our warfare, it seemed to me that one of the great strengths of my relationship with Nicholas was that he made it possible for me to express my own anger without having to feel guilty about it later. I suppose in a way I have always confused excitement with happiness and seen catharsis as a prime ingredient for joy.

So the autumn we bought the shop, it rained a lot. Nicholas was sick, he had got the flu, caught it from me, in fact. I had been laid up in bed for two days while he did the work around the house and gave me precious little sympathy. He didn't believe I was really ill, I suppose, largely because he himself was healthy as a

horse and he thought that if it were a *serious* flu bug he would
catch it from me. Well, finally he did. And he spent three days
in bed, not two, and moaned with frustration at the fact that life
was passing him by. Having been vindicated anyway by the viru-
lence of his sickness, I could afford to be kind to him and brought
him orange juice and water, aspirin and magazines, with a metro-
nomic regularity. By the end of the third day I was getting a little
bored with this, as he seemed to all appearances to be quite
recovered, and I told him I was going out for the evening, to
spend some time in the library and maybe stop in at the bar.

Well, that set it off. He didn't want to be left alone. He wanted
me to stay and talk to him. He felt a lot better. Maybe we could
even make love. Or if not, we could read together. Orion was
coming up soon. Shouldn't we decide what we wanted to do when
he arrived? Nicholas used every means at his disposal to get me
to stay with him, entirely missing the point that what I needed
was some time alone. So it built, as such things do. Didn't he
appreciate all I'd done while he was sick? I said. Couldn't I see
that just this once he really wanted me to stay? he replied. Back
and forth it went, increasing in volume and exasperation until
finally, when he said something about the fact that if I did go out
I could certainly forget about making love when I got back—he
would be much too tired then, probably asleep—I said, "Well,
fuck you, Nicholas. What ever gave you the idea I wanted to make
love with you anyway?" And I finished by giving him the finger.

I was standing in the doorway of the room and he was lying
back on the bed, pillows propped behind him. As I started to turn
my back on him he reached for the nearest object at hand, which
happened to be a glass bottle of ointment, and, his face contorted
by rage, threw it as hard as he could onto the floor at my feet.
It was a very thick glass bottle and instead of breaking it bounced
and when it bounced landed right on top of my unshod foot,
hitting it just between two of the thin bones that run back from
the toes. It hurt like hell; and though it was perfectly evident to
me that Nicholas had not tried to hit me, that the bounce was

purely accidental, and equally evident that he was in a danger- ously uncontrolled state of mind, filled with the peevish self-pity of a convalescing invalid, I felt at that moment that it was neces- sary for me to return blow for blow, that if I let him get away with such things there would be no end to them. Stupid as hell on my part; I actually managed to convince myself—in the four seconds I stood motionless before I stooped to pick up the bottle—that it would be better for both of us if I drew the line right there. So without really wanting to, but feeling a kind of weird responsi- bility to myself and to him, I tossed the bottle back at him, aiming for the covers on the far side of the bed.

Naturally, I missed. Had I been trying for the most excruciating return I could arrange, I couldn't have done better. I hit him right smack in the middle of the shin. With a howl of rage he threw back the covers and came at me, wearing only the bottom of a pair of string-tie pajamas. He hit me on the arm, his fist bunched together like a knot of rope, and though I hadn't really been angry before, I got angry then, and unloosed myself on him like the Furies. A shadow of fright crossed his face. He hadn't realized I was going to be in *this* kind of mood, the totally no-holds-barred mood that came over me, rarely but definitively, when I didn't feel like messing around with words. He wasn't sure he was up to it, obviously. He was still a little bit sick, after all. But it was too late and he saw it was too late, so he decided to make the best of it.

That mood I was in then, it was the same mood, really, that came over me last fall when Nicholas, in a weary, halfhearted attempt to even up the score between us, told me he had invited one of our friends, a female friend, to go climbing with him for the weekend and I found out to my absolute astonishment that I was an intensely jealous woman. I shouted to him at the top of my lungs that if he did, I was going to cut his balls off with a rusty knife, and all I felt about my own behavior was a kind of detached interest—like the kind of interest I felt when I took off my boot in Ghoropani and found it full of blood, discovering thus my first leech and the ease with which it had joined me—that I was, in fact, *that* kind of woman, and not, as I had fairly consistently imagined, the other kind. Well, the mood then was the same, though the astonishment was not present. I *knew* I was not the other kind when it came to a physical fight, and I punched him back on the arm as hard as I possibly could.

But you know, we never really lost it, Nicholas and I. Not then. Not ever. He hit me on the arm, I hit him on the arm—but he never broke my jaw, I never kneed him in the balls; even at our most unhinged we never lost it that much. I never feared him physically, which is perhaps another way of saying that deep down I trusted him with my life. And I could see, even as he brought his fist down on my shoulder, that he was holding back his force as much as he was releasing it; it was a perfect study in kinetic and potential energy. In fact, he looked as if he were about to explode from the conflict, the conflict between the desire to just once really let me have it, slap me around until we were both quite black and blue, and the desire to protect me from harm, even harm that was channeling straight through him. He shoved me against the wall and I kicked him in the shin; we tumbled through the doorway into the living room, where I grabbed his ear and tried to twist it off. He stuck his thumb into my neck and I beat down on his back. We were both panting, audibly, and had our teeth clenched tight, and I was well aware of the way we would appear to a sudden, startled visitor—like two people who were totally out of control.

But we weren't, not at all. I tripped over a chair and picked it up and held Nicholas off with it. When he wrested it away, I managed to pick up another chair and break it against a wall. At that, Nicholas kicked the wall with his foot so that there were two holes in it, one foot-sized and the other the size of a chair leg. His hole seemed much more significant than mine and that impelled me to try and slap his face, though it was a struggle to overcome my own reluctance to really hurt him. As a consequence, the slap was very light and ineffective. But it was enough to give him the excuse to slap my face, and he brought his hand up and then down across my jaw. It was a very feeble blow for so strong a man, but I managed to squeeze everything out of it that I could and spun around with the violence of the assault, letting it knock me to the floor, onto which I fell like an uprooted tree, landing half on the carpet and half across the hard edge of a couch. The next day, when I examined myself for permanent wounds, the only bruise I had was on my arm, where a great patch of blue beneath the elbow marked the spot which had come into contact with the couch, a contact I could easily have avoided had I not desired to fling myself to the floor.

All those feelings, gone forever, wherever feelings go. After hauling myself to my feet and daring Nicholas to come after me, I put on my parka and stormed from the house. A light snow was falling and the limpid circles of lamplight were caressing. I climbed halfway up Snow King that night, and with each step I took above the town I felt more and more pure, as if a clean rain had washed right through me, as if I were almost light enough to float to the top. Halfway up the mountain, I stopped and looked down on the glow of the lamps from the town below, rising through the mist of falling snow like smoke. After great effort, purity descends. Words, spoken or thought, are euphonious as temple bells and the shadows that fall from the trees lie on the ground like purple velvet. When I got home, we didn't talk, but pulled the quilt, tiny roses and baby's breath, over us, and opened the window wide. When I tried to explain how I felt, Nicholas shushed me. We made love into the small hours of the night.

So part of my love for him was all that. The part that was easiest to be sure of. The part that required no effort, from me or from him. And part of it was that he could always make me laugh. Not that he always bothered or found it possible to try. But though a lot of people thought Nicholas was a somber man, he could laugh as deeply and as freely as he could cry and for as little cause. He had an innocence about him, an innocence which was, per-haps, born of never having felt shame. In high school I knew a girl, the daughter of a very wealthy rancher, and something about being born so rich gave her a quality of innocence. It wasn't as if she had never suffered, no, not that, but as if she had never felt shame, as if there were no reason in the world for her to suspect herself of being bad. And Nicholas, though he was ten times more paranoid of authority than the average person—if you could judge by the lengths he went in order to avoid exposure to it—was paranoid somehow not because he felt he had ever done anything wrong, but because it was so incredible to him, it outraged him so much, that he had once or twice been unfairly accused.

But the point, I suppose, is that he figured anything he had ever done had been justified at the time; he could have acted no differently, ever, than he had. So although he suffered many kinds of torments, he never suffered guilt. And that was extraordinary to me, miraculous, if often infuriating. It may have been the reason our fights so often ended as they did, with me at his feet in tears, but it was also the reason he could always make me laugh. In me, guilt has always been ready at hand. If a policeman were to accost me and accuse me of any monstrous thing, there would be a moment, I know, an endless sickening moment before I could deny the charge, hotly calling down vituperation on his head—and that moment would exist because I would know quite well that, whatever it was he accused me of, under some circumstances, given the right conditions, I would be quite capable of doing it. The fact that I had *not* done it would seem to me, in a way, accidental.

I don't know if you can understand this, really. But I've always been aware, ever since I can remember, that I was not a really *good* person, that I didn't have the proper instincts, to help and to love, to give. And though I've always liked myself anyway and made a certain defiance part of my self-image, I have also been afraid of this non-goodness, afraid of the things I might do. Once when I was a child and we passed an accident on the highway, an accident around which twenty or thirty people had already gathered, I slumped down in my seat and hid on the floor of the car lest I accidentally catch even one brief glimpse of blood or death, going so far as to cover my eyes with my hands and press down on the eyeballs so hard that I saw lights in six different wallpaper patterns, one after another in quick succession. I didn't know why at the time, of course. Later I thought it was because *I* wasn't about to become like those others, gawkers, hangers-on at tragedies, sickening shallow people who probably gossiped at home night and day. But it was really because I was so scared of what I might find in myself. What if I liked what I saw on the highway? What if I wanted to poke at the blood? Every time I read about something just too horrible to think about—the Indians flaying a man alive, for example—I would be so absolutely repulsed ("How *could* they do such a thing, how *could* they be human and do it?") that I never allowed myself to answer my own question nor to see that my horror had an element of fascination. Though most people are like that, I have since discovered, and a lot of kindness results from the fear of being cruel.

But Nicholas—he was such an innocent. He had so much blackness, but it was not that kind. He was never purposely cruel. And since nothing came from malice, the deep wells of his love were never muddied by doubt. So when he was feeling strong he could make me laugh until I gasped for breath. And when he was feeling tender I felt as safe as a trumpet in its case. A week after he had recovered from the flu we went to climb Mount Owen and I had a relapse, and when we got up for the climb before dawn I was so tired, just burned out, that I couldn't stop yawning. Nicholas had already gotten the coffee and the oatmeal made, but when he saw the way I felt he took his fingers and put them on my eyelids and closed them, not even talking, just making it clear the mountain could wait. And he had no patience, remember; things never happened soon enough for him. Or when I flew back to Jackson from my visit to Orion in Santa Fe, and I got off the plane totally grubbed and spaced and he was waiting for me with a bunch of flowers, holding them in his hand like a banner. He thought that was what you did, you understand, to show a woman you loved her. Give her flowers. But it wasn't the flowers. It was the way his hand was wrapped around them. If a policeman had ever stopped *him* and accused him of monstrous acts, he wouldn't have paused for a second. He didn't have that tiny tickle of guilt.

But he carried, in a way, the burden of excessive sensibility. He was capable of so much feeling, such passion, such attachment to the moment of pain or ecstasy, and he didn't admit that to himself, except to try and control it, to try and keep it from harming him. Which was futile from the start, more than futile, because it was never the burden of such sensibility that caused him pain—in the realm of emotion, really, nothing is ever laid on you heavier than you can bear—but the degree of his refusal to accept responsibility for that burden, to accept that he was not a simple gunslinging cowboy but a man who was unusually sensitive to the potential for purity in life. He was confused by that potential, the way everyone is confused. He loved to read history, where truth is laid out on a platter like a series of slices of ham, and he, as much as any of us, had imbibed the basic tenet of science on which most modern life is based, that truth is somehow absolute, if elusive. So the ever-changing nature of the truths he sensed, with the deep sensibility he did not admit to, was something that frightened him so much he never even let it past the door to his mind. And the pain he felt was really from that rejection, a self-inflicted wound. I tried to explain that to him again and again. He just looked at me like *I* was the crazy one.

But Nicholas never had much faith in words. To him, I think, life was so much more *real* than the words we use to describe it and his feelings far more complex and comprehensive than the sad little bundle of sounds we use to try and contain them. If the language had as many words for love as the Eskimos do for snow, then we might perhaps be getting closer to the core of things. As it is, though, hell—how does "happiness," for example, relate to the reality of days? How does "hate" suppose it can support the flux that drives it?

And Nicholas saw that. Or rather he did not see it, but he let it rule him, so that feelings came and went across his life like wind across the surface of a lake, undefined, uncaught, unrecognized and then gone. And maybe that's why he was no ripe field for guilt, because what is unperceived when it occurs simply does not exist, and when he tried to look back upon his life, few moments of passion stood out as different from all the rest, and his inability to connect experience with the words that attempt to describe it was not unlike the inability to connect acts with their consequences and had a flattening effect upon his past. His mountains, once climbed, sank down to sea level, and the whole of his thirty-one years became, in memory, a long undistinguished plain of sand. And from that grew a frustration as profound as that of any unhappy child who, living so fully in the present, cannot imagine a future in which the present will be past. No matter how many mountains he climbed, he had never climbed enough. But the funny thing is that once I started meditating, I began to see that Nicholas, far more than any books or meditations, had been in fact my teacher and lived always heartbreakingly near the edge of true enlightenment.

True enlightenment. And what is that? It's something, clearly, that cannot be seen until you're upon it, but according to the dharma, the path to it is marked at the beginning with the determination to admit our emptiness—to admit that all our feelings, multitudinous and variegated though they may be, are nothing but desperate attempts to prove to ourselves that we exist, and that suffering is perhaps the most efficient way to do it. So when I began my study of the dharma, I realized that the very intensity of the emotions that Nicholas aroused in me and that he lived with was perhaps the greatest gift he could have brought me, since I had seen the faces of both love and hate as fully as any person ever could and also seen the emptiness that follows them. It's like giving up cigarettes by smoking them till you're sick—and there are people whose function in life is to force you to smoke them, locking you into a room until you retch and retch and finally are drained.

I tried to tell that to Tina, when the storm was all around us. She told me at the end, though, I should climb the mountain alone.

Nine

It was after we actually saw the mountain that we really started to come together as a team. The hills were getting higher, the gorges deeper, the hillsides far more steep. Little villages would pop out at night like fireflies from the woods above us and in the daytime we passed through settlements built around and between granite boulders as large as the houses they sheltered. Ancient trees were chopped down for firewood and every bit of arable land was under cultivation, although the corn looked poor and sickly and often the terraces were washed away. Sometimes we came to pine forests that reminded me of the Wind Rivers of Wyoming, while the great sweeping curves of the Marsyandi—growing tougher and stringier as it retreated to its source—seemed to bring the nine of us together in common cause, giving us a familiar setting around which to stage our evening meetings and to organize our acquaintance. In the evenings we talked about climbing, past and future, until Naomi left the campfire with one or another of the Sherpas, and Margaret and Taffy Anderson—who were friends, I gathered, even before Taffy's newspaper had sent her to Katmandu—went off to talk together, and then Dervla would tell us stories, her enormous wide gaping smile gleaming in the dusk so brightly you almost felt she had caught beauty from her beautiful black husband. She plied Sibyl, the one full-time adventurer among us, with questions about the Amazon country, where she hoped someday to study, and Sibyl told us about crossing the Sahara with camels. Robin played the flute, her long blond braid hanging all the way to the ground. Sometimes Tina and I went bouldering after dinner and when we came back we sat and stared for a while at the coals of the fire, which looked like phosphorescent paint on the bottom of the pot that rested in their midst.

One evening it was raining out, cold and stormy, and we sat around the dining tent quite late. Tensing kept popping his head through the flap like a worried mother to see if there was anything we needed, and the Coleman lantern had to be adjusted several times by the porter who lurked outside waiting for just that necessity. With the heat of the lantern and nine large bodies, it was very cozy and some of us dragged our ensolites in to lie on. We were talking about climbing, of course, and after the usual quota of personal anecdotes—most of them tales of disaster—Tina said she had always found it strange that most of the metaphors people assign to mountaineering are warlike ones. People talk about an expedition as a siege, a thrust, an assault, a penetration, though actually the reason a lot of people go climbing is that they can achieve on a mountain an intimacy, a kinship, a cessation of the competitive that they can't find in many other places today. So of course Naomi drawled, "Except in a war," and Tina got very excited trying to explain that it was *different* from war, because it didn't involve any killing, that the only thing that was at risk was *you.* And Margaret, partly to avert an argument and partly because she had obviously thought of it before, said:

"Of course, those metaphors aren't exclusive to either mountaineering *or* warfare; indeed, they simply reflect the Western conception of reality."

Well, we talked about that for a while and the fact that yes, there was no getting away from it, on the face of it climbing a mountain did seem a perfect symbol for the kind of logicality that admits no boundaries, that it reflected an almost childlike belief in progress, the idea that there is a long, thin line of time leading in one direction, into the golden age of the future, where all happiness is found. At least, most of it did. Robin seemed to be dozing, and Laurie was reading Messner's book on Everest. She's such a fanatic that she doesn't just read mountaineering books when she can't be in the mountains; she even reads them while she's climbing. And I was feeling so good, so absolutely *there*, that I never wanted the evening to end and started wishing that we didn't have to climb the mountain at all but could just stay warm and cozy in that dining tent forever, getting to know each other and proving, to ourselves at least, that summits are not the important thing, the important thing is starting toward them. After a while, everyone left except Tina, Naomi and me; for once Naomi had decided not to sleep with one or another of the Sherpas, which made me feel uncharacteristically fond of her, and really quite at peace.

The next morning we all woke early, full of renewed vigor. The rain had stopped overnight; the mountain was in sight. The breakfast porridge was thicker than usual—Hakpa had outdone himself, with that and with a kind of white-bread cake, iced in playful curlicues of peanut butter and jam—but we hardly had time to enjoy it in peace, as everyone seemed especially eager to be off. The Rai porter who carried most of the wicker stools settled himself about five feet from the table, eyeing the stools as hungrily as if they too were edible, and the moment anyone stood up, he whisked her seat away before it had time to cool off, and tossed it onto his load.

As usual, the cook crew had taken off even before we sat down to breakfast—all except Pasang, who waited at a good distance until he was sure we were finished, then deferentially gathered up the remaining pots and pans, the teakettles and the serving trays. When his basket was packed, only two frying pans protruded from the neatly tied rope that held the load in place, and he slipped the tumpline around his head and set off quickly so as to reach the lunch site before any of the expedition members. But

Tina and I followed him and with us came Ang Nima, who had been deputized by Tensing that day to be the "Membars' " mother hen and make sure that none of us got lost or mugged or ran away.

I was beginning to feel a great security in being with the Sherpas, the confidence that comes from spending time with people who do not expect from you anything but what you can give, who accept you as the person you are and do so because they have a wholeness themselves, an air of being rooted firmly in the present moment, able to deal calmly with anything that moment may reveal. We walked along in happy silence, and when after an hour or two of walking we all stopped at a stone chutora to rest, setting our packs on the slabs beneath a pipal tree, Tina and I picked up the Sherpas' loads and set off up the trail. By the time the Sherpas realized we were not planning to turn around and come back, they had to move fast to catch up with us, wearing *our* packs—and had difficulty doing so, since apparently the spectacle of two memsahibs struggling with baskets was so ridiculous that they were convulsed with laughter, which made them weak in the knees.

"Buyhini, buyhini!"—"Little sister!" cried Ang Nima piteously. After they got their baskets back, they were careful not to let them go again and soon had left us behind.

After that we went more slowly, wandering up a long series of stone steps, grateful when for an interval the trail turned into sandy soil, easy on the boots and feet. We passed a porter carrying a load of great square tin cans which banged rhythmically together when he walked and from which issued the sultry, heavy smell of oil. A startled water buffalo, tethered very tightly against the wall of his byre, looked up at the porter, aghast. A Gurung woman, dark and intense and wearing a flower-shaped stud in the side of her nose and a ring through her septum, seemed absolutely astonished at the looming height of Tina and stared at her open-mouthed until we vanished from her sight. But some dark young men dressed in Western clothes showed off their sophistication by saying from the coolness of a porch:

"Do you have any medicine for headaches? What is the time now? I love you!" not pausing for any answers, not even to the last remark, but calling after us as we left them, "Thank you. Bye-bye!"

We were getting into Buddhist country now. Villages had prayer wheels set into their entry gates, and chortens, small and white, were set on windy corners of the trail. Prayer flags were stuck beneath the slats of fences and above the thatch of roofs, and the incenselike smell of burning juniper lingered above the villages. A boy picked large fresh mushrooms and placed them in his cap. Hand-axed boards as wide as king's boards were drying in stacks held down by large white rocks. Tibetan traders coming from Manang rode by on horseback, shouting and laughing to one another; almost everyone who passed us asked simply, "Manang?" meaning were we heading in that direction, and we said just, "Manang." A bevy of girls, beautifully dressed in a rainbow of colors, called out, "Chocolate, chocolate?" and the boldest smiled in my face. But when Tina said gaily, "No chocolate," they didn't seem disappointed, but went off smiling as if they had never really wanted chocolate at all, did not in fact know what it was. Chocolate, medicine—perhaps they are worth a try, but in the end the Nepalese will settle quite happily for wild mint, dung plasters and the clouds beyond the mountains. Even the Brahman who stood so sadly by our luncheon cloth was not beset by greed—only by wonder, at the way in which life overtakes you and the limitations with which it rules your days.

Sometimes I think that having too many choices is the curse of our civilization. I've never felt so sorry for myself, or so bereft, as when I could clearly perceive the multitudinous tangle of paths that sliced the future. The Nepalese don't have to think about those paths. They eat rice and lentils three times a day and they put on the same white sneakers with the same shiny bottoms every morning of their lives until the sneakers wear out, and then they step from them as easily as a bird steps from a nest and leave them behind on the smooth stone steps. It isn't so much that simplicity brings happiness as that it allows clear-sightedness. When you have only ten possessions, you have so much more freedom to see past them to something else; and if you don't have to take responsibility for the appearance of those possessions, all the better, because you don't have to make your expression match theirs and your face has only two aspects, eagerness and repose.

It's like—when I am in Jackson and walk down the street. I keep my shoulders squared and sometimes mince when I walk, my eyes straight ahead, because I don't want people to see me. But in Nepal when we first got to the hills I never felt like an egregious woman, a dancing girl, a clown, a whore. That's what the mountains do for you anyway, of course, make you feel just like yourself, as simple as a candle flame, and there, even though the hills are as full of people as Jackson ever was, it's all right, because it's the same for all of them, the path to the mountain has been laid out for the last six hundred years and the long brown legs that move in front of you as you climb it—purple cloth shot with gold thread falling loosely around the knees—are so firmly muscled because they have gone up and down that mountain path every day, twice a day, since they were old enough and strong enough to support their body and a copper pot of water as well. But there it is. In the West, the very first time you eat outside your house, you're handed a menu that's bigger than you are. No wonder you're confused from that time forward, and walk down the street like a whole parade.

Well, somehow, what with this and that, Tina and I missed lunch that day. Though everywhere we walked there were people walking with us, the villages were growing more widely scattered and as the morning went on, the trail at times was carved from the rock of a sheer cliff; far below it, the green river wound across pebbles and clean white sand. There were lizards about, large lizards with yellow spots on their backs and bluish-purple legs, flushed as if by some strange alchemy. The butterflies were black and yellow, mottled, and flew with their wings sharply canted. Because of the growing steepness of the terrain, the trail now followed a wandering course and we crossed the river several times as we got higher into the hills. One suspension bridge was very long and fairly rotten and Tina and I hurried across it along with several goats who were going the same way we were. The smell of the goats was so strong and the sound of the river so loud that we neither heard nor smelled the preparations for lunch there on the other side, and by the time we realized that lunch must be behind us, we had gained more than two thousand feet of elevation. Since neither of us had any desire to lose them again, we went on.

Whether it was the effect of the higher elevation or the effect of desperate hunger or simply the effect of walking with Tina, I don't know, but as we walked, the day acquired a hallucinatory quality. Tina, because we had missed lunch, was sure that we were lost and asked everyone we passed whether we were on the road to Tal. Of course, everyone said, "Yes, yes, to Tal," and finally Tina began to see the humor of this and when a very sophisticated and bored-looking Japanese man laden with cameras passed us, she said to him, "What's the name of the place we're going to, again?" then went off into gales of laughter when he said politely, "Tal," as did I, clutching my stomach to keep from falling down.

Before long we were laughing at everything we saw: a little girl, saucy and showing off, who said "Hello," then tripped over her plastic thong sandal; several men carrying enormous bundles of greenery down from the hills, looking like moving trees to which had been attached small hands and feet and buttons; three women in saris, twirling parasols, who looked so cool and clean and pleased with themselves that they might, as Tina said, have been going to a presidential inauguration. Finally, too weak to laugh anymore, I told Tina to walk in front of me so that I could look at her boots.

"Perhaps," I said, "they will have a sobering effect," and even that seemed hysterically funny, so that by the time we got to Tal we were total wrecks and collapsed into the first teahouse we came to, where we ordered whatever was ready—which turned out to be dhalbat so heavily spiced it made our eyes water, and lemon tea so strong it looked and tasted like pee.

Some cuckoo birds outside the teahouse were letting loose their songs with vigor. Tears running down her face, Tina said, "Somehow I keep taking the cuckoos' message more and more *personally*, Temis," and if we'd not been sitting on the floor we would have fallen there, where we remained, in stitches, until a young girl wandered in.

The girl was dressed in rags. Her face was dirty and her hair was matted and her eyes in her face were as bright and happy and alive as a pair of bluebirds winging in the sun. She had the dark curly hair of the Manangi and the light coloration and pink cheeks that make those people so lovely. She was electrifyingly beautiful, no more than seven years old, and with an absolute lack of self-consciousness she walked over to where I was sitting cross-legged on a woven rug and began to touch my face and body, to play with the toggles on my wind pants and the Velcro on my sleeves. Although she had a bad wet cough that racked her periodically, she took no notice of it at all, simply went on learning how toggles worked and caressing my barrettes with wondering hands. She played with Tina too, but soon came back to me, untying my boot, then tying it up again.

After a while the woman who ran the teahouse spoke to her sternly, ordering her to be gone. Disappointed, she turned toward the door, then looked back at me, her eyes so full of invitation that I told Tina I was taking a walk, and got up too, and followed the girl to the street, holding the hand that she proffered. When we came to the smallest and leakiest house in town, she drew me inside it, conspiratorial, and once my eyes got accustomed to the dimness I saw that it was full of children and one lean woman with pendulous breasts who sat at a loom, weaving. Baskets of unwashed, untreated wool sat on a chest with an old-fashioned iron padlock, above which hung a yak harness and a bundle of folded blankets. On the wooden bed next to the chest were pillows and more blankets and on the floor lay a beautiful though

very worn Tibetan rug with orange and pink flowers in its center
and a geometric scarlet mazelike border. At one end of the house
a fire burned on the floor. Four thin straw mats lay beside it.
Other than these fairly meager furnishings, the house contained
only a huge sack of rice leaning against a pillar and a smaller
basket of rice with a heavy cup inside it for a dipper.

The girl, oblivious of her mother's disapproving stare, led me
over to the bed and sat me down upon it. The other children
clustered around me, but she was always the one that sat nearest,
and eventually she climbed right up into my lap. She didn't say
a word, although she made small mewing sounds and although the
other children, delighted at my unexpected advent, brought over
several tattered schoolbooks, intent on teaching me in an hour
their language and its splendid manifestations on the page. When
I asked each child's name he or she was ready enough with the
answer, but when I asked my lapmate hers she just looked puzzled, and it was one of the other children who said, "Lyti."
"Lyti?" I asked her, pointing to her chest. She nodded solemnly,
then broke again into her enormous breathtaking smile and
squirmed around on my lap.

I've never been what one might call maternal. Children tend
to frighten me or disgust me or simply, often, bore me. But
holding that little girl on my lap was like holding, not a child, but
a lover. I leaned my face against her hair, breathing in the slightly
acrid smell of her scalp, and rested my palms against her small
round legs as if I was touching the source of all my happiness. For
almost an hour we sat together quite contented while the other
children came and went and Tina popped her head through the
door to say hello and Ang Nima, who had finally realized that we
had missed lunch, came running into Tal with our food in a small
tin pail.

I shared mine with the girl, not that she ate much. But colors
and shapes and textures delighted her, and the challenge of deter-
mining how things were put together and how they came apart.
By the time the main body of the expedition arrived in town, the

girl and I were inseparable and we went together to watch the tents being put up. When Tina's duffel bag arrived, Tina took from it a set of watercolor paints, which she gave to the girl to play with, so after the dining tent was up we found some paper and went in there, and I taught her how to mix water with the paint and apply it to the paper. Entranced, she sat at the table until dinnertime, filling page after page of my notebook with bursts of color and lines and spirals, never repeating a pattern.

What a bright kid she was! And with a physical presence as powerful as any adult's. But still she did not speak and it slowly began to dawn on me that she was set apart in some way from the other children—not just by that lack of speech but by her clothing also, because no matter how poor a family may be in Nepal, they always manage to dress their children in colors and deck their arms with bangles, and this girl was all in black, as thick and dusty as a tent. Yet she moved like an actress, wrapping the shawl around her head and peering out from under it, draping it across her shoulders like a piece of mink, trailing it from one finger like a queen on her way to an assignation. When Pasang came in to lay the table for dinner, I took her to my tent with me, and left her there with Tina while I went to find Tensing and ask him if he would look into her story.

He did. He told me she was a Lyti. That was not, it seemed, her name, but a term used to describe people who were either deaf and dumb or retarded or sometimes both. He said that they were respected but that since they were nonproductive and different, people never felt quite at ease around them. He compared her to Changpa, one of the porters, whom Tina and I had befriended. Well, actually, Tina had befriended him, as she befriended everyone, and I had simply noticed him through her.

Changpa was a small man, with a flat Mongolian nose and short spindly legs, but with an intelligent face and eyes that seemed to understand everything that went on around him. Tina didn't believe that he was deaf, simply that he was mute, and she talked with him as freely as with me. But he never made a sound; there was no rasping in his throat, no groan or strain, nothing at all that made you feel he would have liked to talk. It almost seemed that he had chosen silence, taken a vow as a monk might, and was no less wise because he could not share his wisdom. The Sherpas seemed uneasy around him, as if he were an unpredictable and therefore rather dangerous animal, and were quite content to leave him alone.

Tensing smiled sadly—that bodhisattva smile of his—and went off to dig trenches around the campsites. I went back to the tent. Tina was writing in her notebook, and the girl was watching her do it, one finger outstretched to the pen. I must have been quite mad, but I took her on my lap again and started to try and figure out what it would cost to buy her from her family and how I could adopt her and how long I would have to stay in Katmandu to get the paperwork straightened out. It was quite incredible to me that anyone could think her retarded, and I felt both angry at the stupidity of such blindness and also somehow grateful, as it would give me a good excuse to take her away from her home. My Lyti —she would *never* become like Changpa, not if I could help her find her voice. Never since I'd met Nicholas had I felt such an instant attraction to another human being, and since Nicholas and Orion had died I'd thought that I could never love again. After the avalanche, for months that merged like empty journeys, I'd felt that I was not, had never been, a giver; that whatever came from my hands had the vacuousness of air. An all-encompassing lethargy had ruled me, and though I'd talked to people in the shop, packed gear and eaten my meals, I'd felt as embarrassed by my own gratuitous existence as if I had been truly shaped of clay. Sometimes I even had resented Nicholas for not having left me a child, and sitting in Tal with a child on my lap, I felt closer to him than I had in ages, even before he died—felt as if I had found once more something I had lost long ago.

That little girl, that Lyti. Of course, I didn't adopt her. Though I fell asleep talking with Tina of kidnap, when I woke up I simply told her goodbye. I left her the paint set and two of my barrettes, but I knew that even before we were out of sight the other children would have them and she would be again as she had been before I came, a Lyti, with eyes and heart as full of life as a river, but no paint set and no words.

After that . . . nothing went really wrong. But nothing went really right either. I kept remembering the girl, a child without even a name, and every step I took away from her seemed somehow like a betrayal. Not a betrayal of her, perhaps, but a betrayal of myself.

Ten

We were daily getting nearer to the mountain, moving up into higher, drier country, the rain shadow of the Himalayas where the land is stark and arid even after the monsoon. Everything was dull and thirsty; at the bottom of the cirque on Annapurna Three the gravelly rock ran off in a sullen rubble and wisps of dirty cloud obscured parts of all its faces. I imagined myself made suddenly giant, striding to the mountain in two long steps and laying myself down as if on a coverlet, nestling my head on a pillow of rocks and leaving the earth for the sky. A flock of doves flew by, black and white and gray, and I stared at them jealously, coveting flight. I wanted to put myself right out of the accessible world. I wanted no responsibility and in truth no contact with the other members of the team. Although we had begun to get pretty friendly and to feel some real team spirit, after I left the Lyti behind, a lot of that feeling was gone. In fact, the other women began to irritate me exceedingly; I saw embodied in them all the excesses and neuroses of Western civilization. Not always. But often enough so that it made me feel weird.

Sometimes, I mean, I would like them—Taffy for her feminine charm, Dervla for her unfailing good spirits, Laurie for her dignity and skill. But other times . . . it wasn't just that at other times I wouldn't like them, or would be annoyed and turn it over and dislike Taffy for her excessive femininity, Dervla for her false good humor, Laurie for her standoffishness. It wasn't as simple as mood swings around a center which was relatively untouched. Rather, there were times when I'd sit like a visitor from another planet, judging, analyzing, practically taking notes in a loose-leaf: thinking, for example, that the fact that Robin didn't want to climb anything but simple routes—nailing a wall straight up or doing a long undeviating jam crack—was clearly a sign that she wasn't interested in climbing for its own sake, that she only wanted to set out on things that could be written down on a résumé and instantly recognized as worthwhile; in other words, that she was basically a coward and manipulative. And all the time I was thinking this, I was listening to her play the flute. Something felt very wrong to me, that I could sit in a group and be part of it and yet not be part of it, be a little person in a control station somewhere, making judgments, always judgments, unable to be with the others. And I had been looking forward so much to reaching the high mountains, not just because they were the mountains but also because they held the followers of the Buddha and in some inarticulate and illogical way I had hoped that without really trying, I too might become a genuine follower when I trod such well-worn paths.

Of course, when I joined the sangha in Jackson Hole, it wasn't because I knew I would be going to Nepal. Indeed, I somehow assumed that whatever passed for Buddhism in Jackson Hole could scarcely be the same substance, the same reality, as what one might experience in the mountains of its evolution; yes, the mountains might be similar, the high thin air of elevation, but that was likely to be it, the only resemblance, though we all have a way of giving old names to new corruptions.

I joined it after Nicholas was killed. While he lived, it never would have crossed my mind. But when he died I needed something, anything at all, that was different from what I'd known with him. Besides, they had signs up in every store in town. Suddenly I could scarcely take a step without tripping over a Buddhist, and even among climbers who came into the shop it

seemed to be the new concern, promising not answers but a way
to make the space to look for them.

In that, of course, it seemed to me to resemble climbing itself:
both methods for abandoning the buzz, the noise, the badly
constructed machinery of the mind, of journeying to a quiet place
where everything you do is careful, not because such care will lead
you somewhere but because it will let you be where you already
are. I didn't think it could ever become my center, but I thought
it might at least distract my mind, help me to cope with that
echoing sense of bewilderment that I felt time and again after the
avalanche, the sense of what in the name of heaven am I doing
here at all? And once I started sitting with the sangha I did see
the connection more and more clearly, the similarities between
climbing and the Hinayana path. Both bring a heightened state
of concentrated awareness; both are the way of a person facing
death

We've all been brought up to believe, somehow, that our lives
have an ultimate purpose stamped out upon our birth and that
each of our actions should be directed toward that end. Ask ten
different people what that end might be called and you will get
ten different answers, but very few people will say that the end
is here and now, that life is just a finite series of disconnected
moments with the best path through its changes being no set path
at all. But when Mallory said that he wanted to climb Everest
because it was there and the phrase went down in history as either
evasive or inspired, he had in fact managed to reach out into the
pool of truth which the Buddha also tapped and to lift out of it
a coda for existence which, if embraced completely, could lead
one finally to peace.

The sangha was a small one. Eleven people on a good day, we
met in the house of the oldest and most experienced member of
the group. He had just that winter taken the bodhisattva vow—
which affirms that you will, through compassion for others, sur-
render the possibility of your own enlightenment, since only when
you aren't seeking it will you find it in the end. That's nice, don't

you think? A beautiful turnaround on the idea of seek and you will find and a hell of a lot more logical if you ask me, since the one thing that is clear to anyone who has lived beyond the age of three is that whatever you find, you can be quite sure it's not the thing you were looking for, and even when you climb a wall direct, the summit is never just where you thought it would be. So that instead of labeling everything in advance, on a set of neat and sticky white address tapes, and carrying them around with you in a basket, reaching into it constantly to affix a new definition to whatever it is that surrounds you, you try and cut through that impulse, the impulse to break things into pieces, discrete enough to deal with one by one, and instead learn to be open, truly open, to the place where you are fixed. You see how well I managed. Well, at least I tried.

The newfound bodhisattva was a tyrant. Not like Tensing at all, with his smile and his endless cheerful service; not like Pasang, with his deep and limitless compassion; Mitchell asked from each of us an absolute commitment to the Way, and when we were in sitting meditation his physical presence flowed over us like an admonition. Even an itch on my nose or ear would remain unscratched until it went away—although my ears seemed to itch all the time when I was sitting, and I got the illusion that it was because I was listening for something I could never quite hear, a very good example of the kind of self-entertainment you are supposed to learn to let go when you start to develop mindfulness.

Sadly, there were no voices to be heard. I could hardly believe the effort involved in constantly bringing my attention back to my breath, the sound and feeling of my breath as it left my body, which is what sitting meditation begins with. As I sat there cross-legged on a cushion, breathing in front of an altar with seven little glass cups of water on it, it seemed ironic that I had to sit down on a pillow and cross my legs to pay attention to nothing but my breath, since half of every climb I've been on, my breath became my world, and there's nothing in life a climber knows more intimately than the sound of air going into and out of his lungs.

But try to tell that to Mitchell. He didn't climb. He sat. No, that isn't quite fair. He worked too, and lived in a house he had built himself, piece by slow piece, and the exactitude of every cut and the perfect placement of every nail in the staircase was an unmistakable demonstration of the fact that when he was making the cuts, sinking the nails, what he was thinking of was the saw, the hammer, the wood, and not life and death and bewilderment, whether he was going to get laid that evening or the fact that his father had spanked him unjustly as a child. He seemed in many ways like Nicholas's diametric opposite, with an ego as strong but turned ten times more inward—a monk at heart, with all the fear of love that Nicholas never felt and the concomitant need for finding truth, which is the only conceivable alternative to indiscriminate passion.

Nicholas could never have become a Buddhist. And it wasn't that his ego was overpoweringly strong, because that is not important in the end; because that would in fact, if anything, have been an asset. The ego is all that you have, after all, and before you can try and transcend anything you have to have something to transcend. That's where some people go wrong, right from the start, in thinking there are shortcuts to peace—that all you need is a flower in your ear and a kind of easy humility, which can be nothing but another word for a lack of self-respect, in order to gain enlightenment. They think enlightenment is a kind of present you get, for being good, perhaps. They think that if they can simply never desire anything at all, they will never be destroyed by grief. But you don't fall onto summits from the clouds.

No, the reason Nicholas could never have been a Buddhist was that he couldn't bear to think about the darkness at the heart of light. And yet he lived, somehow, much more closely to the mystery than I did, than most of us ever do. He felt with an intensity I have never seen surpassed, and one of the things that composed the pool of his deepest feelings was the enigma of the jointure between himself and everything around him. For him, I am convinced, climbing really was a mystical experience. In climbing, as in nothing else, he simply trusted to the connection to take care of itself, he placed his actions on the altar of otherness and was rewarded by an unsurpassable intuition of his own organic relation to the world. That was what made him a great climber. And he was a great climber, greater than Ryan, certainly far greater than I. Without him, we would never have been what we were. Without him, I would never have really lived.

Until after his death, though, I didn't see it thus. Because the flip side of his ability to become one with the rock was his absolute inability to become one with anything else. Into every encounter with a box, a room or a person he put all the intensity which worked so well for him in the mountains and didn't work at all for him anywhere else. Engines fell apart under his hands. Roomfuls of people disintegrated. He insisted on making all repairs, all confrontations, by himself. The result was that we spent twice the money and energy on maintenance that we otherwise would have, and that I used to have to watch him take on several antagonists in more than a few barroom brawls. Well, maybe that was his background. His father was a roughneck; who knows the kinds of things he had to prove?

But at the time, I felt nothing but contempt for his inability to cope, not only with the world around him but with his own powerlessness to ultimately change that world. Now, of course, I do not feel contempt. Far from it. For I have come to realize that the inability to cope is in fact the most precious of gifts, because only when we can perceive and admit our own bewilderment can we begin to touch the mystery of life. Before Nicholas, I coped perhaps too well. And afterward—both from feeling, through the medium of my love, all the frustration that Nicholas was born to, and also through experiencing my own inability to help him, to change him, to have, ultimately, the slightest effect upon his pain —afterward I knew with every fiber of my being that there is, finally, no way at all to cope, except to try and open yourself wide to the demon hosts around you, letting them pour through you like light, letting the absolute illogic of existence fill you. Because then—then, perhaps, you will intuit sometimes the oneness that was Nicholas's reward when he leaned upon the point of his ice hammer, his crampons thrust into the thick blue ice, his Karrimor warm and heavy on his back, and his hair, curly and touched with fine white mist, falling softly around his face. He was brilliant when he led the first ascent of the Northeast Ridge of Mount Reconnaissance. Brilliant. You have no idea. That was always his reward and mine.

Why on earth I should have thought that getting to Nepal would let me experience that feeling again—that here, if nowhere else, I would trip over revelation, intersect epiphany on the trail —I don't know. But though I was in Buddhist country now, and climbing toward the mountain of my dreams, not only did I not discern an answer but I felt a greater sense of disconnectedness from the possibility of answers than I had felt for months, perhaps for years. Each hour that passed on the trail seemed to bring me closer to the brink of desperation. There was a quality of inattention about everything I did, as if I were only half a person and the other half had been left behind on the road somewhere, like a pair of worn-out sneakers, like the little girl in Tal.

Yes. Yes. There was really something wrong, I see that now. Behind everything it lurked, like a hallucination, a cloud, a veil across my mind. I would start to speak and be unable to finish my sentence. I would look at Tina's face and then my eyes would glaze, would wander, and whatever it was she was saying would go so totally unheard she might have been talking to the wind. I did imprudent things. I crossed log bridges with my waist belt fastened and my shoulder straps drawn tight. I went bouldering alone, without a spotter, and got twenty or thirty feet off the ground just as darkness fell. I climbed to the edge of a waterfall where a granite slab quivered over the void, and lay down flat to watch the water rushing by, losing myself in its motion, feeling that I shouldn't move, couldn't move, until someone came along and called out my name. I kept setting up these arbitrary rules for myself as I went along, tests of courage not unlike the ones I had set myself as a child—if I don't go over that wall without stopping once I'm not going to get an A on my exam—perfectly ridiculous linkages of two quite disparate realities, giving myself rewards which were inappropriate to the achievements, if achievements was what in fact they were.

So I started doing this again, but in a bigger way. I took risks which were essentially as unnecessary and therefore as foolish as unroping before you reach the end of a glacier—when there are, perhaps, only thirty feet to go, each one of which is quite sufficient to kill you. It was as if there were a stone inside me, a stone that wanted to be shattered by a hammer big enough to fell a mountain, something hard and knotted, cold and glassy. And I went from place to place alternately forgetting about the stone, feeling its weight not at all, and letting it rule me completely, letting the desire for its fragmentation rule my life.

It wasn't really new to me, this sense of being split in half, this feeling that I was two people: the one who could get so high on sense itself that I thought I could float right out of my body and into the air above my head—and the one who hid inside like a rock waiting to be shattered.

I had felt this, in fact, all my life; I had felt it and gotten used to it—when I was ten years old, or twelve, or seventeen. I had felt it, really, even when I was with Orion, though I had never noticed it then or seen it for what it was. And then? And then I had met Nicholas and the two halves had come together with a snap, since he was a hammer big enough to shatter that rock and gather the gravel that was left and with it pave the way to anywhere. He made me whole—and when he died, I thought that the incongruities of my existence were because he had *died,* because he had been killed—not because he was gone. But now . . . now I was beginning to feel that maybe there is something to this business of your other half. Because that wholeness had to do with moments—moments when I knew what I'd been born for. Whenever I watched Nicholas breathe, or climb, or sensed him behind me on the rope, then that was the reason I had, by a series of miracles, escaped death when I fell down Teepee's Glacier and lost my ice ax, and stopped only twenty feet above the rock band at the bottom; the reason I had swung my horse tightly around a hundred barrels set in sawdust, my thighs wet with sweat and sticking to the saddle; it was the reason I'd opened a jar of kosher pickles and spilled all the juice on the floor; the reason I'd been called to the principal's office by mistake on the day I'd finally dared to wear sneakers to school; for that moment, I had never been able to hold a tune and had slept in Orion's arms. No matter how murky the matter had been before and was to be again, at that moment it was always plain why I was alive. It was to watch Nicholas and let out the rope while he climbed.

He was so beautiful, really. So pink and so brown, so alive. When he set his hand on the edge of the table as he stood beside it—not conscious of his hand and the small cup it formed on the wood—the veins just under his skin filled with blood and became rounded and soft and blue. When he put on his headlamp and the elastic strap, frayed at one edge, clamped his balaclava to his head, his face was as smooth as a tree stripped of bark. Sometimes he would sit by the trail, his shoulder straps loosened, his bright-orange wind pants stretched taut across the muscles of his legs, and spread a map across his lap to study it, not even using his finger to trace our route. And when he climbed, he moved from hold to hold as fluidly as a branch bends, and his fingertips—even just two of them, the very top joints—would rest on a shard of rock as if it were ineluctable, would be drawn to the stone as confidently as the roots of a ginkgo seek water.

And so I started dreaming. I had had dreams about death, lots of dreams, right after Nicholas and Ryan died, but they were simple in a way: I'd be standing looking down at a black river just entering a cave, aware that though it looked quite still, as firm as steel, obsidian or ice, it was actually rushing by as fast as bombers and I was dizzy and tilting toward the edge. Well, now I started having dreams again, and they weren't simple, though they scared the hell out of me, and I would wake in a cold sweat and be unable to sleep again for hours.

There was one that I remember clearly. I had it just below the town of Braga. We were camped on the plain there, exposed as an army before a siege wall. The city loomed above us like a medieval fortress, its crazy pueblo houses leaning against the cliff as precariously as the log ladders used to reach them. The paths leading into the town were as slick and steep as logs across a stream and the rubbled rock slope that marks its base seemed like a runoff from the fortress itself, the slow accumulation of ages of decay. A policeman lived in Braga, a policeman singularly well matched to the bleakness of the town. His big moment, he reported, was when he stopped a party of nineteen Germans and all their porters who were trying to slip quietly and carefully up the Nar valley into Tibet. Two hundred people, quieter than mice, and he stopped them, single-handed. But he was university educated and spoke good English and was terribly hungry for conversation. Except during the trekking/mountaineering season, he said, the snow is up to your chest in Braga and only old people, blind people and idiots remain there. He served us good coffee in filthy glasses which he wiped apologetically with filthy fingers and showed us a book in which he had all the climbers who passed sign. He had noted the deaths opposite their names, in a beautiful archaic hand. "Died," he said, "on expedition. That is the world beyond these walls."

Tina and I had visited the Buddhist gompa just after we met that policeman. The monk who unlocked the big steel padlock was dressed in dirty robes, yellow and maroon, and he practically tapped his foot while we looked around in the dimness, and then indicated that it would be very holy indeed if I put my offering on the altar along with the rice and the butter, rather than in the locked strongbox by the door—to which, evidently, he had not been given a key and into which, therefore, it would be a great deal more difficult for him to get his hands. Well, I put ten rupees in the strongbox when we left, watched by the great smiling Buddha that lurked in the shadows, and that night I had the dream.

There was a great locked warehouse in my dream, a dim building full of objects, all of them out of my past. Old toys were pinned to the walls like bats, worn-out climbing shoes sat in long rows on benches against the walls, sleeping bags were slung in hammocks from the ceiling like Malaysian paper kites. A policeman stood by the door to the warehouse, a policeman who looked and sounded like Orion, and after a time he let me in—unlocking the big wooden door with a flourish and then standing back, his face full of foreboding. He warned me not to stay too long. He warned me not to take anything out of the hall.

So I went in. I felt a great affection for the warehouse, a love for the objects of my past, mixed with a great, half-hidden fear —a fear of the blackness, the cobwebs in the corners, the places I couldn't quite see clearly. As I was leaving, I noticed on the floor a blue-black seed. Of all the objects in the warehouse, it was the only one I couldn't remember having seen before, and it looked so small and innocent, just carelessly left behind, that I picked it up and put it in my pocket, then bowed once and went out. Ryan still stood by the doorway. He locked the door behind me and then said:

"I'm glad you didn't bring anything out. I couldn't warn you before." His voice dropped and he added in a whisper, "The seed. The seed that grows in the dark."

I tried to put my hand in my pocket and get the seed and fling it away, but I couldn't find it, it had slipped through a hole or changed its shape, so I started running, running through long cobbled streets full of stones. But the seed pursued me and transformed itself, changing first into a bat, then into a gargoyle, and finally into an old, old woman dressed in black, who flung herself onto my back, wrapped her arms tightly around my throat and whispered, "I am the seed, the blue-black seed, the seed that grows in the dark."

I woke up trembling and crying. Tina was sound asleep. A little drop of spit had run from the corner of her mouth onto her pillow, and her hair was soft across her head. She looked so young, so handsome, so gentle and unmarred, that I wanted to cling to her tightly and beg her for release. I remembered that when Nicholas and I had first started living together, perhaps only two or three weeks after we moved into the trailer in Jackson, I had had a nightmare and woken up crying out in terror, and without even fully waking he had turned to me and clutched me as tightly as a python and said in a voice heavy with sleep, "It's all right, love. It's only the morning."

It's all right, love. It's only the morning. A strange thing to say, meaningless in itself, but with the deeper meaning that is given to the messages of the night. As if, left to my own devices, unloved, unprotected by Nicholas and his arms, I would naturally misinterpret the meaning of the morning itself, would see it for something other than what it was, granting to the morning, the chance of a new beginning, all the menace one normally attributes to the night—as if, in the deep truth of his sleep, he knew that the thing I feared most was the future, not the past, and that all nightmares, once they were done, had power only if you let them rule tomorrow.

So I lay there and looked at Tina in the moonlight, touched her hair and moved a tendril on the pillow and kept crying. Not because I had lost Nicholas; but because when he had died I was getting ready to leave him, because when he was killed I was already convinced that all was over between us. Now that seemed like nothing but psychosis. In truth, I had loved him so much that it still hurt, so much that it would hurt forever, and all my mornings would be full of the shadow of the past since I would never have the chance to go back and love him as he died. Because when the avalanche was over, it was Ryan I found first. There was snow in his mouth and nostrils and I couldn't find a heartbeat. But he'd been close to the surface and he was still warm. I don't know how long I worked on him. An hour, two? Maybe more. I forgot about Nicholas as if he had never been.

Eleven

Memories are peculiar. They can be so recalcitrant sometimes, when you're trying to line them up. You can't approach them as if you were unrolling flypaper or something, twisting it carefully as it comes out of the tube, so sticky you might as well cut your hair off if it ever brushes your head. You think the past is there, all fixed and stable, but it's really chock-full of surprises and endlessly susceptible to change. Once, in the foothills of the Wind River Mountains, Ryan and I came across a house that had been abandoned and had tumbled down, the furniture still inside it, the plates that survived the crash intact. We spent a few hours exploring the wreckage and, perched on a rotten beam, eating tuna fish sandwiches. But when a year later we went back to look for the place again we couldn't find it, though we combed the woods like a search party. It was gone as if it had never been. And this so fascinated Orion—the way in which the present swallows up the past—that he really convinced himself that we had made up the house between us and that we had the power to create and destroy our world. When we were older, stuck on a belay ledge one night with nothing but bivy sacks between us and the snow, he told me he believed that nothing and no one in the world can hurt you: you can only, if you want to, *choose* to be hurt. There was a mountain sheep bleating somewhere below us, a sheep that was also stuck on a ledge. We listened to the sheep for a while and then he said that anyone could go back through the leaves of his own past and choose not to be hurt by the things that had already hurt him: not just go on, not just put yourself in a position where you never again open yourself up to such a hurt—but remake your past in a fundamental way, and open yourself ever wider. I couldn't believe that then. I said there were limits to any strength, that your life is something you accumulate, your baggage, something you carry around. There's no left-luggage room where you can deposit it forever, there's no unloading avalanche, no forgetting short of death. But maybe Nicholas never hurt me, and I, through ignorance, only hurt myself. Sometimes I really believe that if Nicholas had appreciated me from the first, I never would have stayed with him. He used to say, you see, that all women are alike. So sometimes—now, only now, it's all now, always now—I wonder whether that wasn't why I stayed with him all those years: because ultimately I was stubborn enough to want above all else to prove to him that all women are not alike, not in the sense that he meant. That there was one woman who was capable of mastering him. For all that, of course, he mastered me. In the end, I had no choices left; my emotions were no longer under my control.

But I wonder if I can really change that now. Of course, I was just as responsible as he was for the patterns of our life together —but how to sort out where my own mistakes were made? Probably in thinking I was somehow good by virtue of the fact that I wanted to help him—when perhaps, without such meddling on my part, he would have coped much more adequately than he did with the vicissitudes of life. But the corollary of his impatience was the fact that he always seemed to respond to my touch too late. If he was, for some reason, sunk in depression and I tried to urge him out of it by every suggestion and encouragement I could command, he would be obdurate, hopeless, until I was quite wrung dry and had accepted that this time too there would be no happiness at the end of our encounter—until I would, in fact, be feeling that anyone who placed such a burden of failure on me (the failure, that is, of my own ability to help him) was someone I would just as soon be rid of—then and only then would he suddenly emerge from behind the walls of his dejection and say, "O.K., you're right, let's do it, shall we?" in a tone that was suddenly bright, and I would be left with the choice of either saying, "Forget it, jocko, it's too late now," which would in effect make me a hypocrite since the burden of my message to him the whole time had been essentially that it was never too late for anything; or against all my instincts wresting from myself a cheery "Fine, great, let's go," when I no longer felt in the least like going wherever it was or anywhere else, but away, as all the pleasure of anticipation had been sucked from the plan by the obstacles he erected and all the pleasure of helping him had been destroyed by that immeasurable and seemingly endless delay between the time when I had stopped hoping he would respond and the time when he finally did.

So maybe that was where my mistakes were made. By trying always to fling myself between him and the realities he didn't want to face, I gave him a crutch he could not refuse, a crutch that partly crippled him. Sometimes I think it's power, all power, in the end. And I wonder now whether I was not as manipulative as the worst women of my fantasy world, wanting him to behave as I wanted him to behave, in fact, and stopping at nothing to bring about that end. Although I *thought* I was never physically afraid of him, the threat of force always latent within him may have made me try and defuse it by verbal games that I believed were love. The flip side of unrestrained violence is controlled violence, after all, and the kind of encouragement that I engaged in was perhaps a passive form of warfare. Still, I never wanted to hurt him. I merely wanted to win.

And I guess what kept me with him was the fact that I could win—sometimes, in various ways. And also the fact that I could never know when this would happen. There was an element of chance in all our undertakings which kept me interested. The gambler in me, the climber who takes unnecessary risks, was

fascinated by the unpredictability of the outcomes of our strug-
gles. I remember one fight we had. It was slow in building, like
most of our conflicts. We'd been talking about selling the shop.
We'd only owned it for a year and it was becoming pretty clear
to us that neither of us wanted to be a businessman. We didn't
have the aptitude. We didn't have the self-image. We would have
been better off working in the coal mines all winter and climbing
from spring to fall.

So we were thinking about selling the shop. We were up to our
ears in debt and the winter hadn't been good. We'd moved to a
little house in Jackson, but we didn't see how we could manage
to get the time off to climb the Grand, much less go to Patagonia,
as we wanted. I had been urging Nicholas to relax; whether we
sold the shop or not, Ryan would help with cash for South America. Nicholas was having his biannual go at rejecting this; he
wasn't about to take charity, he wasn't the kind who lived off
other people. He would, in fact, stay at the shop all summer if it
killed him.

I see now that I should probably have let him do just that. But
though the instinct for independence is, in general, one that I
admire, in this case it interfered too radically with my own wishes
for me to countenance it. Rather than encouraging him to make
it on his own, to make himself independent of financial charity,
I maintained that his reluctance to accept Ryan's generosity was
simply stubbornness and rooted in false pride, a macho disdain for
the fruits of love. I was very persuasive. I was, even after four years
with him, unthinking enough about the way Nicholas worked to
fear that he would actually stick to his guns and let Ryan and me
go off alone. And I wanted him along, more than anything in the
world. As a climbing team the three of us couldn't be beat. In
fact, our moments on the rope were the still points of peace
around which our relationship revolved. I didn't want to find out
what would happen if we lost them.

So there was this fundamental tension in our life. Had it happened two years later, it would have been increased by my own

irritation at the knowledge that in the end, of course, Nicholas would give in and go. I would have perceived as hypocrisy the stand for independence. But at the time the tension stemmed simply from my own fear that I would be unable to convince him (plus the classic by-product of that, my underlying sense that if such were the case, he could not really love me) and from his inability to reconcile his image of a real man as one who "pulled his own weight" with his desperate desire to climb.

Well, that was the background. After a week of this back-and-forth, in the dreariest days of late winter, one Sunday the weather dawned beautifully sunny and there were spring smells in the air —sagebrush and jack pine, water running over rocks, the steamy odor of melting snow—so we decided to go for a ski. You know how you feel in the springtime: that nothing on earth can stop you now, when everything around you is sensuous, touchable, desirable once more. It's like coming down from the alpine zone, from a tent in a storm, and on smelling the flowers, just having to run, with big squishy leaps in the air, from sheer joy at having your senses back once more. Well, this was *that* kind of day. We set off for a new place, a road that a friend had told us about, a long winding road which turned into a trail above Togwotee Pass, where it went over the rim of the Absarokas and down into a bowl on the other side. We didn't have a map. But since it was spring and Sunday, we had absolute faith when we began that we would find the place and that it would be quite untrodden. A white place that waited for marking. How could we miss it? We would find it right away.

Of course, we did not. The roads off Togwotee Pass are a maze and no one's directions are ever exact. We set off up one road, which turned out to be a skid trail, nothing more. So we skied back to the truck, took off our skis and drove on until we located another road, one we were sure—with the grateful conviction of uncertainty—resembled in every particular the one we sought. And after three hundred yards that one dead-ended also. At that point we should, of course, have left and gone elsewhere. It was still early in the morning and there were plenty of places to ski. But we tried once again, in that fatalistic way we had, each of us filled with a sudden foreboding that we were not going to enjoy the day after all and each of us doing our best to ignore it. Halfway up the third road, which I had been excitedly maintaining was the proper one at last, I began to be doubtful. I commented that it looked awfully new. Somewhat sardonically, Nicholas agreed that it did look awfully new.

Our skis had started to stick a bit and I was getting hot and frustrated. Stubbornly wanting to wrest enjoyment from the day and from the woods which had so often given me peace, I suggested that we simply go on, bushwhack up to the teeth of the ridge and ski along it until we found the trail. Nicholas said that he wasn't interested in "thrashing about in the bushes" and told me we should call it a day. He then went off into the woods to take a shit and while he squatted in the snow we bickered

I told him I wasn't about to go back to Jackson, that we'd been stuck there long enough. He told me it was my fault we were stuck there—that he had never wanted to buy the shop in the first place. There was an element of truth to this; he had been terrified of getting into debt, even to my brother. But that only made me more irritated, and through the lens of my present frustration it appeared to me that far from being *my* fault that we had done less mountaineering since we bought the shop, it was *his* fault that we had let it tie us down. Nicholas might want to go back, resign himself to mediocrity—play, in fact, the dying martyr on the cross—but I was damned if I was going to give in so easily. When Nicholas pulled his pants up and we started back for the truck, I was determined to ski all day if it killed me. Nicholas was reluctant even to speak to me, but we managed to argue about who should get the truck and who should hitchhike back to town as we glided down the wet snow with the sounds of woodpeckers and chickadees quivering around us and the mournful groaning of some cattle coming from the road below.

I don't know why it was, but Nicholas always had a horror of trespassing on private property. He would go to great lengths to circumnavigate any bit of woods that looked likely to belong to someone, or where there was any evidence of human habitation. I suppose in a way it's not so odd; it tied in with his underlying fear of being caught out somehow, of being found in a position where he was required to defend himself from the inquisitiveness or demands of other human beings. I suppose in some ways he had a child's paranoia of being made to look foolish—and what could be more foolish than to be on someone else's land, especially to a man who did not want to believe in the right to private ownership of land and yet desired to have whole mountain ranges to himself? There was a time when it made him nervous that I plucked a stick to play with from the top of a barbed-wire fence. He said that if the owners of the fence saw me, they might think I was stealing.

"Stealing? A stick?" I asked.

When we got back to the truck I took the wheel. We both refused to hitchhike and I refused to go back home, maintaining that our original agreement was to spend the day, that this was incontrovertibly proved by the fact that we had brought a lunch, and that I intended to hold to our agreement. Nicholas closed himself off at this as definitively as someone shutting down a faucet.

This was one of my most effective tactics—to hold him at his word—since he believed that a man of honor should always do what he had agreed to do even though his mercurial nature made it almost impossible for him to know what he wanted long enough in advance to gain much happiness that way. But the longer I used it as a tactic, the less satisfaction I got from it, as he simply became less and less willing to commit himself to anything until the last possible instant, and I picked up this trait from him by a kind of osmosis and as a form of self-protection, so neither of us had any security about our future plans. Anyway, having shut Nicholas off, I hadn't the strength to turn him back on, though once he had withdrawn into the boundaries of his body I saw instantly that this was the last thing I had wanted to have happen and I longed to pick him up and slam him against a wall, move him bodily from where he sat to somewhere else; anything to disturb his stiff self-righteousness.

Perhaps that's why I tried to find the road again. By now I knew that even if I found it I would not enjoy my ski, nor would I be able to relax, with Nicholas waiting in the truck. But I had more of a chance of stirring him up if I pursued the road and I could not let it end without at least an apparent victory for myself— me skiing, Nicholas waiting—even when such an outcome would give me no pleasure and would give Nicholas the pleasure of putting me in the wrong by not considering his changed feelings about our plans. I didn't intend to park on private property. I had no idea that any of the land near Togwotee Pass was posted. The fourth road had been plowed and I drove up it with an utter disregard for the question of how I was going to get out; I assumed there must be somewhere to turn a truck around.

Two hundred yards up the road we passed the sign: "Private Property. No Hunting or Fishing." It was nailed to a tree by a particularly steep bit of road and just as I was sensing that the wheels were about to start spinning, Nicholas barked that we were on private property and to let him out of the truck at once.

Well, I couldn't possibly have stopped. I would have lost all momentum and had to back down the road again. So I kept going, imagining it must be apparent even to Nicholas that I was heading for a flatter stretch of road before I stopped. It was not. With the truck still moving, he wrenched open the door, threw out his rucksack (with all the food) and leaped after it. Out of the corner of my eye I could see him stumble and fall and then pick himself up again and take off, almost running, for the roadhead. The door of the passenger seat was swinging open. It slammed suddenly with the movement of the car and, distracted, I let up on the gas. My back tires spun wildly on the snow.

Backing down the road again was hell. There were high snow-banks on either side of it and it twisted and curved much more unpleasantly than it had appeared to on the ascent. It took me ten minutes of high tension to reach the highway; by the time I got there I was absolutely furious, on the ragged edge of explosion. I got onto the highway and headed for Jackson, intending to leave Nicholas on the road if I passed him—but when I did, almost against my will I stopped for him. I didn't want him to have anything to use or hold against me.

He got into the truck in stony silence, as if he were doing me a favor to grace it with his presence. He held his silence like a shield and, with a lightning reversal of intention, I felt suddenly that *any* price was worth my freedom from this. I told him to take the damn truck himself, that I wasn't about to ride back to town with him, then or ever.

He didn't respond. The snow-laden trees, the sunshine, the moose tracks that meandered across the field far below the highway where it ran by the edge of the cliff—all these called to me with their stillness. I had so many memories of graceful, peaceful woods and hills. I longed to be a child, with my brother once again.

I braked hard and stopped the truck. The tires squealed and Nicholas was flung forward in his seat. Without stopping to consider, without thinking for an instant, in one of those dry heats of rage which transform the world into a fragile bowl, easily broken, easily lost, I put the truck into neutral, and even as it started to roll, like thick liquid spilling from a jar, I jumped to the road and slammed the door behind me. Gathering speed, yet moving with almost arresting slowness, an elephant, a bear, deceptive in its strength and speed, the truck rolled driverless toward the edge of the cliff. Nicholas sat as still as someone already dead. There was a moment in which my whole existence hung by a thread, and then, elated, I saw that I had won. Nicholas leaped for the driver's seat and wrenched the truck back from its passage toward the cliff. As surely as if I had picked him up in my hands and slammed him against a wall, I had forced him, at last, to move.

Yes. I know. What an asinine thing to do. Not only was I playing Russian roulette with a lifelong load of guilt but I was giving Nicholas a weapon against me which could reach around corners, through water, even into the mountains if he cared to carry it there—the knife which proved that I was a dangerous, idiotic woman, out of control, unreliable, not to be trusted with life itself, her own or anyone else's. Much more than that, I was handing over my mind, like a turkey on a platter, to the darkness that lay beneath it and saying I could not help myself. I felt at the time an absolute inability to connect my act with its possible consequence.

Well, whatever I'd done, I surely suffered for it. For three days, Nicholas would not speak. He skirted me in the house and in the store as if I were a perambulating piece of furniture. When I spoke to him there was a silence as insignificant and complete as a lull in the traffic noise. And I was *bound* by that silence—as porters carrying a cable up a hillside are bound by the weight of the steel, held in place by its dimensions, forced to move by its speed. Such silence. Such stillness. I seem to feel them still. After a time I even doubted my existence; I looked in the mirror to make sure that I was real. And time and again, though I tried to make up with him, tried to apologize, tried to get through, I felt that I was talking in the dark. Each word as I spoke it fell to the ground before me, a tiny stone into a cup of cotton. The cotton held them, each one only a word, the collection just a group of words, meaning nothing. After a time I could scarcely think; there was no chance at all of action. Yet Nicholas was not being purposely cruel. He was stuck in a moment, not noticing it had passed. And I, in noticing its passing, felt too that this could not go on. Felt for the first time that soon I would have to leave him.

You know how kind it's supposed to be to tell someone you can't see him again, as soon as you realize that he is in love with you and that you'll never be able to love him back? I suppose in retrospect it often does seem a kindness—when you were on the receiving end of such outrageous news—to have gotten it all at once, rather than in dribs and drabs, in fits and starts, in talking and in silence. But at the time? My God! After all, we could all be dead tomorrow. Why not at least die hoping? What now we see as kindness, then was nothing but a sword. So maybe it's true that we are constantly rewriting our own pasts; they are not something fixed and unchangeable for all time. There is a basic structure, of course, a canvas stretched across boards, which cannot be remodeled at will, but the surface of that canvas can be shaded, rearranged, touched up, continually worked on to correspond to the needs of the present. In fact, the present moment is largely the focal point from which you shape the direction of your future and juggle the implications of your past. So at the time, with Nicholas not talking, who knows what I really felt. I think I felt despairing. I think I felt it was the beginning of the end. I think that in a strange reversal, I decided that Nicholas loved me more than I loved him. Otherwise he would not *dare* torment me as he did.

Nicholas was sitting in the living room, reading a mountaineering book. I had asked him one more time to be my friend, the tears running down my cheeks as I spoke, and his eyes had raked my face as if it were a traffic sign and then passed on to the clock on the bookcase, exhausted, timing my appeal. Wildly, I looked around. The .22 hung on the rack on the wall and without thinking anything through, knowing merely that I had to go outside, to act, to move again, I grabbed the rifle, pocketed a box of bullets and the clip, and banged out into the night.

The thaw which had started on Sunday had continued over the hot spring days and the snow on the ground was wet and pulpy, like snow bridges just before they break. The moon had not yet risen, and the night was starry, the air quite sweet and cold. I drew it into my lungs in great deep gulps, and climbed the hill behind our house. For a while I stood there, just looking at the sky, then I took out a single .22 shell and thumbed it into the chamber. The bolt closed with a soft little snick. I aimed the gun toward the brightest of all the constellations and pulled the trigger. In the

stillness of the evening the shot was like a whiplash. On and on
it rang, endlessly, a flick of a hand from a hunter in the sky.

A minute passed. Then two. Before the third went by, however,
a door slammed against the darkness, a truck engine started, and
the sound of tires spinning on gravel echoed on the road. Up to
that moment, I did not know what I had done—but then, like
a naughty child, I suddenly saw the implications of my act, and
was as scared of punishment as if I'd broken all the rules and
more, the rules they'd never even thought to make. Terrified, I
froze, then moved, then moved again, finally gliding down the hill
like a convict. The truck was coming back just as I reached the
ditch, and in a state far beyond that of reason, I slid into the gully
and lay there on my side, my heart pounding in the back of my
head like something trying to escape from bondage. When the
truck went by again the lights grazed the dirt embankment just
above my head. Then the truck stopped, the door creaked open
and Nicholas started to call out my name.

He searched for me for an hour, while I lay there in the ditch.
Over and over he called me, his voice high and wild and often
cracking with the strain. The truck went back and forth six times.
Each time it seemed more frenzied, and each time Nicholas
combed the woods he moved with less control. Thirty times I
thought of putting an end to it. And thirty times I stayed where
I was, unable to move, hardly daring to breathe, afraid, with a
deep and unexpected fear, of being caught—as if I were truly
being hunted, truly trying to escape, as if I were a refugee from
pain. The night was full of latent danger and every move I made
increased it. I had turned into an animal, hiding in a hole.

When I finally emerged, Nicholas was past the edge of panic.
He had moved, by ragged stages, into grief. He was kneeling in
the driveway, crying. When I came up, I took him in my arms.
For a while we cried together, then we went inside and went to
bed, and loved each other all night long. We actually saw the sun
rise. And there was a wholeness about Nicholas that morning, a
completeness to his shape and sound and smell. For once he was

all there. So you can't really call it winning. I have never loved him more. And maybe *that* was the disaster, and the avalanche only the end. Or maybe the disaster came long after—in Nepal, the day we reached the mountain, when I thought, perhaps, that I'd escaped from Nicholas for good.

Twelve

Maybe five days out from base camp, a lot of the porters got sick. We were scheduled for a short march the next day, to allow the dysentery to take its course, but I could hardly stand the idea of hiking for only three hours, with the snow mountains now so near. I longed to get away from the crowds and villages, if only for a day, so I suggested to Tina that we take a short detour upward and climb to the base of the Chalakota icefall. We could meet the team that evening at our camp; it would be fine and reassuring to climb high.

We were sitting in the dining tent when I spoke; the meal was cleared, the lamps had just been lit. Tina was sprawled out on the ground, wearing her bright-blue wind pants and a shell that came down to her knees. She had washed her hair in a bucket before we ate, and it stuck out around her head like a bundle of fire or wind. Margaret was doing mapwork at the table; Naomi, I thought, had already left for the night. By then, it was clear we would never be friends. Even her breathing could sometimes drive me wild. When I thought of the mountain, my feelings were mixed. I certainly didn't want to traverse it with her.

"Of course, let's do it," said Tina, just as Naomi walked back in through the door.

"Do what?" said Naomi. "Have you seen Ang Nima?" then she nodded her head when Tina explained.

"Sounds good. We should all go." Ang Nima appeared, and Naomi drifted away.

When I got up the next morning I had a mental commitment to the idea of gaining the icefall but I felt lazy at first, bemused. What I'd envisioned as a private hike had turned into an expedition, since Margaret and Laurie had joined the party and Pasang was coming too.

The terrain got very hard and steep almost immediately; at first we climbed through rhododendron forest and then through oddly bent, stark trees. When we stopped for lunch, three hours after we'd started walking, we had gained over three thousand feet of elevation. I picked some flowers and put them under my hatband. Then we sat on rocks and ate our eggs and bread and biscuits and no one talked for a while; we just inhaled our food. The snow mountains thrust up into the blue before us with an unarguable distinctness, an almost mocking clarity of light and shadow; far below us, on the floodplain of the river, the sluggish water curled like gray smoke. The mist rolled in shyly—although the sky was blue below us, above us it looked like rain—and then darted away again, and paths, yak-carved, crossed and crisscrossed the soft red earth. Small green plants like folded hands lay flat on the ground, misted with a silver the color of bells, and tiny flowers, blood red or sun yellow, popped their heads up through the mat of silver green. Even the spots that should have marked the villages below were merely green and brown and shadowed, and for a time it was a mountain's world.

I was sitting just below Pasang. Though Pasang spoke very little English and I'd hardly ever heard him speak Nepali, of all the Sherpas it was him I felt most fond of. He had, I think, a special kind of gravity, as if he had suffered greatly and still survived, and so not only did he know enough not to call every stranger he met "Darling"; he knew enough to listen to them when they spoke, even when they used no words. One morning when he brought the wash water, I was for a change already awake, sitting on my bag cross-legged and naked, combing my hair and yawning at the morning. He unzipped the fly of the tent, steaming kettle in one hand, pile of bowls in the other, and when he saw that I was naked, dropped his eyes instantly and did not raise them again, though he poured the water in the bowls as deftly as ever. The only difference my nakedness brought about in his morning routine was that he didn't say, "Good morning," not only because there was clearly no need to wake me up, but because once you have met the eyes of a person unclothed by anything but light, there is no need for the approximations of words to greet them.

So when he suddenly spoke to me this lunchtime, in a fluid, muted sentence, I was startled out of my stupor, as if I'd just been given some great gift. "The mountain, Temis. Perhaps there is something here you want to find?"

Before I could begin to form an answer, Naomi moved her feet and spoke.

"Why don't we go right into the icefall?" she said. "I'm so damn tired of just walking around these hills." She stared blithely at the tips of her sneakers and thoughtfully chewed her final egg.

Had I suggested that myself, I would have thought it a fine, enticing plan. Had Margaret suggested we do it, I would probably have gone along. But the fact that it was Naomi who spoke, and with her eyes fixed on her shoes, meant the idea was not only unappealing but foolish and even quite unsafe. In somewhat more guarded language I said as much, and to my astonishment found that both Tina and Margaret wanted to go into the icefall anyway; and that Margaret thought Pasang should go along. Within five minutes I had surrendered my rope and my ice ax to their cause and been left on the hillside alone.

I sat there for quite a while before I saw the yak. Motionless, he was standing on a small green ledge, and though he was white and brown, with soft belly fur that reached almost to the ground and sharp gray horns that could be mistaken for nothing but an animal's crown, I had thought he was a rock and missed him until a patch of mist obscured him and in clearing away, pointed by its absence to his form. Almost as if he felt my eyes upon him he started, then, to move and as he did I got to my feet and began on the descent. Together but separate, almost as if we were roped, we followed wet paths through the meadows and put behind us many steep feet of pasture until we came to the foot of a ledge-riddled cliff and the yak, leaping lightly onto the first and nearest shelf, paused only long enough to crop some grass before he made his way up the slippery verges and disappeared over the top. Somehow I felt deserted, which was odd. I turned back, to find that I was lost.

Getting lost, of course, is something that you can't do all at once. Rather than a sudden meeting, a pattern that you trip over, a maze to whose terminus you suddenly come, it is like a shadow that darts beside you through the trees, hiding gingerly, crouched along a bush, then popping out and startling you, though you can only see it from the corner of your eye. You are lost, in fact, for quite a while before you focus on it squarely, and when it hits you that you don't know where you are, part of the panic you feel is at your own stupidity not to have seen the fact before, not to have realized that the shadow that ran beside you was something that bore watching.

Well, we had climbed the east ridge of the mountain and were supposed to go back down the west, where our afternoon's camp would be set up and waiting for us to arrive. But inexorably, it seemed to me, all the trails down led east, and after an hour's struggle I gave up and decided to retrace my steps to our old camp and from there wend my way around the mountain.

From the treeless subalpine zone of the yak trails I came down at last to the upper reaches of the forest. But underneath the trees the ground was thick with cover and there were few untroubled trails; brushing my way through the wet and tangled bushes, I lost all sense of direction except for up and down. When I came to the top of a slope that seemed to head directly for the floodplain, I headed straight down it, walking backward on the tips of my boots as if I were front-pointing on crampons, so steep was the terrain there, so soft and slippery the brush. Faster and faster, more and more unthinkingly, I climbed down the slope, holding onto trees as I passed them, gripping long green branches with my fingers and letting them snap back above me. The sound of the snapping was loud in the stillness, though beyond it and below it there was a muffled roar, like a bull trapped far beneath the surface of the earth.

In a little less than twenty minutes, I descended through more than fifteen hundred feet of rain-soaked forest. The roar was growing louder and what with the deepening mist and the tree-created twilight, the seeming imminence of night pushed me on even faster than I was already going. The slope was really so steep that I could easily have rappeled down it, had I not given away my rope and my ice ax to the others. I was hungry again and very wet, and suddenly my feet slipped out from under me and I was skidding down the pine needles and brush, trying desperately to catch hold of one strong bush. Several of them tore out by the roots and I started gaining speed. I remember thinking that this would be the fastest way I could get down, after all, and then the roaring grew very loud and I realized I was falling toward a gorge, where the river was breaking thunderously over the rocks—and I just had time to think disgustedly that it was certainly a kick in the pants that I had lived through the avalanche, if this was what would happen in the end, when my feet struck the back of an enormous tree, a bone-jarring shudder went through my whole body and I came to a stop not twenty feet from the edge of the cliff and against the last big tree that had held its own against the precipice it grew on.

For quite a while I lay there on my stomach, my face buried in the ground. People talk about survivor syndrome, with that true delight they have in cataloging chaos, but sometimes I wonder how much they understand. As I lay there on my stomach, my fingers bruised and bleeding, I knew that what I had feared most was not, in fact, chaos—sudden death—but rather the inexplicable order of life, the way the sun rises each day and seems to expect the same from me, a rising, a going on, a self-created pattern of existence, seems to expect from me that I give something of myself to help create the order of the world. But now, given back once more my life, I felt both lost and hopeful. There seemed no longer any hurry; my destination was something that would wait. Life was the gorge and the river and the wind sweep and the tall dark trees creaking in the air like thin applause.

Slowly I climbed back up the hill. I knew I would have to retrace my steps all the way to the spot where we had eaten, if I was ever to find my way back down and onward, but now I walked carefully, placing each boot with precision. Just as I came to the top of one steep gorge, where I thought I could start back down, it began to rain again, so I buttoned up my coat and carefully made my way down the slippery rock, and the earth as wet as dung. I half expected to be overtaken by the others, who should surely be done in the icefall by now, but no one appeared in the mouth of the gorge and halfway down it I stopped and sat, my parka wrapped about my knees. You know how when you are coming down something fairly steep you feel you have to keep moving just so that the momentum of your descent will prevent you from rushing headlong outward into the space that tilts before you? And then, when you manage to stop, it is as if you have stopped at the apex of a Ferris wheel and you wait, breathless, for the movement to roll you onward once again, even as you are held in a state of suspension, like a boat at the top of a great green wave?

Well, as I sat on a beveled rock, my feet tucked neatly beneath me, the green that started up through the rain light with a surreal vividness was framed by the dark-brown walls of the gorge. For a long time I looked down that stretch of listing earth, as precipitous as longing, with a feeling there was something there I had to find. So suggestive was every patch of gentle green in that continuous fall of meadows that I almost wished I had it in my power to tilt the earth and so shape any landscape through which I chose to travel. In that green moment, I remembered why I had come there—to climb, and feel the power which catapults the world.

That would have been quite enough for one day. But at the bottom of the gorge I found a shrine. Although we were in Buddhist country now and the shrine was built of rock and square, like a chorten by the trail, there was about the place an air which was neither Hindu nor Buddhist but older than either, older and more spontaneous both, as simple as the stone that formed it. In the little window of an altar—which had no back wall but was rather a stage looking out across the earth—were set three beautifully formed balls of dung, each with a thumb-sized indentation in its center, the indentation filled with yak milk, fresh and thin and a little blue, poured carefully just to the top of the dung, so that you could see a slight convexity in the surface of the liquid —so that both the dung and the milk had a roundness and a wetness which mirrored the form and texture of a mountain in the rain. The offering was fresh and above the dung, on a flat wooden shelf, were laid three new-picked flowers, a blue, a pink one and a white. I took the flowers from my hat and set them on the altar with the others, full of a sudden, serene conviction that if there were in fact a God, he did not demand from me more than I had it in my power to give; he would never ask for flowers that were not already tucked beneath my hatband.

▲

I kept on walking downward until, coming to the crest of a hill, I saw below me a long cylindrical structure set in a hollow out of the wind. It was a yak herder's hut; from its thatched roof, smoke issued like a hand waving in greeting. I stopped and wondered if I should return the hello, but as I stood there a man came to the door and smiled with a face as wrinkled as the sea.

He was dressed in little but rags, a brown loincloth wrapped about his crotch, a gray shawl stretched tight about his shoulders. I didn't even say "Namaste," but merely smiled a return to his smile and when he gestured me inside the hut threw back my hood and ducked beneath the lintel of the door. The herder made his way to the back of the hut, where the bare dirt floor had been piled high with a layer of clean straw and where a neat fire was burning under an iron trivet on which was set a small tin pot. Four wooden posts, set on the four sides of the fire, supported a supply of wood, and more wood was piled all along one thatched wall and against the stone wall which was the only permanent part of the house. With a regal pantomime the man invited me to cross my legs and be at home. Then he thrust a few small sticks into the fire to make it blaze more brightly, and lifting a ladle from a stick that leaned against the wall, stirred the pot with two quick gestures, scooping up its contents once and letting fall a stream of hot blue milk. When the milk was scalded, he lifted it from the fire and took down from the same forked stick that held the ladle a pair of well-worn leather pouches stuffed with spices, each in a twist of leather or cloth. Carefully he drew out bundle after bundle, setting each one on the ground until he found the one he wanted, which he untied, shaking from its folds a lump of salt as big as the knuckle of his thumb. Tibetan salt. With his fingernail he broke off a sliver from the lump, pulverized it in his palm, then added the sprinkle to the pot of milk. Dropping a smooth symmetrical droplet from the ladle to the center of his palm, he tasted it, pronounced the milk complete and poured it into two cups. With both hands, he passed me one.

The salt seemed to make the milk more sweet. I drank it greedily, inhaling both its richness and the soft bread smell of the straw, and just as I drained the cup and set it down, the sun came out of the mist around us and threw its light into the hut. The smoke rising through the pinpoint holes in the roof looked like a hundred tiny laser jets of light, pushing not upward but downward toward the ground, as tangible as something you could gather in a cup. And at the end of each stream a golden penny lay, tossed all around us like the notes of a symphony, happy to bedeck the straw, the wood, the tiny leather pouch. The hut, light-strewn, was as much a shrine as the chorten in the gorge and I drank the second cup of milk as if it were an offering.

I spent the night with the herder. I knew the kind of anxiety it would cause the expedition to have me not return that evening, but somehow at the time I couldn't think beyond the moment. That place, that hut, that man: they were what I had come to Nepal to find, as much as any mountain. I had, I suppose, grown used to loneliness and begun to see it as my fate, fearful perhaps of the desperate intensity that two people such as Nicholas and I could manage to create between us; but with this man there was neither loneliness nor intensity, just the same kind of communion I had felt with the little girl in Tal, the same kind I was to feel with Tina in the storm. Though after a time he and I talked a little, each in our own language, our talk was no more intrusive or less restful than the singing of the birds or the strange and earnest groaning of the yaks when they gathered about the hut as evening fell.

We watched the sun set over Annapurna and the whole massif grow red as blood. I sat by as he milked his animals and I helped him tear the greens to pieces and put them in the pot to cook. He had a lovely smell—rank and smoky, old and rancid—and after we had eaten the greens and rice spiced hotly with red peppers, we stretched out on the straw and he covered us both with his blanket. Through one of the pinpoint holes in the thatch I watched a star shining and I thought then that yes, as long as you do not *try*, you can tilt any landscape through which you choose to move and make it into one that will allow you both to fall and to climb toward any point you see. When, during the night, I woke, suddenly cold, and watched my breath steamy on the air, without even thinking I turned and wrapped myself around him. He did not wake but moved in closer, sharing with me unconsciously his heat. Yes. I was more than glad to be alive. I felt beautiful on the straw. Sharp pieces of grass and wood stuck into my thighs, delightful as the pins and needles of feeling new returned.

THE WALL

Thirteen

In the morning, after we had eaten but very early still, when the dawn was orange in the sky, the herder walked east with me a ways until we came to a trail much broader than the rest of them. There we stood together and looked across the fall of meadows; I noticed one lone stalk with a round burr at its tip, bobbing against the backdrop of the sky.

My mood of . . . call it reverence, lasted all that day. I was back in camp within the hour and luckily before the search party was sent out. I had expected Margaret at least to be angry, but she was nothing but relieved. "Well, Phillips," she said, "let's just hope you didn't pick up lice from him." Tina, I think, felt guilty —as if she should have supervised me down—and Naomi, if you can believe it, was jealous that I had had an adventure which she had had to miss. It was the Sherpas, though, whom I was happiest to see, and in particular Pasang. We hugged each other, lightly, though we were both embarrassed, and he smiled, it seemed, for me alone.

That day we walked together to the city of Manang. It was an absolutely glorious morning, and a small boy pushing a homemade bamboo hoop ran along with us for several miles before he gave up and turned for home. Because of my night on the mountain, we had gotten a very late start, but even the porters seemed to have caught some of the gaiety which grows in the void of catastrophe averted, and the whole expedition moved fast, reaching the medieval village by early afternoon. I suppose it was nothing but happenstance that we got to the town when it was right in the middle of its annual five-day-long Buddhist celebration—but to me at the time it seemed like a fulfillment, inevitable as noon. After the tents were set up and the duffel unpacked, Pasang asked me if I wanted to go with him to the gompa. Although the streets were narrow and winding, a rabbit warren of doorways and tunnels, passages and alleys, I would have had no trouble finding the temple even without his guidance, since the music that issued from it spread out all over Manang like a pool of clear blue ink. Prayer flags fluttered from a hundred rooftops and almost everyone we passed was twirling a prayer wheel between his hands. At the bottom of several steps Pasang turned ceremonially and offered me his hand, which I took as ceremonially, feeling as proud, somehow, as if I were being chosen for a dance. When the two of us stumbled at last from the brightness of Manang through the doorway to the gompa which lay at its heart, I felt that I had finally come home.

Even today I can't describe the ceremony well: the chanting, the music, the drums and the incense, the cool wood floor and the all-pervasive peace. From time to time the chanters would toss rice into the air, looking up from great bound books, the canons that they read from in the dimness, and rice would fall on the floor, on the books and the chanters, and on the banks of lighted candles that lined the walls. Three lamas sat on high stools at the back of the temple near the altar, and the chanters —some of them in maroon and saffron robes but some of them in jeans, in loincloths, in great white shawls—sat at three long tables that ran the length of the floor. With thin, curved sticks tipped by tiny wads of cloth, they banged from time to time on the drums which hung before them, and some of them piped on long silver horns with flared mouths that reached almost across the narrow aisles. Baskets full to overflowing with torma, a blessed and air-baked bread, stood by the front of the temple, next to the long wooden bins in which the torma had been made.

Cross-legged, Pasang and I sat beside the chanters. Sometimes they recited words in low, guttural voices and sometimes they keened in wordless sounds, the music soaring louder and louder until it reached a crescendo and then died. Rhythms would rise and fall and harmonies enter from the rear, and all without a visible sign of control. Seemingly magically, the music changed pitch and volume and tone, again and again and again, once in a while coming to a full stop in which the silence dripped like water from the drumbeats, and then a lovely throaty mumble would lead the way again to sound. Many of the chanters looked up in greeting as we sat.

An hour passed, or two. Margaret and Tina arrived with Tensing, and the two Sherpas after a brief consultation went over to one of the benches, where room was made for them to sit down and where they too began to read from the canons, singing and tossing rice from time to time. Some women, five or six of them, in wraparound Tibetan chubas and with their hair in braids wrapped twice around their heads, came in now from the courtyard, where they had been cooking chapaties and brewing tea and sometimes desultorily spinning the enormous prayer wheel, big as a truck, that loomed brightly by the entry to the temple. In a cluster of giggles and chatter, they made their way around the room, serving each chanter with a cup of tea and offering a chapati from an enormous stack on a wooden plate.

Some of the men took the chapati from the top of the stack. But some of them poked and probed through the pile until they found one that suited them best and then they tugged it out and laid it on the table with the holy books. When all the men had chapaties, the women went round again with little bowls of dry spice and piled a spoonful of the spice in the center of each one. One monk gestured vigorously to his server for more and she piled five spoonfuls on his cake before he was satisfied. Then, breaking off a bit of wheat he dipped it into the pile of spice and stuffed it into his mouth with a great smacking and sucking noise. All the monks ate happily for a time, burping and farting as the spirit moved them. When they were done, they went back to chanting, renewed by their meal, and some of them left the gompa for a moment to urinate in the courtyard.

Tina and I stayed at the temple until late in the evening, until long after Tensing and Pasang, and finally Margaret too, called by their duties at the camp, had had to bow and leave. I don't remember that we said much, although once, when a great moon-faced, moon-bellied monk in official robes but wearing brand-new eyeglasses gestured to Tina to get up and then picked her off the floor like a sack of potatoes—lifting her high in the air above his head before he set her down—neither of us could keep from laughing aloud. We didn't laugh as loud, though, as the monk himself, who went back to his place at the altar looking very pleased indeed. But that evening when I got back to camp, though most of the Sherpas were sitting around the fire—where Tina started talking with her silent friend Changpa—I found that Pasang and Naomi had gone off together for the night, and somehow *that* I could not process through me, and just as if I had never found the gompa, just as if I had never lost my way and found the herder's hut, I started dreaming terrible dreams again.

Now we were getting very near to the mountain, and the terrain was turning far more difficult and steep. Although the monsoon rains had stopped, the river near the headwaters was still swollen and torrential and some of the bridges had been washed out and not replaced. Not only that, but there were several sets of trails on both sides of the river, and at several crucial points it wasn't clear which trail to take. I walked alone. Once I traveled a thousand vertical feet up a hillside, only to find that a stone wall had been built across the trail and that beyond the wall a landslide had taken a bite out of the hill a hundred feet across. But I didn't care. I really didn't care. Not that I was apathetic, or numb; quite the opposite. I felt full of life, but my energy was erratic. It would overtake me in waves of desire, the desire to prove that I was invulnerable, that nothing could hurt me now. It wasn't that I thought I couldn't fall; I just felt that if I fell, if I slipped from a boulder or landed in a river, at least I might finally learn something. So, like an idiot, I crossed the river all the time alone, by slippery boulders just close enough together for me to leap them or by fallen trees, slick and wobbly and perturbed. Somehow it all seemed so hopeless, and avalanche the one thing I was sure of. Too much, that single flower. Too much, the crunch of crampons on the snow. I might be able to reach out into moments; but people? That was something else again. And underneath it all I was worried, I think, about my behavior on the mountain, where like it or not, I was going to be responsible for other people, holding their lives in my brake hand. But though I was worried, I longed, as we all did, for the mountain to simply *arrive.* It floated like milkweed in the distance. It was so near, elusive. It seemed so far away. Yet finally we approached it. And that day, Changpa drowned.

Undoubtedly the confusion of splitting the expedition contributed to the delay in missing Changpa. We had come to a gorge near the mouth of the Marsyandi, and the easiest route from there on up lay on the far side of the river. One of the Sherpas, Ang Dawa, was convinced that he could throw a log down across the river and wasted a lot of time trying to do just that, with the help of some of the other Sherpas. One of the logs as they dropped it rolled suddenly toward us and before going over the edge into the river knocked off with its tip a porter's load that had been set near the edge of the bank. The load contained a bunch of ropes, and its loss caused instant consternation among us all. Rather than risk any more such losses, we decided to set up a Tyrolean traverse and Tina went half a mile downriver, crossing where the stream widened to a considerable degree, but even so compelled to get into it up to her waist at times, belayed by Margaret and with several Sherpas standing near.

By the time they got back and we had the traverse set up, it was midafternoon and the advance guard of the porters had arrived at the edge of the gorge. Since it was clearly going to take hours to get them all, and all their loads, across the river, the expedition members crossed over first, along with most of the Sherpas and the porters equipped with high-altitude clothing. We were going to eighteen thousand feet that evening and put several miles behind us before we camped, leaving the main body of the porters on the far side of the river. And although Tina, of course, noticed that Changpa was not with us that night and probably Per Temba, who was running the rear encampment, was aware that he was not there, naturally both assumed that he was on the other side of the river, and it was not until we came together at lunch the next day, not far below the apex of the pass, that we saw that he was gone. Some of the Sherpas were willing to believe that he had taken off with his load, to sell it in Manang. But most of us, the moment we heard that he was missing, knew instantly that he was dead. For Tina's sake, however, and our own, we pretended to think he had simply twisted his ankle and, being mute, had been unable to call attention to his plight.

We found his body in a side stream. Really, it was a miracle that we found it at all, in that vast expanse of rocky debris, where the five moraines controlled us like the fingers of some huge hand. We had divided into nine search teams, each team composed of one climber and two Sherpas, and each carrying a walkie-talkie. Changpa himself, of course, was carrying the radios—an irony the dimensions of which did not strike us fully at the time. Once we spread out across the valley, I could only occasionally glimpse another searcher, wandering along a vein of water, disappearing behind a knuckle of stone. There was a desultory look to the figures at such a distance, a halfhearted, hesitant air. Everything was so colossal. The land engulfed us like a storm.

As luck would have it, Tina found him. Her voice was very careful and controlled over the walkie-talkie when she said she had sighted clothing in a stream. I was not far away, and when I reached her side she was just stepping into the water, bracing her boot soles against the bottom of a large boulder near where

Changpa had come to rest. His yellow rain slicker—Tina had given it to him and he was so proud of it he wore it even when the sun was shining—had been pushed up by the stream of water, off his back and almost over his head. One of his feet kept bobbing up like a waterwheel, a buffalo scarer, a millstone grinding wheat. His arms were underneath.

I pulled Tina back and two of the Sherpas lifted Changpa out. Tina was sobbing uncontrollably by now, and I put my arms around her and said anything that came into my head. I said that it wasn't her fault that Changpa had drowned, that such accidents could happen anywhere, anytime, and that they were no one's making, though everyone's grief. But she didn't hear a word I said and my own voice sounded hollow, so hollow, in my ears, because I didn't believe, myself, what I was saying, even then, I couldn't believe it, though it isn't as if I *caused* the slope to slide and no one asked me if I wanted to survive its passage. So even while I held Tina close, breathing the perfume of her skin and tasting her small salt tears, I felt that there was only part of me engaged with her, and I envied her, somehow, her pain. The Sherpas laid Changpa on his side. His face was fixed and grave as it had been in life, and his eyes, wide open, were infinitely sad.

Fourteen

The day of the avalanche was hot, a hot spring day. It was early March, but a chinook had blown in the night before, and things were starting to melt in the valley. Ryan was up from New Mexico again and I was feeling very high. The invitation to the expedition had come only two months before and those two months had been, in many ways, the best that I had ever spent with Nicholas. Now that there was an end in sight—and, then, I saw the entrance into India as an end, those hot, hot hours as a flower-covered arch at the end of a thirsty journey—I could relax again and feel at ease and I saw Nicholas as someone who would always be dear to me, and whom I could allow to love me without the fear that he would thus rule me, as if by remote control. I see now that although I knew our renewed happiness was the direct result of its anticipated end, I also started, despite myself, to let myself believe that there was hope for Nicholas and me together, that our love was in fact a lifelong conversation on which it was foolish to attempt to gain perspective, because I was and always would be part of it. And—perhaps—I let myself believe that because it was the only way I could continue to respect myself. I had said goodbye to Beckett, after all, and in a different way to Ryan, long before, and yet I still believed that I should, somehow, be able to give up all I had for love. I didn't know how close I would come to succeeding.

One day the autumn before I'd been walking back from the store to our house. Nicholas was away for a week or ten days. He had gone on a buying trip. He hated those more than anything else, not because he didn't like buying—he was as fascinated by shiny gadgets as anyone else and didn't try to conceal it, an endearing trait—but because they took him to dismal places and he had to stay in hotels. The aspen leaves had started to turn and the mornings were frost-crisp, so that you walked then very fast in order to keep warm, though in the afternoons the sun seemed strong as summer. I was so happy to be outside that I wasn't thinking of much but the weather. Things with Nicholas had been peaceful for several weeks and at the time that did not mean that they were getting boringly repetitive— we kept making the same mistakes, though less frequently, and having the same good times, though less frequently—but just meant that I could relax into myself for a time, reconstruct to some extent the independent world I'd inhabited as a child, a world of fantasy and fairy tale, where bites out of red-tinted apples could put you to sleep for a hundred years until a prince came by and kissed you quite insane with life. I was thinking also, maybe, of Orion, since the day was *our* kind: sleepy and crisp, full of surprises, stirrings, everything latent, skipping weather, leaf-leaping weather, fall.

I turned the corner past the monument—quite a few tourists were sitting on the benches there, eating picnics out of paper bags —and somebody grabbed me by the shoulders, bringing me to a sudden stop, and said:

"*Please* don't walk off like that again. Look, I'll pay you anything you want. Just sleep with me, for God's sake!"

Well, it took me an endless moment of staring into his teasing eyes to recognize Beckett and by the time I did it I must have looked to the spectators as if I was seriously considering his proposition, because a dead silence fell on them and they waited interestedly for my answer. I burst into laughter and fell into Beckett's arms. I hadn't seen him for a very long time, not since just after high school, but he hooked his arm through mine and led me triumphantly away.

You know when something happens that you suddenly realize you've been waiting for for as long as you can remember and you are so astonished by the simultaneous realization that you've been waiting without knowing it and also that you need wait no longer that you can't think of a thing to say or do? For five minutes I was rendered utterly speechless by the extent of my own happiness at seeing Beckett again. Then, of course, the dam burst and I talked with him nonstop for hours, taking time out only to call the shop from the Wort Hotel to tell them I wouldn't be back that day. And I knew even as I dropped the dime into the slot of the pay phone that I would sleep with Beckett, that nothing could stop that now—that I needed Beckett badly, his giddiness, his irreverence, his irrepressibility. When the waitress brought our order he leaned across the steaming plates, took my hands in his own and said in an intense reverberating tone, which could be heard throughout the room, though Beckett wasn't raising his voice:

"Look, I don't care *whose* it is. Just have the baby!" I saw several old people look at Beckett admiringly and at me disapprovingly, as if to say that here was a right-minded young man, though clearly more of one than a woman such as I deserved. I kicked Beckett under the table and drank some water to clear my throat.

Jesus. To have the chance to fool the world again! Not to feel, as I always felt with Nicholas, that I was transparent as I walked down the street, more than transparent, naked, and walking on eggshells, picking up my feet as carefully as an Indian fakir walking on red-hot coals. But to muck around barefoot, up to my knees in mud, knowing that whatever people saw in me, it was a projection of their own desires and not *me* at all—that Beckett and I together could create an illusion as big and colorful as a hot-air balloon and float away together before the eyes of a hundred gaping spectators. I needed to live out fantasies, a hundred of them, a thousand, and to feel that I was strong enough to make the rules myself and not have to obey a list of regulations which I'd been handed at birth, a list printed in invisible ink but which Nicholas could always read and interpret for me when he thought I was stepping out of line.

"Don't pick up that stick! Someone might think you were stealing."

"Stealing? A stick?" I asked him. And even then I doubted. Maybe he was right. But Beckett . . .

"Excuse me, sir," I can imagine him saying to some irate rancher, "but this is our pet stick, Ricky. He ran away this morning and my wife has been so worried. Luckily, we know his habits. He likes to climb on fences. Come, Ricky. Darling?" And he'd give me one arm and hold the stick in the other like a child.

Of course, if we had stayed together long enough, our relationship would probably have been nothing but companionship in the end. That was the way our friendship started out, after all, in high school, as a friendship, nothing more, and things like that usually revert in the end to what they are. In the old days, we had never thought of making our friendship into a love—or I, at least, had not—mostly because I wasn't at all attracted to Beckett as a male. And my idea, of course, was that either you fall in love with someone and follow him to the ends of the earth, or why bother seeing him at all; you might as well go climbing, or read, or run, or anything but feel the loneliness of being with someone, even lonelier than you'd be alone.

But really, Beckett was one of the most thoroughly kind human beings I had ever known. He saw himself as a potential dragon-slayer; he wanted to be the world's ace number one hero and he made a better start on it than most heroes by being the type that actually helped little old ladies cross the street. And it all came from the same root that made him want to tease me and the world; he created his life from the stuff of fantasy and wove around him a universe in which virtue was triumphant and moments could be shaped according to any rule you chose. After we started sleeping together, he named his car after me; it was an unpredictable, unreliable beast, but beautiful, a 1960 Porsche with a dark-blue finish. He called it the Greek Witch. When someone asked him where he had got the name, he said it was named after the best fuck he'd ever had. Which was dangerous in a town as small as ours.

But that was typical. He figured that since he'd met me before I met Nicholas, anything went, as long as I liked it. It was typical also in that he always treated me like a woman—the same breed that wears white tea gowns in novels and that men regard with adoring eyes and say: "No, no, I am quite comfortable sitting beneath a leaking drainpipe. Any spot on earth is comfortable, as long as it faces toward you." That kind of woman. One whose clothes move on her like slow-motion liquid and whose hands lave men's foreheads with long, cool fingers, or bind up the wounds on their chests as they sit, pale with loss of blood but upright in wooden kitchen chairs, their faces dusty, their hands gripping the edge of the seat in silent pain. And other kinds of women too. Women who pull on black lace underpants and walk casually across the room to draw the curtains back and let the early morning sunlight fall slanting across their breasts, or look at you from behind sudden shocks of black hair that have drifted imperceptibly across their wet lips, their sultry eyes. All kinds. Beckett, in fact, saw my sex as an inextricable part of me and not, as Nicholas always did, something that had been tacked on at the end, when the item was almost finished, a final touch that was more cosmetic than anything else. I wasn't compartmentalized to Beckett; there were no contradictions allowed. Practically in the same breath he might tell me that I made his cock so hard it ached, that I was wetter than a sailor's wet dreams, and that my skin looked like alabaster in the moonlight, my breasts like two small pears, ripe for plucking. Two different modes of reality, two different stories, had been raided for the stuff with which he stroked me—and somehow that made me, for the moment, whole.

I don't know why I talk about him in the past tense. He's still alive, for Christ's sake, although not any longer in Jackson. He had joined the army, of all things, two years after leaving high school, and had finally been stationed in Wyoming, where he'd wanted to be all along. He stopped in Jackson on his way to his post. He intended to do some climbing. But he met me instead and fell in love with me, though it was only in the first ten days, while we worked our way by small degrees toward absolute abandon, that I felt for him an affection unmixed with deep repugnance. And the repugnance was never his fault; it was my own and Nicholas's doing. It was our jealousy that came down on Beckett in the end. That and Beckett's own need for me, which grew too intense for him to handle lightly. Once he became a hero-worshiper it was more difficult, as I tended to transfer to him all that was negative about the men who hung around the shop admiring me, the famous woman climber. That admiration is hard to resist—for the moment. You bathe in it, respond to it and find out only later that it has a way of cloying in record time, of getting nothing but boring. Those men don't see you, after all; it's all projection, like the headlights of a car projected onto the wall of a cliff on a high mountain road, so you turn aside quickly to avoid a collision and find yourself going over the cliff instead. Where did *that* one come from? Some mystery I read once, I suppose. The perfect crime. No perpetrators can be traced.

Well, anyway. Beckett admired me, all right, but somehow it was healthy, without that strange projection. He *saw* me, I think —my ambition, my greed, my destructiveness, perhaps. He loved me anyway. So it wasn't fair to mix him up with those groupies who broke chunks of me off to hold like natural chock stones, in case they ever needed such a tool, to help them up, or down. And it wasn't fair to blame him for the guilt that Nicholas made me feel or for the chains that I let Nicholas drape me in, after he found out. I let myself be sucked back in, no doubt about it, even though after the first time I slept with Beckett I felt as if a part of me had come loose and was floating somewhere in the air above my head, the same feeling I had sometimes when we were coming up the Marsyandi Khola and saw the top of the mountain through the clouds—a total release, the sense that school was out for the summer, that nothing could hold me back but lack of courage, that anything was possible if I only believed in it enough. And he believed that too.

▲

But though we had this—this faith together, if you want to call it that—and though I treasured Beckett's kindness and his hope, still, right from the start, I feared too much involvement with him. If I had known why, perhaps things would have gone quite differently. Because such fear, the nature of such fear, was something that up until then had been quite foreign to my nature, something I didn't know I had in me. Caution with my feelings? I might as well have been cautious about walking down a trail. I had always wanted absolute commitment, absolute passion, absolute everything. Now not only did I not want it but I actually feared it. I saw in it a potential for disappointment and despair. I developed a sort of paranoid awareness that permanence can drive all ecstasy to boredom. Is that what aging does to you? Or Nicholas, perhaps. Not everyone has a Nicholas, though. I knew too, intellectually, that this awareness was not something which was unique to me, but something that lovers throughout the ages had held close or pushed away. So what did that say about love? That it is just a chimera, an illusion, that it exists only when the elements of fantasy are present, that when you have found someone who may in fact be the perfect man to share your life with, you had better not give him the chance to do it, lest you find out that he bores you?

Or if not about love, then what did that say about me? Part of me desires to be scintillated always, to go on and on, endlessly, to the next mountain, seeking the brilliant gold light of the sunrise, the mist like rich incense on the rock. And part of me wants nothing but peace and silence and the quiescent movement of day, the sluggish clarity of a low-lying river in autumn when leaves, red and brown, drift aimlessly on the surface of small pools and eddies. And luminosity is *always* veiled by the rising of desire. But I had let such times come as they would, sunrise and autumn, with the natural changes of life, not seeking the changes exactly but entering into them as they came. Now . . . now I was trying to control them, as much as Nicholas had ever tried to control them, trying to keep Beckett at a distance, to make myself invulnerable to pain. Was it a disease I had caught from my husband? Or had we simply reversed our roles, like alternating current, at some point unknown to me, when I was mainlining the force of our passion?

Yet it did not seem like a disease. It seemed . . . it seemed like grandeur. I felt that it would be a mistake for Beckett and me to overwhelm each other, then or ever, for the very reason that there is something lovely about the ever unfulfilled, the ever possible. The very first boy I ever thought about loving, I never even kissed. He came to my window at night and talked on the other side of the screen. The nights were brilliant with stars, the sage was wet and sweet, the little sounds in the darkness rustled like birds' wings. We would touch hands, lightly, through the mesh of the wire and feel each other's fingers, rough and scratchy as the copper, divided into tiny squares of flesh. When one night we met without the screen, on a desert hill in summer, we did nothing but touch each other's hands all night long, feeling each finger, each knuckle, over and over until dawn, when we could see each other's pupils, dark and round as the bowl of the sky. The morning was delicately transformed, by my exhaustion and my arousal, into loveliness so great that it verged on terror, since I felt it could somehow destroy me.

Maybe it was the same thing, the same thing I felt with Beckett. Or maybe I just feared it would destroy *him*. To keep it delicate for a time . . . but it was too self-conscious. I wasn't fourteen anymore. I knew. And though I knew, I found that I instinctively tried not to repeat myself with Beckett, to do everything with him just once, so that in memory it would be easy to sort things out, to think of the time we ate pizza on the sidewalk, the time we jumped in the pile of leaves, the time we made love in the treehouse. I didn't want to get burned out. But when had I become so flammable?

I don't know. It's hard to remember. Sleeping with Beckett was one of the finest experiences I've ever had. That sounds so cold, so clinical. It wasn't. It was just that Beckett—he truly loved to touch. He was sensuous. He was sensitive. He was—Christ almighty, he enjoyed everything about his body and about mine. And he talked to me constantly, painting pictures with his tongue, putting me into a hundred Renaissance settings, perching me on top of forty Romantic chasms, carrying me into the bedroom farces of the eighteenth century. It was all there, all at his command, and when one morning after a night of little sleep he woke me with his movements and I lost my temper, shouting, "Fuck it all, Beckett, what the hell are you doing?" and leaping to my feet to drag one of the quilts with me to the doorway of the next room, he just lay in bed complacently and watched me, then said:

"The trouble with you is, you never went to summer camp. But Lord, you're beautiful when you're angry." That—it didn't threaten him. I had to laugh, but I gave him the finger also and went to sleep on the floor.

All this couldn't last very long. Nicholas was still away, but although I didn't really think it through, I knew that when he got home I would have to tell him about Beckett. I found it quite impossible to keep *anything* from him, had, actually, a compulsive need to tell him all my thoughts, my acts, my feelings. And though whenever Nicholas and I had discussed the possibility or desirability of one or the other of us sleeping with someone else, Nicholas had always, very brusquely and definitively, made it clear that he would consider that to mark the end of our relationship, I somehow couldn't take this latent threat seriously, couldn't imagine getting from where I was to the point where I would have to be for that to happen.

And more. I was playing with dice, throwing my life on the waters. Things had been predictable too long. Would Nicholas kill me, leave me, love me? I would tell him. Then what would be would be.

You've got to understand that. Things hit me. I mean, I may sound as if I'm very self-analytical somehow, very in touch with my feelings, but really that isn't quite true. I can't *imagine* very well. I can only reconstruct. Maybe that's what Nicholas and I had most in common, an inability to understand the commonly accepted truths of life, an inability to see the validity of other people's wisdom until it hit us like a ton of bricks. I once had a conversation with my mother; she was trying to give me some little bit of advice, to impart some of her life's learning to my recalcitrant brain. I listened. But I told her I couldn't possibly accept her direction, not because I didn't want to, but simply because her words had no meaning at all for me. They were as empty of substance as cotton candy, as gas, as sea fog. Exasperated, she inquired sarcastically whether I intended to find out *everything* for myself, just as if no human beings at all had lived before me?

"Of course," I told her. "How else can I possibly live?"

The first time I kissed Beckett I got a shock I was quite unprepared for. Kissing him was as magnificent as I had ever imagined a kiss could be. It was the universal kiss, the one that wrote the book on union. And this with a man I had hardly before that moment even considered as a man. After that moment, a whole universe of truth seemed to open: you can be attracted to someone you don't consider handsome, you can be blind to all sorts of latent power in people.

So anyway, you've got to understand that things hit me like this, out of the blue, and things that the rest of the human race take for granted without having to experience them simply don't exist for me until I do. Sure my relationship with Nicholas was doomed from the start—but how was I supposed to know that? Sure it would tear him apart to have me sleep with someone else

—but I assure you that it never even occurred to me that he would be really hurt. I thought it was all an act, that possessive trip of his. I thought, even, that it might be good for him to see that it was all hot air, his jealousy. What a joke. I should have known better, after Orion.

Not that I wouldn't have done it anyway. I wanted desperately to free myself of his bondage. That bondage was very simple, very classic, really. Nicholas and I, though we shared so much, could not share everything. And what he mostly could not share with me was my essential optimism, my underlying belief that things in the end turn out for the good. If you don't try to mold them too fiercely. If you try and let them evolve. So there was a whole part of me that wanted to breathe again, to float away in that hot-air balloon of faith in life itself. But Nicholas—Nicholas didn't have enough faith in *himself* to really believe it was possible for *me* to float away like that, and his disbelief, however unconscious, however unexpressed, had a crippling effect on me and pinned me to the ground. That was what I wanted to be free of, and Beckett was a prayer flag, fluttering in the breeze.

Why do you *have* to understand that? What an absurd thing for me to say. You don't *have* to understand anything, except that another day has passed. You don't *have* to understand anyone, not even your mother, your brother, your wife. The higher you climb, though, the deeper you seem to see into yourself, and after a while no one seems too different and strangers are only people who will not admit their kinship. The truth of the matter is that we rest heavy, burdened with the load of time and space. The truth of the matter is, perhaps, that there is no truth of the matter—but why do I remember things so clearly? The day of the accident, so hot. Like Bombay, hot at midnight. Like Delhi, hot at dawn. And when the first spring thaw came and the sagebrush poked up through the snow as sweet as birthdays, weddings, I didn't want to smell it, I didn't want to know. So what is love, from all that? Naomi screwing on the mountain?

Fifteen

The mountain. The mountain. There are so many things that that one word can mean. It thrust up into the sky with the purity of a dagger. Spindrift dusted the sky around it like a veil. Beyond the mountain a cloud hovered, a strange long lenticular cloud that didn't touch the summit but stood above the stillness of its upper reaches, a ghost cloud waiting, like me, to be sucked back in, to the spell of the mountain, by the incantation of dreams. We had buried Changpa in a mound of rock and climbed to the col above its hidden valley, and its vastness and its grandeur could almost have blown me away. A wind tore off its tumbled slopes, the sun was tickling its ruin, and I took out my binoculars and studied the route up the face. The icefall looked very tricky and the rock wall just damn hard, but it was climbable, no doubt of that, and the sky above it was blue as dye.

So we began, at last, the climb. In retrospect, no one could say this was exactly an auspicious beginning. Changpa had just drowned, and I was thick with memories, we'd lost some ropes and all our radios and the nine of us hadn't begun to form a team. Still, there is something in action, and in labor no matter how hard, and the tents were blue in the morning and the sunsets silver at night. After we set up the base camp, most of the porters were paid off and they left the mountain in a straggling stream, thrusting ten-rupee notes into their pockets and waving with great relief. One of them, on his face a grin as wide as a river, repeated over and over again, "Sorry, so sorry," as if he felt he was deserting us to our fate, and all of them walked about thirty times as fast when they were leaving as they had when they were hoping to arrive. The Sherpas who remained got out their high-altitude clothing, some of it debris from other expeditions, most of it equipment we had brought, and set up their tents on the perimeters of ours—a little puzzled, some of them, that their services would not be needed on the mountain itself, but seeming quite contented for all that. Perhaps Naomi contributed to their contentment; though her voice and her lovers I'd decided to simply ignore. Since that one night in the dining tent, when the three of us had been at peace, as one, we had not again achieved such closeness, so I had tried to put her out of my mind.

But Tina, even then, was getting sick. The swim through the icy river, to set up the traverse across the gorge, had left her chilled and somewhat weakened, and Changpa's death had been a genuine grief. In fact, when I saw how it affected her, I realized that for Ryan she must have grieved much more, and just because I hadn't been there to see it didn't mean it wasn't something that we might have truly shared. Every night when we lay in the tent she seemed a little shadowed, dampened, in need of reassurance, and she wrote in her journal less often than before. During the days, however, she refused to let it slow her down, and she seemed from the start to have magic on snow and ice. Within four days we had driven a route through the icefall, and on the fifth we all made a carry up to Camp One.

We had stopped just above the icefall to eat lunch. Naomi and Laurie were supposed to sleep in Camp One that night—to straighten equipment, put up two reserve tents and generally make the camp a more livable spot on the mountain. The rest of us were going to make a second carry up that afternoon, so we were eating rather hurriedly and talking very little. Robin was absolutely exhausted; she had been at the end of the last rope on the ascent and we had stopped several times to allow her to catch up with us, but it was pretty clear already that she was going to be a problem even in a support role. Margaret seemed a little worried about that. I was tired and hungry and gloomy, and Tina hadn't been herself for days.

All of us were staring down through the icefall when we saw two figures slowly making their way up through it. We couldn't imagine what they were doing and all of us had instant premonitions of disaster. They didn't seem to be carrying loads, merely light summit packs. Margaret got out her binoculars and said quite grimly:

"It's Per Temba and Ang Nima. What in God's name can have happened now?"

"Nothing at all, I don't suppose," said Naomi. "I told them they could spend the night in Camp One."

There was, of course, a resounding silence. By now, nothing that Naomi did in relation to the male sex should have surprised us, but we were all as stunned as Margaret at the blitheness with which she imparted this plan.

It was Margaret who spoke first.

"Miss Thompson," she said sternly. "I can only imagine you haven't thought this through. We'll have to send them back down. You know that we want no Sherpa support."

"Why?" said Naomi. "They aren't here to support us. This isn't affecting the team at all."

"You sleeping with anything that can pee against a wall?" I said. "That isn't affecting the team?" My sudden rage surprised me. I guess I was thinking of Pasang.

"At least I can *climb* without men to help me. That hasn't been proven yet with you."

I will say for Margaret that she tried very hard to keep the lid on. One of Naomi's oldest friends, she still had good reason to be furious at the risk Naomi had put the Sherpas to, sending them through the icefall for no reason. But though she tried her hardest, it was no longer any use. I would have gladly killed Naomi, had I had the means at hand. I realized then that I hated her—

hated her competence, hated her invulnerability, hated her hands. Hated her, I suppose, in the same way that I often hated Nicholas, and felt something of the same way that I often felt with him: that I wanted to win, to triumph, to be the one victorious. Though the battle, both with him and with her, is one I cannot even now define, it had something to do with courage and with writing all your own rules. For it has always seemed to me that courage is the one value that makes all other values possible —and that when I meet someone braver than myself, he becomes an obstacle, both loved and hated, that I have to overcome. And in this case, I see now that I too would have liked to sleep with a Sherpa; to have the kind of courage that would bring me relief from pain.

Well, we all of us got angry. We spread out on the snow and shouted and by the time Per Temba and Ang Nima arrived we had actually unroped. I was threatening to go down through the icefall alone and Naomi was urging me on, when suddenly Margaret snapped, "Shut up, you two," and we all fell silent, except for the murmuring of the Sherpas, who could hardly have been more amazed. Tina kept saying, "Temis, for God's sake, ignore her. Temis, for God's sake, calm down."

Somehow we finished the carry up to Camp One, then all returned together to the base. The whole team was seething and upset, but though all of us wondered, perhaps, why the hell we had ever come to the mountain, all of us also wanted to get to its top. So we spent the evening in conference, trying to straighten everything out, and some form of peace and order actually got restored. Naomi said she was sorry, looking astonishingly contrite.

The following day it was foggy, and ominously warm. We were carrying up to Camp Two now and found when we began that the route through the icefall had been effectively destroyed by the collapse of a serac. Before we could go anywhere, we had to decide whether to make the new route to the left, where the glacier was more jumbled, or to the right, where the path would have to be longer. All of us were pissed at having to go near *either* edge, close in to the valley wall where things could fall off on us, where the odd five hundred thousand pounds of snow or ice might drop, and we stood for a long time arguing, until finally Margaret decided on the right, the avalanche chute. We kept having to go closer and closer to the valley wall. There would be cones of avalanche snow, sometimes flat, sometimes angled, across the route, and it was so damn foggy we couldn't really see a thing.

Margaret was staying on course, however, by guiding off a dark rib of rock. From time to time the fog would clear and we'd all see this dark smudge against the white. None of us felt too terrific, but Tina kept cracking jokes to try and raise our spirits. We were about three-quarters of the way through the icefall when suddenly there was in the distance a sound like an old-fashioned express train, rapidly coming closer.

Finally Tina said: "Here comes the three-fifteen express."

We all laughed nervously and then a large patch of fog split away and we could see a huge mass breaking off the ice cliffs on the northeast shoulder of the mountain. Sizable pieces kept calving off the face, but the main mass disintegrated into an elephantine mixture of ice and dust which—gathering more mass in the shape of snow and large seracs—was blasting its way across the icefall, heading, it seemed, straight for where we stood.

Since there was nothing at all that we could do, we stayed and waited to be engulfed. Then, at the last possible instant, the billowing cloud of snow seemed to change direction and veer away and downwind of our route. Five minutes after the last of the dust had settled down, the fog cleared too and we could see that the slide had obscured our tracks for fifteen hundred yards. For me, with that, the day turned into a nightmare.

It wasn't just the avalanche. It was the snow bridges, the fog patches, the crevasses, the seracs. Everything was getting soggy and I kept hearing bridges collapse behind me with a squishy, plopping sound—like someone getting hit in the stomach and gasping in surprise. On the ascent, I was the last in line so I thought at least I was safe from crevasses, until, crossing one that no one knew was there, I stopped and looked at my feet and saw a piece of snow between them fall away like a piece of skeet, like a badly thrown Frisbee—white light turned to golden light and then to the deepest of deep blue, and I could see two hundred feet or more of space below me and no real bottom, but a curve and shadowed dark. The skin all over my body started registering heat and cold in flashing alternation and it felt as if my body were being controlled from a point at the base of my stomach. There was a solid wall in my mind between my feelings and my actions and I held onto my will like a ball between my hands.

I know, I know, I know. Why then, of all days, why then? I wish that I could tell you. All I know is that I kept thinking of Nicholas and of the way he looked when he was dead—so blue, so still, like a stranger, like someone I had seen once, years before, a face on a subway, a face across a countertop—and wondering why on earth I had come to the mountain, the mountain we'd always wanted to climb together, wondering whether perhaps I was mad, to do this to myself, to put myself in a place above all others where it would be impossible to forget and impossible to remember, where the best I could hope for was to survive one more hour, one more minute. If what I felt could be called survival at all.

Each boot as I set it down had an unnerving quantity of mass to it: it seemed heavy, so very heavy, to try and lift it up. I wanted to walk as lightly as the mist, but the only lightness within me was the lightness of my breath, which couldn't seem to find room to enter my lungs, so that, instead of a frame pack full of food, I wished that I had brought with me a balloon as light as air, in which perhaps I could float to the top of the mountain.

Somehow I made it to Camp One. Once we were out of the icefall, my fear should have ceased, since nothing could be safer than the route across the lower bowl. Even there, however, I felt like sitting on the snow and crying. I was right on the thin edge of abandon and I was remembering one time when Nicholas and

I were climbing Mount Baker in a total whiteout and three-quarters of the way up I sprained my ankle and he wouldn't just turn around and go back with me, I had to *ask* him to please turn back. God, how I'd hated him then, for doing that to my pride. Well, this time there wasn't anyone I could ask and no one whom I could even *tell* the way I felt, and the wall between me and the women around me was as high and impervious as the iron curtain, as unnegotiable as a mountain of glass.

By the time we got back to the icefall it was midafternoon, and things were hotter and squishier than ever. The mist, at least, had cleared and we could see that the route Margaret had chosen on the ascent was both winding and unsafe, right below some of the most treacherous of the seracs. Margaret wanted to get another load up to Camp Two that day, but she also wanted to improve the route, so she deputized Naomi and myself to find a better one and mark it with wands and set up some fixed ropes where they were needed. Naomi had already proven herself rather brilliant in setting up a ladder across a bergshrund in the lower icefall, and since we were, together, the best she had on rock, Margaret certainly hoped that we would pin the big rock wall. So her theory, I suppose, was that if we had to work together now we would also have to become friends. What she didn't realize was that Naomi had entirely forgotten about the shouting match of the day before, and that I was far too concerned with my own fear to have much energy left for animosity. The others dumped out all the long ropes they could spare and then took off and left us.

Well, at least Naomi didn't hesitate to lead. We roped together and I belayed her across some nasty snow bridges, while she probed and poked and came to five dead ends and then another one. Whenever she got close enough for me to hear her, she narrated episodes of a long and hair-raising story about almost getting blown off Carstens Ridge on McKinley, twice, when she went out at night to take a shit. She was wearing only overboots on her feet and she didn't have an ice ax, so when her legs slipped out from under her she had to do a self-arrest with her elbows and her fingernails—not an easy thing to do, as the crust on Carstens Ridge was thick. Then, when she had finally taken her shit and was almost back in the tent, the wind blew her over again and this time she slipped *at least* fifty feet down the ridge, according to her tale, before she was able to stop; from the terminal point of her slide she could clearly see the upper glacier, two thousand feet below. I'm sure that none of this was calculated to make me feel insecure, but every time I moved a step I felt that I was walking on something as thick as a soap bubble.

By the time we finished wanding the route, there was literally not a cloud in the sky. Spindrift was curling off the upper slopes of the mountain like pencil shavings twisting in the breeze or old-fashioned ringlets on a girl in a white starched dress. I was hot, sticky hot, and my cheeks were flushed with sun and windburn. The purple and red of my harness were brilliant through the smoke gray of my goggles and my double boots were dark with wetness, my socks glistening with beads of water. Everything, in a word, had taken on that startling tactility that is generated by sunlight on the snow and the clarity and thinness of air in the high mountains.

With one accord, Naomi and I stopped and simply drank it in. I don't know what Naomi was thinking, but I was remembering a girl I had seen once, a girl in the mountains. She came down the glacier, glissading, her hair in the wind behind her. It was brown and it flew like her ankles, all right, all together, a picture of beauty, and I felt . . . it was something like terror, that something so lovely could be. I looked at Naomi and felt that again, just as strongly—that the line between her and my panic was nothing; that beauty is just as terrible as fear.

I don't know if I can make this clear. Naomi's blue-black hair curled gently around her cheeks, and her fingers, so lean and clever, were hooked through the purple straps of her pack. She was wearing a white sweater and gray French knickers and those deep-purple gaiters that set off the color of her eyes. And though, in a way, I wanted her to be there—or rather, perhaps, I wanted her to *be*—I was thinking again of courage and of walking fearless toward a crevasse. That Nicholas died in the avalanche—it was something I had not forgiven him, a final, dreadful proof that he would always dare a test that I could not. But not just that; if possible, I hated him even more because, before he died, I had never ever been as scared as I was now, and I blamed *him* for the transformation of my world into something fragile, easily shattered, soap bubbles floating through space. But he was gone, gone to a place where I could not punish him; and so I wanted to punish Naomi instead.

With an intense compelling need to move, I turned my back on her then and started through the lower icefall toward our camp. The route through the lower segment was well marked and indeed quite churned up by countless passages through it. The tracks seemed ugly to me—harsh and brutal—and without consulting Naomi I started to break a new trail, through white and virgin snow. Though the snow was soft and mushy and consequently following a new trail would be much more exhausting than sticking with the old, I plowed ahead, filled with a kind of anger, and daring, in my mind, Naomi to come after me.

We had not gone twenty yards before it happened. Not even a tug or a slackening of the rope occurred to warn me; suddenly there was just a sickening, splintering crash and then an earth-shaking thud, and when I turned, neither Naomi nor our route was to be seen but instead a huge block of ice—which a moment before had stood quite tall and regally above us—was buried deep in the surface of the glacier and little cracking noises like the reports of a BB gun against a stone wall were echoing all around me and under my feet.

But that, though ghastly enough, was not the thing that astonished me most. What absolutely dismayed me was that when the ice came down it fell upon the rope and somehow not only severed it like a knife but tossed it outward in a whiplash motion so that it piled itself quite neatly at my feet. There were still crevasses all around me, lurking like mouths beneath the smiling snow, and here was my umbilical cord, stern and contemptuous, leading to nothing at all but air. Guilt and panic flooded me. Tracks do not lie; how could I explain this death? Then I heard Naomi call me, her voice sodden, muffled, cracked. "Temis?" she said. "Are you all right?"

You know, it's funny. I don't think she'd ever called me by my name before. Hearing her say it, as tentatively as a child—not only was it a victory, as clear-cut as the final step to the summit, not only was it a relief, but it was, most important, like discovering again who I was, like discerning in a moment of sudden clear perception that even if the rope around my waist led nowhere, my name would always hold me tight. My name—my history—was something both of us could cling to, and if followed, like a thread within a maze, it would lead us once again into the sunshine. I was Temis Phillips, of Phillips, Phillips and Rhodes; I was here on the mountain I had always wanted to climb. And yes, not only was beauty as terrible as fear, but fear could be as beautiful as grace, and lead me once again to action. I called that I was fine. "And you?" I said.

"Stuck," she answered. "A crevasse. I don't think I'd better move. And . . . hurry."

Well, I hurried, all right. I hurried. I gathered up the broken rope and struck out around the great serac, watching each boot as it sank deep into the snow. Once, one of my feet broke through and this time I watched the snow as it spiraled down the maw of the crevasse with an almost aesthetic appreciation of its passage and of the inevitable end, its dissolution. If I went after it, I went, that was all. No sense in worrying about things before they happened. I could certainly think of worse ways to go than checking out in a wedge of dark-blue ice, as fine and shadowed as a pair of eyes, on a day when spindrift dusted off the mountain like the wild hair of a child. No ghats, no rotting corpses, wild dogs. But a mountain; to be part of it forever.

Naomi hung just below the lip of the crevasse. Though she had managed to jam the tip of her ice ax into the soft ice at the edge of the chasm and had wedged one of her crampons somehow into the wall, the other crampon hung free in the air and her whole upper body was trembling like a leaf. The ice was still making noises and at any moment the noises might herald another shifting of the block, but she did not even look up as I approached. One slip and she was gone and she knew it and I knew it and though speed was all-important I hardly dared to breathe, and she just clung and clung, supported by nothing but her will and fingers, trusting me to pull her out and soon. I tied a knot in one end of the rope and stretched myself flat on the snow at her side. Then, with a caution born of desperation, I slipped my hand down in front of her, trying not to touch her with even the lightest touch, and somehow got the rope clipped through her harness while energy poured from her trembling body like light. Still she could not move, and I backed off with the rope to a distance of fifty feet and sunk my ice ax into the snow and set up a boot-ax belay and braced myself with everything I had, then called out, "O.K." And she let go and fell into the crevasse, and the force of her fall was nothing compared to my relief.

No more than five minutes later, she jumared over the edge. When she was finally standing on the snow once more, she looked at me and said, "You've seen one, you've seen them all"—though her face was so pale the beauty mark on her cheek stood out like a small black hole.

As for me, I felt so lighthearted I was almost singing. This time, there had been something I could do. The rope as it ran through my hands was as clean and dry as penitence and I felt that even love itself was something I might survive.

Sixteen

Three weeks after we reached the mountain we finally got to the base of the big rock wall. The weather had been holding clear and steady, though each morning a cloud lay in the valley below us, and at night the wind would rustle like a song. At times it almost seemed like music, like scraps of harmonies torn in tiny shreds. But the sun glittered on the diamond snow, tents bloomed like desert flowers after rain, and at night the tent seemed like a ship to me, its ridge a keel that nudged among the stars. We climbed, that's all we did. We climbed. We carried packs and dropped them, untangled ropes and tied them to our chests. Though life was hedged about with ropes—the span that fell from tents to the snow, the harnesses stretched about our waists, the lines that pegged the mountain like a pencil, crayon, wand—all was subsumed, at last, in action, in steps, in moves, in endless hopeful breaths.

Four of us were at the base of the rock wall. At twenty-two thousand feet, everything slows, and we thought it would take us three days to climb it, and another day or two to dig a high camp. The band was dark and full of chimneys set with ice and rock that was too rotten for comfort, but it looked climbable to both Naomi and me. Since the accident in the icefall, she and I had reached some real peace; whenever I had a choice about it, Tina was my partner, but when I was left to climb with Naomi, we honestly got along. That she respected me now was part of it, I guess. And then, the Sherpas had long since been left behind. Actually, I loved to watch her climb. She moved against the mountain like a cardinal, a bright-red dot against that world of towering blue-gray cold, and the paradox of her subjugation to that great bondage—a subjugation entered into willingly and with great grace—was constantly reminding me of the subjugation of all of us to something beyond ourselves, and the fact that graceful sacrifice can sometimes see us through. I didn't *want* to like her, but I liked her more and more, and saw that perhaps I'd been wrong in my judgments, that she wasn't flighty, just smart. In fact, the ease with which she concentrated on her breath—the sound of the air going into and out of her lungs—made me think that *she* didn't need the dharma to teach her how she should live.

So Naomi and I were at the base of the rock wall, along with Laurie and Tina. To all intents and purposes, the expedition had split in two. We were short on ropes, and we had no radios, and the other five climbers were down at Camp Four. As soon as we got the high camp ready—on a slope above the rock wall where the granite turned to snow again, and where we thought two Whillans boxes could be squeezed, and stocked with food and fuel—they planned to move up to support us, but for now we were there alone. Though the high camp would scarcely be perfect, since the snow bowl above it was a natural avalanche chute, we didn't plan to be there long. By then it was plain that Dervla, Robin and Taffy would never see the summit. We hoped that six of us could make it to the top. As long as the weather held, we saw no problem. We knew we could pin the wall.

But four days passed while we did it. Naomi and I alternately led, with Tina and Laurie alternately belaying. I'd never done work so hard before, or seen so few results for labor; each evening we would stagger down the ropes we'd fixed that day, each morning we'd roll out of bed, ascend them, and go on. Small things impinged on consciousness: the sounds of stoves, the smell of tea, the crunch of crampons on the snow. But once I set an ice screw which pulled out at the lightest tug; and once I lost an ice ax down the echoing windy ridge. When things are going well in the mountains, there is mostly just being and nonbeing, and the line between now and all other time is as sharp as the line of the sky. This time, though, perhaps they were going badly. There seemed to be something to remember, something I needed to know.

I led the final pitch on the rock band late on the fourth day. Standing on a ledge, both Naomi and I were chilly, and the ledge was only three feet wide, and covered with shards of ice. A wind was blowing off the rock, and water was running down from somewhere up above, and it wasn't a place where you wanted to talk, or do much but get away. So though I couldn't see where the route went, really, I just clipped in and started off, and once off, was instantly in trouble; the wall was much steeper than it had looked from down below. What I had imagined to be holds were simply colors in the rock and the water had slicked the surface to a ghastly rainbow sheen. The route not only wouldn't go, but it seemed to be driving me backward, so I angled out and to the right and almost started back down. I was fifty feet beyond the ledge before I finally found some rock that was sufficiently solid to take a piton, and my heart was pounding by then like a hammer in my chest. I got the piton in, and climbed straight up above it; by now Naomi was far away, below me and over to the left. She shouted something, but her voice was lost in the wind that was blowing, and though where I stood the rock was bulging out in a sneaky, satin coil, I thought that just beyond it there was a jam crack that led to the top. If only I could reach it, from there on things would be easy; it was clear enough to me that at last we'd reached the crux. I put my foot on a solid hold and paused for a second to rest; but when I looked below me, I almost fell off the wall.

I hadn't clipped the rope through the running belay. It dangled below me, then curved off into the air, and the first point that it touched down at was the spot where Naomi stood.

I don't know how long I stood there, hearing nothing but my

breath. I had the absolute conviction that I was going to fall, and
that the longer I stood there, the harder the fall would be, as if
any fall could be harder than total, any ending more final than
death. The air smelled strange, like something singed, and each
tiny flake of rock as I watched it became a climb in itself. I wasn't
scared, but the mountain seemed suddenly alive, a thin bright
edge of shadows and of wind. Each tiny col, each huge arête, had
become too sharp to hold; but for a minute I managed to hold
on, while I thought of a number of things. I thought of the guide
we had had in the city, and the tour of the Rammadir temple that
day. "To the truly religious," Banni had said, "it is best to come
here to die." My brother rubbing my small wrists with snow. "Is
it worth it, Temis? Are you glad?" I thought of my father, sitting
in his tower, solving the puzzles of our lives. To be born, I
thought. And what is that? Something that made you a god? I had
no time, less than no time, but the moment I stood in stretched
like thunder, and ate me, dreaming, whole. I had been trying to
make things simple, manageable once more, no falling in love
again, no convolutions of human relationships, but something I
knew, something that had defined whatever self I had—a mountain, golden and silver in the first light of morning, not an obstacle
in my passage over life but the journey itself, complete, carved
plain and hard in the backdrop of the sky. I shifted one foot and
got ready to fall, at last completely alone. And then, from somewhere, Naomi's voice came floating. "Below you, Temis. Climb
down."

So I climbed down. I'll never know how I did it, since down-
climbing even at the best of times is twice as hard as climbing up,
and this was not the best of times; I was trembling in every limb.
But I climbed down, not knowing why or how I found it in me,
and if I ever said that Naomi had saved me only once, it wasn't
true, she saved me three times, each more clearly than the last.
I climbed down to my protection, and clipped my rope through
the piton, and then just simply collapsed on it, letting everything
go. I fell then, and dangled in the air, turning slowly, looking up

at the mountain, and the cone of light beyond it. I knew that I'd
been given back my life.

When I could breathe, I started off once more, feeling my
energy returned. As neatly as a dancer, I climbed to the top of
the wall, and stood at last on the snow I'd longed to see. I drank
some water, put in a snow fluke, then climbed to the point of the
ridge. There I shouted loudly, and heard the mountains carry
away my voice. I didn't have enough rope with me to continue
the line to the ridge, and though even in my elation I noticed that
the slope had a weak layer, ice under which some softer snow still
lay, it had been such perfect weather for so long that I thought
the slope was stable; and tomorrow I'd be back there, and could
set the anchor again. I shouted once more, pretending I was
flying, then rappeled back down the rope. Naomi was waiting and
she actually hugged me. Together we walked back to camp.

I was very tired, actually, having eaten almost nothing all day,
and consequently everything was taking on that delicate significance that makes you think the night is full of signs and symbols
and even the simplest occurrences are portents of things to come.
There was something wrong with Naomi's headlamp; it kept
dimming and then brightening again, erratically, for no reason
that either of us could see. And as I watched it flash across the
snow, it slowly acquired a reason and became like a signaling
device sending out mysterious Morse code messages across the
mountain's flanks. When I turned off my lamp for a second, I saw
two bright stars—one below the other one—making a line that
seemed somehow incomplete without a third, a third that would
form a triangle. I couldn't decide where the third one would be
—to the left, to the right, or in one of the planes below it. Then
I saw another lamp, not Naomi's and not mine, bobbing below
the bottom of the wall. Slowly it came nearer and turned into
Tina. She said she had been shooting pictures of our headlamps.
But she'd really been waiting for me.

That night we had a party in Camp Five. Sibyl and Margaret
had come up from Camp Four to see how things were going on

the wall, and when they found we had finished pinning it, insisted
we celebrate. They had brought with them Robin's tape deck, and
a bunch of old swing music, and Laurie had a special bottle of
wine. The day had been unusually warm, and as the sun had set
it hadn't got much colder, which was strange, all right, but pleas-
ant enough at the time. Below the mountain a cloud had been
hanging, looking the way pictures of clouds do from space, folded
around the earth like phantom hands, but dancing, with blue at
its edges like the blue at the heart of a fire, and wisps of white
tinged red like foam on the sea. Though we had seen the cloud
rise daily from the valley and then by evening tear and disappear,
for three weeks now the weather had been holding so steady that
we had really ceased to associate the cloud with weather at all. By
the time we got to camp, it was gone with the daylight, and we
were intent on the night.

Maybe it was the liquor, or maybe it was the heat, but the night
turned electric as soon as we started to dance. We had pulled out
some pads to sit on, and Naomi and Laurie had stamped out a
platform around which they molded a bench made of snow. Large
white candles were set into the bench, and they burned quite
steadily in the still, thin air. To me, the women seemed burning
too, like so many sharp white flames.

I was standing looking vaguely toward the summit, but Tina
had started to dance. Each evening for the last three nights she
had been falling into the tent after dinner, a tree that had been
axed. Her face painted with exhaustion, she would crawl into the
tent, unlace her boots and set her cameras carefully to one side.
After a time she'd move and smile, but she seemed to be running
out of steam. Tonight, though, from somewhere, she had found
new strength.

"Hey, Phillips," she said. "Want to dance?"

She had never called me Phillips before, and for a moment I
didn't respond. I thought she was talking to Ryan, or someone else
who wasn't really there. She wore a shirt with the slogan "It's
better on top," and though she moved slowly at first, she drew me

toward her, her grip as firm as any man's. Her eyes were shining, and her cheeks bright red, and after whirling me round in a wild circle, she pulled me in close to her neck. Pulling me forward, pushing me back, she guided me through my steps, and impossible gestures untangled themselves, till we moved like two sides of a swing.

"Chicken wing," she said, and I twisted under her arm.

"Sweetheart walk!" and we promenaded around. We danced closer and closer and more and more quickly, till we fell in a heap to the side. Tangled together, we watched the others, and Tina put her arm around me.

The next morning the cloud below the mountain was bigger than it had ever been before, and the red on it was more distinct; it seemed a day of reds. Tina had tied her hair back with a piece of bright-red avalanche cord, and she clambered around taking pictures of us all, saying, "Red, red, why isn't anyone wearing red?" All of us, including Sibyl and Margaret, climbed the fixed ropes with heavy packs, and late afternoon found four of us still high. We had hauled up two tents, along with food and fuel enough for seven days, for two, and we even had some oxygen, cached at the edge of the cliff. We didn't yet have ropes, so I couldn't move the anchor up the ridge, but that night it didn't seem to matter; the camp was dug in, the summit was in sight. The blue of the icefall below us, the blue of the sky up above us, we sat, we four, as if waiting, but waiting for no one knew what.

Naomi was the first to move. She wanted to get back to camp. Laurie was more than willing to go with her. Tina seemed utterly exhausted, and leaned against her ice ax, unable to decide whether to go or stay. Ravens were wheeling in the air below us, riding the updrafts like butterflies, staying poised, motionless as prayer flags, their feathers spread. And God knows why, what possessed me, but I wanted to stay there for the night. There was no doubt that Tina should get lower; she needed her strength for the next two days of push. But I asked her to stay with me, and of course she said she would, so we watched Naomi and Laurie go down and stayed on the edge of the world. After dinner, we sat together in the door of a Whillans box, and Tina put one arm around me and I put one around her, and everything was lovely to me, for though I knew I would feel again the desire to move onward—the longing, the hunger, that has been my reason for being—at the moment I was perfectly contented and I stared at the icefall in the sunset as if it were fine torma on an altar, and at the changing shadows on the cornice as if at prayer drums twisting on the air.

Again and again these things are glimpsed. Again and again they stay unknown. We come and then we go. We climb and then we fall. And that evening while we slept, a storm came on the mountain, and we could hardly get out of the tent at dawn. When I woke, Tina was curled against me, but Nicholas spoke in the wind.

Seventeen

It had been a long and nasty day, with a high incidence of confusion. Some climbing groupies had hung around the shop for hours, talking about clean climbing and chocks as if they had just discovered these concepts themselves, and with their self-obsession and admiration exhausting me more thoroughly than a long day on the rope. I had misplaced the key to the cash register and was madly searching for it when Nicholas said, out of the blue:

"I wish you wouldn't encourage those guys so much. You don't know what it does to me."

"What it does to *you,* for Christ's sake, what it does to *you!* What the hell do you think it does to *me?*"

I found the key and jammed it into the lock, swinging the side of the register viciously open, feeling already that this was probably going to be harder than I had imagined, to tell Nicholas about Beckett—and glad, I suppose, that he was giving me an excuse to feel self-righteous, since nothing can make you feel more self-righteous than uncalled-for jealousy. Some joke. And also, I did feel truly sorry for myself, to be the subject of such thoughtless adulation: It seemed to me unfair that I should be tempted toward corruption of the soul when other people were never subjected to such a test. But though I had planned to tell Nicholas about Beckett very soon, I had planned to choose my own time to do it, a good time, a time when it would not threaten him to know. So I also resented the fact that he was apparently going to press the issue of other men right now, in such a way that, inevitably, not to tell him about my affair would seem afterward to be indistinguishable from an outright lie. And I had never lied to Nicholas. So already I was feeling stuck with it.

"I don't know," he said. "But I just know that it's one thing *you* never have to worry about—me and other women."

That was true, of course. Then, it was true. And maybe that was most of it from the beginning, my love for Nicholas, the fact that he had given his heart to me wholly. If he hadn't always known it, I had, and he knew it now, just when I was starting to be less his. I had put up with a lot for that, that totality of togetherness, that surety of power. So it was true. I never had to worry. But it made me angry that he stated it as if it made him good, as if it were a conscious choice, as if it were anything on his part but something he couldn't avoid. He didn't *want* other women. He wanted me.

"Oh, for Christ's sake," I said. "You think I'd have anything to do with those jackasses?"

"How do I know what you'd have to do with? How do I know? And how do I know you'd tell me if you did?"

"Tell you what?" I said, aggressively cleaning out the cash drawer.

"You know damn well what."

"All you have to do is ask me."

"I won't. I expect you to be honest."

Of course, that was just what I intended, to be honest. If I could. If there was such a thing to be. But at the time, his demand, his expectation—it seemed like another power game he was playing, like that time we were climbing Mount Baker in the whiteout and he wouldn't turn back until I asked him to; he wanted so much to go for the top that he didn't care if my ankle broke beneath me as long as I didn't speak out. Don't ask me why, but this seemed like the same sort of thing. In this case, he didn't care how hard it was to tell him I had slept with Beckett, how many barriers he himself had set up to make it hard—over the course of the years, over the course of the day—how much the rules had been created by him, defined by him. From the start of our relationship I had told him, after all, that I wasn't making any promises not to sleep with anyone else. It was he who dictated the outcome of that purely speculative freedom. Because, of course, for years I had had no desire for anyone but him and my stance was quite abstract, a principle, not a reality. No longer. And it wasn't because of me, it was because of him, the stand he had always taken. Maybe that too was galling me, the fact that now that it came down to it, I thought his stand would fall apart, like a duck blind after hunting season. How could he be so weak?

"Right. You want me to be honest?" I said. "Fine. I have. I've slept with someone else."

Nicholas started to tremble. I couldn't bear to look at his face, but I saw his body and it trembled all over, it was shaken like wheat in the wind. He was holding a rack of hardware and he dropped it to the floor; it literally fell out of his fingers and just afterward he followed it to the floor, he sat down suddenly on the carpet. The only other time I have seen someone go so fast into such deep shock was after an avalanche in the Cascades. It was a slab avalanche and this guy—I didn't know him—got hit with a lump of snow as big as a pickup truck. It rolled over him, pushing him into the soft snow beneath it and then rolling on; and when he picked himself up he looked as if he were made of rubber, one of those toys you can bend every which way, contort their legs into knots, hang from the edges of tables, from lamp-shades and chairs. That was what Nicholas looked like.

He didn't speak. He didn't say a word. And I felt sick, as if I had been burned, as sick as I had felt once when he almost cut his thumb off with a penknife and we went to the emergency room of the hospital and I asked the doctor if I could watch him sew up the wound—to learn how to do stitches, in case I ever needed to in the mountains. The doctor stuck the novocaine needle into Nicholas's thumb. He didn't make a sound, but his face contorted with pain; it was one big grimace like a death mask and I nearly fainted. A nurse had to lead me away and stick my head between my feet. Only this time there was a remnant of anger in me and a great big welling of fear that any second, guilt was going to flood me like water in an arroyo. I tried to speak, to tell him he was taking it far too seriously. But I just looked at him. After a minute he managed to croak: "Leave. Please leave."

And I did. I walked out, stunned, through the front door of the shop; for once in my goddamn life I did just what he asked me to do, just when he asked me to do it.

What Nicholas went through the next week was hell. Pure hell. We had to keep working together in the shop, but about once an hour Nicholas would suddenly turn on his heel and go into the back room and turn the radio up loud. Then he would sit in a chair with tears streaming down his face, withdrawn into a world of unmitigated pain. I didn't see him put food into his mouth for six days. He lost fifteen pounds and his jeans started to hang on his hips as if he were a kid again, all bones and numinous energy. He had never looked so beautiful to me before. His skin had a tone to it, a luster like raw silk, and his eyes were huge and black. In fact, I fell in love with him again, and though I did manage to tell him that I didn't regret my relationship with Beckett, that it was one I had *had* to have, that even knowing what it would put him through, I would still have had to act the way I did— and the fact that I could never do it over, that the inability to envision the consequences of my actions had been the largest element of its joy, was something that I then did not perceive— I also found myself telling him with every other breath that I loved him, that I needed him, that he was my man; that I did not love Beckett and never could.

Did saying this make it so? I think there is a power to words, a power as strong as that of any acts. Because by any reasonable standard my relationship with Beckett was a hundred times more nurturing than my relationship with Nicholas. All through the next week, a week of incredibly convoluted workings through, I turned to Beckett again and again and he was always there when I needed him, he was always just what I needed when I needed it. When I needed a lover who could kiss me quite insane, he was that to me. When I needed a friend on whose shoulder I could cry, there he was. When I wanted to be told to stick to my guns, he told me that. And when I wanted to be told not to be afraid to love Nicholas, he told me that as well. And yet even so, it was not the saying I couldn't that made me unable to love Beckett. The truth was, I wasn't ready to love *anyone* anymore.

No one, that is, except perhaps Orion. He'd been my man, long before the rest. One night, when I was maybe twelve years old and he was just fifteen, he came in from playing soccer after school and found me at my desk doing my homework. He was wearing gym shorts and a T-shirt, as was I; but while he was still sweaty, I had gotten chilly from sitting in the house. I was rubbing the sole of one foot against the calf of the other leg, in an effort to generate some warmth, and struggling with some math problems, percentages or fractions. Ryan came and crouched beside me and told me about his day; we talked about what we'd do that evening, and Ryan helped me with my math, and all the while I was rubbing one leg against the other and feeling on the verge of shivering. Ryan put his hand around my ankle, and though it was very warm, it somehow made me feel even colder than before, though I stopped rubbing my foot over my calf, and set it on the floor, away from Ryan's hand.

"You should take a bath," he said, and moved his hand up from my ankle to my calf, which he rubbed with his palm—first the back of the calf, where the muscle begins to curve inward to the knee, then the inside of it, where the muscle doesn't seem to matter, and the hairs are very soft and long if you brush them toward the sky. Though he started off with a firm pressure on my skin, and just his palm upon it, at last he spread his fingers wide and stroked me with each one of them; five points of fire that made me ache with cold.

I clenched my teeth together, and kept on doing fractions,

while he moved his hand by slow degrees to my knee and then
my thigh, and I felt I had to hold my body rigidly in place, so
intensely did it want to jerk from such a deep severity. There was
a numbing quality to Ryan's touch, in that it seemed sedation to
the flesh around it, seemed to make wherever it was *not* just half
alive. We didn't look at one another then, or for a long time after,
and the reason was the same as it always is, that we feared at first
the power of us two together. I kept my eyes on the page while
he kept on stroking my leg, and I could scarcely believe that we
had never before stumbled to this place, this tumbled sanctuary
which hurt as much as the pains that drove us to it. And whatever
confusion started in me then, confusion about the realms of pain
and pleasure, of happiness and sorrow, it was no more Ryan's
doing than my own, just the fact that rules all human life, that
the things that absolve us can also destroy us, which is perhaps
why we invented gods. Finally, his fingers reached the seam of my
shorts and traced the lines of thread and cloth like fingers leading
music for the blind, each note a sharp reminder of the loss of
something far beyond it, and echoingly sweet for that reminder.
What it was I was losing I had no way to know, and that it was
my immortality I couldn't have cared less, then or ever, for since
it was my brother who taught me that love is irrevocable, like any
action taken and not dreamed of, the line between birth and
death seemed finally erased. So if only I'd gone back, then, to
Orion. We might have tried it, made it, who can say? But maybe
I just wasn't ready to love *anyone* anymore. Not Orion. Not
Beckett. And not even Nicholas Rhodes.

Though Nicholas changed daily, before my eyes. One hard kick
to the balls; it was all it took to make him grow ten years. And
yet. And yet. It was all too late, too late for me. Because now I
was so full of fears and because now, though I wanted so desperately to be loved, I wanted even more desperately to be free. And
both of them—Nicholas and Beckett—needed me so much it
made me sick to my stomach. Quite literally. I had never known
that being loved could make you feel as if you had twenty-four-

hour flu. Well, much as I saw or felt the danger to my soul of building walls of parting, I finally saw that there was another, even greater danger, which left me no choice but to part.

No choice, in fact, at all. Free will? Ha. You stagger along, just stagger along. You can do the standard route or the direct. On the direct, you'll need a lot more hardware and perhaps a lot more skill. That's the only difference between them. They both get you to the same place in the end. But though that is not *free* choice, choice it is all the same. And the moment finally came when even in Nicholas's presence—within the sphere of his influence, that monumental current that carried me along—I could revert, like a Martian, to my own true nature and stand apart and see myself and him and know with blinding clarity that I had to leave him, whatever the task I set myself in rewriting my own past. I no longer cared about winning. No victors, only victims. I can even pinpoint the end.

▲

Beckett had finally left town and Nicholas and I had somehow reached a tenuous state of peace. At least, we thought it was peace, but it was closer to exhaustion, the momentary respite from inevitable movement which happens also to low-lying pools on quiescent autumn days and to leaves when they hang motionless in a sudden breach of wind. We had decided, that is, quite firmly and finally, that we would stay together always—and Nicholas may have believed with all his heart in the validity of this decision but I most certainly did not, although my doubts were buried so deeply that the only way to release them in the end was by explosion, a volcanic eruption of truth. I suppose, really, that I put off making a decision of any kind for the time being and wandered along as nerveless as a frog, not only because I have enormous trouble making negative decisions of any kind—decisions, that is, to reject—but also because I knew that with us there could be no happy ending and that no calm friendship could emerge from the waters of our separation. Finally, I wanted to climb with him still; I wanted to climb with him forever.

One morning, a Sunday soon after the first big snowfall of the year, Nicholas was sitting in the big chair reading, though the sun was glittering on the ground. I was lying on the bed chewing gum and waiting for him to make up his mind to go skiing. When, by ten o'clock, he still had not moved from his chair, I stuck the gum on the corner of the daybed, gathered up my gear and took off for Teton Pass. I spent several hours practicing telemark turns where the powder was deepest and most dry, and took some big falls, returning home determined to train very hard that winter. I had given up wearing mittens when I went out just for the day, although and because the frostbite I had contracted on Mount Saint Elias had made them very sensitive to cold.

My hands had still not thawed out when I opened the door to the house and found Nicholas asleep on the daybed. He woke at the sound of my entrance and rolled over from his back onto his stomach. Taking off my parka and gaiters, I was careful to make plenty of noise—partially because he was already awake and partially to wake him up further, since I had no desire to spend the rest of the day creeping around the house like a wombat while he tried to withdraw from existence. But gradually I became aware that he was staring at me with a look of incredulous disgust, and then he said, "Jesus Christ, Temis, will you look at this?"

I saw that he had rolled over on my gum while he slept and it had melted, crisscrossing the back of his shirt with a network of fine strands. The way he took the shirt off and picked at the gum as if it were a visitation from another planet struck me as funny and I started to laugh, trying to choke down the laughter but utterly unable to do so, even when I sensed quite clearly that it would lead to nothing good.

Well, it did not; Nicholas was furious, and I, having had enough of fury to last at least a hundred lifetimes, was left with no option but to ignore him. I took out the Sunday papers and lay down on the floor. It would have been easy to apologize, of course, but it was my daybed too, and I hadn't asked him to sleep on the gum. Moreover, it seemed to me vaguely disgusting that he had been so weak as to fall asleep in the middle of the day. Disgusting and even more, disturbing. Such lassitude in such a man was far from a sign of future happiness. For him or for me.

I had actually managed to turn to page two of the paper, however, when I became aware that Nicholas was sitting behind me on the floor, rubbing his hands across my back. What in the name of hell was he doing? I didn't want to know. I shrugged my shoulders irritably and shoved the paper away. Craning my neck, I saw that he was removing the gum from his shirt and rubbing it into mine. He had already managed to deposit a good deal of it into the loose cotton weave of the cloth.

I was, for once, quite speechless. My only thought was that *this* I would ignore. Never had we descended to such idiocy. Never had I imagined that we would. I felt a dead heavy weight behind my eyes as I strove to simply wipe the incident from existence, as I tried, without at all knowing what I was doing, to practice the dharma, to let the moment wash away like rain. My hands were just beginning to get warm, and I rubbed them together, delighting in the pain of the burning heat even as I struggled to disregard my own irritation and perhaps using the sensation of pain to distract me from the deadness of mind which was my only option other than sudden rage. I chose, in other words, quite definitely, not to be angry. I chose not to give way to hate.

And perhaps because I had chosen, so clearly, to be calm, and because therefore the part of my mind that had the freedom to choose was quite convinced that I was fully in control, there is a moment in this memory that is lost to me forever, the moment when I rolled over and attacked Nicholas, shoving him to the ground and wrapping my hands around his throat. That moment I cannot remember. One instant I was lying still, firm in my resolution to resist his invitation. The next moment I was trying, I discovered, to choke my husband to death.

It's not that I'm so big on choice. It's not that I believe in perfect freedom. But never in my life have I felt so frightened as

I did when suddenly I saw Nicholas's face above my hands, his eyes wide with fear—not with fear that I would kill him, as that was clearly never a possibility unless he himself allowed it, but with the fear that is the raw ingredient of all human striving, the fear of one's power to control the world, the fear that we can *each* become as gods, making other men serve our basest lusts, our most destructive instincts. His fear was at unleashing me. And mine? Mine was at the fact that he could do so.

Even with all that has happened since, that moment seems so recent. His face, reddening slightly from the buildup of blood. My hands, hot with returning feeling, wrapped below his chin. I sat astride him, rigid. I felt that I could hardly breathe. I felt, quite literally, possessed, the battleground for two competing forces. I hung there, stretched out between them like a rope, unable to stop, unable to go on, until, like a cloud lifting from a mountain-top, the battle lifted above me and I was free once again, though only for a moment, to choose what I would do. I wrenched myself free of Nicholas's neck and, breathing as if released from suffoca-tion, flung myself out the door of the house, crying aloud as I did so, "God. Oh, God, please help me. God, oh, God, please help."

Strange? Oh, God, how strange. Because if there is one thing out of all the conceivable variants on truth in which I have no power to believe, it is in the possibility of divine intervention, and probably the reason why Buddhism has such strong appeal for me is that it is nontheistic. Tensing relies on no one but himself, and prayer flags flutter out our loneliness. I ran down the steps to the front yard and, though bootless, kept on running down the street, running, just running, up to my knees in snow, crying over and over again for help as if at thirty thousand feet and moving higher.

Well, that, as they say, was that. From that there was no return. Tina and I, we were pretty extended in that storm, and most inhabitants of this globe would think we were quite insane to have gone so far out on a limb, and all for the sake of a summit. But I, at least, did not feel as extended then as I had a year before in Jackson, sitting finally in a shaking heap, in a snowdrift covered with dirt and dog pee, right at the edge of town. And though I went back home at last and we patched it up once more, from then on it was nothing but deceit and I was using Nicholas only until I had the chance to get away from him; if there is one thing of which I'll always be ashamed, it is those last two months I spent with him, after the invitation came to join the climb and before the accident occurred.

Because afterward—and when I say afterward, I don't know *what* the hell I mean: the only afterward there really is is now, and all the other afterwards are just as much befores as anything else; there's no beginning and no end to it, just pieces, which I arrange and rearrange much as a child plays with blocks—but afterward I felt so frozen, helpless. I would think of Nicholas when we were separate, think that I needed him, think that he was what I needed. Then I would see him and I would freeze, become so suddenly still, be suddenly jerked to a stop as if my self-belay had accidentally caught me, as if I had set it up wrong so that the slip knot was just too far above me for me to reach it and release it. I would hang there, unable to go on, unable to get back up, caught by my own protection and knowing that I had only minutes before the weight on my diaphragm, *my* weight, choked me. Sometimes when we were first together we had made love on sunny afternoons, and having made it, like a cake, had felt this perfect contentment in inaction because just being together was action enough, and if one of us had had to go somewhere else the only way to separate was to actually tear the moment apart as if we were ripping Velcro. Well, now, with Nicholas, it was again the same and for much the same reason; because we were uncertain of the future together, we wanted to prolong the pause before the future came to be. But in the old days when we'd ripped that bond I'd felt energized, hopeful, ready for action, whatever might occur, and now—afterward—I felt deadened, dulled. I only knew that I had lost the capacity to be *myself* with him and that coming together was just as unsatisfactory as being apart.

Although I desired him still. God, how I desired him. He had only to touch me for me to grow excited. I wanted him to take me, endlessly, over and over again, until I couldn't think, I couldn't move, I could sleep and be at peace. Well, sometimes he did just that and though I felt no guilt—he was Rhodes, after all, and I was Phillips—no guilt, that is, at the physical action, no guilt at what it might do to his mind or mine, I felt a profound sense of loss that sex had come to be separable from love and that, like a stereotypical male, I wanted nothing afterward but to roll out of bed, drink some orange juice and, later, sleep alone.

All sorts of fears emerged then, fears I hadn't known I had in me, fears that overlapped and edged one another like rice paddies, a perfect patchwork quilt of fears, all of them off, disconnected, each one seeming at one time or another to be quite as true as the next one but each contradictory, really, to the one before. I feared that if we stayed together long enough, Nicholas would truly cease to love me. I wanted to leave him before I saw this happen. I feared that if I continued to live with him, not loving him as I once had, he would come to hate me and that in turn would make me doubt he had ever loved. I feared that if I let him go, he would end up thinking it was all for the best or be confirmed in his original perception: all women are alike. I feared that if I gave him the chance to make up to me all the bad times he had given me, he would, once the balance sheet was clean, expect more from me than I could give. I feared that if I let him go I might need him again someday, desperately, and he would be there for me no longer. I feared that staying with him would bring out the cruelty in me and that I would use him like a beast of burden until I couldn't bear myself, my face. I feared that I would discover, through the process of staying together, that I was incapable of overcoming the anger and hatred I'd been accumulating for years and that that would make me feel worthless and totally out of control of my life. But it was the all-or-nothing aspect of our relationship that added to my caldron of fears the bitterness I feared the most. Since he insisted on a total marriage or nothing, and since it was doubtful that we could be consistently honorable to one another, the only relationship we were likely to arrange was one in which there was a steady alternation between bickering and peace, a gentle obsession with all our own worst instincts, a broad-based opportunity for indulging disappointment and contempt. And that I held against him. I needn't, though, have bothered. The avalanche took care of things for good.

It's funny about grieving. I always thought it was something you did afterward, after the bad thing had occurred. But I did most of my grieving long beforehand, and when the bad thing actually happened it was more an ending than a beginning of pain. Because nothing could have been more real than the grief I felt each time I thought that Nicholas and I were breaking up. And when, each time, it turned out we were not, the grief I felt was not lost but just put aside, pushed down, stored once more until the day it would be needed, so that when he finally died, there seemed only a very little more to feel. Nicholas and I—it was always as if we were the survivors of a disaster. Only we two had been left when the ship blew up, the volcano exploded, the mountain fell into the sea. The inexplicable accident of our continuance was only slightly less mysterious than the bond which forced us to stay together, trying to grapple with guilt and joy. When the disaster finally occurred, long years after we met, it only proved to the world what I—and we between us—had sensed and carried with us all along. "Died," he wrote, "on expedition." And that was the world below Tina and me, the world outside those shaking tent walls.

Eighteen

I woke to the sound of Tina's breath, as ragged as a wound. I was lying on my side, my knees drawn up to my chest, and my feet were so cold I couldn't feel them, with one whole leg quite numb. Tina was curled in toward me, all six feet two of her quite small; her short blond hair, harshly whitened by the sun, was spread across the pillow of her boots and pack and parka. Her bangs were damp with fever sweat and her lips were open wide. A little drop of spit had run down from the corner of her mouth onto the nylon of her sleeping bag, where it froze, a tiny smudge of darker blue; when she woke up, though, even then, her face was an explosion of expression. But my lassitude was a kind of pale-gray sea that I was floating in, and though I noticed I could scarcely breathe, I just lay and held my toes in my hands until Tina said, "Aw, shit."

The tent looked like a hurricane had hit it. The wind was blowing so hard and the snow was falling so fast that it had knocked one end of the tent quite out of kilter, and the storm was driving snow in through the back seams of the walls. There was frost dust on the sleeping bags as well, and in the night I had rolled on a bag of raisins, which had burst and scattered frozen pellets all over the white of the frost. Tina looked like a martyr in a medieval painting, all angles and shadows and smudges, with an expression of wild surmise, but it didn't take a martyr to know what had happened, which was that the cloud had grown up. I hit the sides of the tent with my arms and large clots of powder snow jumped into the air and slid away. Although it was clearly past dawn, the light in the tent was dim and for quite a while we both just lay there and groaned.

But I was very thirsty and finally I moved. There seemed to be hardware covering every available inch of tent floor and I felt permanently encased in my sleeping bag, but at last I managed to unearth the stove, which started with a roar. I had the strange feeling I was underneath the sea, a place I had been only once. When you put your mask to the bright plane that marks the ocean's ceiling, you are lost to all activity above you, and the magnification that the water effects is joined to the fierce push of the tide to create a world without referent. Below you, tiny translucent fish in astonishing magnetic clusters move together in ripples as if in a wind, and tidal patterns are etched on the sand like patterns in a Zen master's garden, and somehow, there in that world transformed, no warning sense remains to you.

So peculiar did I feel, so sea-changed, that when the stove, with a gasp, went out, without pausing or thinking I thrust out my hand to touch its burner, just as that time I had dived, when I saw a little feather duster waving—a cone of filaments that was like a cluster of stalks, no flowers—without pausing or thinking I had put out my hand to touch it, at which it had drawn away, was sucked away, disappeared in a flash into a small round hole in the sand which, except for its taut black rim, looked simply like the remnants of a single pouting breath. So filled with astonishment had I been that I wanted to shriek like a child, and though I found out later that the duster had been a sea anemone, as common almost as the sand it grows in, having it draw away from my exploring finger was—in the magnitude of its effect—precisely what it must be to see a volcano erupt when no one has informed you that they can. But the stove did not draw away. It burned my hand. "Aw, *shit,*" I said then, and at that I truly woke up. Tina found a pot and gathered some snow and I started the stove once more. Then we lay on our backs and let it melt snow until we had water to drink. We gulped it down in long loud bursts, then lay on our backs some more.

"We've got to get down," Tina said finally. "You know that we've got to get down."

Get down? Go down? Until that moment, such a thing had not occurred to me, and yet as she spoke I saw, of course, that the only thing was to get down. But like a tapestry, a rug woven to hang upon a wall, the reversal of expected actions in the prospect before us was so bizarre that it was enough to slow my thoughts even more, and just as you study the unicorn, the maiden and the tree more carefully because they hang upon a wall, so I studied the suggestion more carefully because it seemed so strangely askew. I was here at last, on the mountain I'd come for, and the only way up it was down.

"So we'll go down," I said. "Let's do it. God knows how long this will go on."

"What do we do first?" Tina asked.

"I think we warm up our feet."

It took us an hour to do that. First I stuck my feet on Tina's stomach, and then she stuck hers on mine, and though you could hardly have been jammed nearer to someone else than we were to each other in half a functioning Whillans box, and though I had to pee quite badly and couldn't find the urine bottle, we still believed that it was just a matter of time before we could get out of the tent and down again out of the death zone, because it never occurred to either of us that a snow slide had taken out the anchor I had set and that the fixed rope from the top of the wall had slid into the abyss, and so we were really in pretty good spirits while we fumbled with all those feet. Tina's breath was still quite ragged, but as we got warm I tried to reassure her, and at last we were ready to emerge.

The wind had hardly died. If anything, the storm seemed more furious than it had when we woke up. We crawled through the storm tunnel at the good end of the tent and fought our way out through its maw. Outside it, the world seemed as wild as the anteroom to hell. I almost got frostbite just taking a leak; the whole slope above us looked dangerously unstable and I really thought the wind might blow us away. I thought of the Japanese women's expedition to McKinley, where nine women, roped together, had peeled off Carstens Ridge like banners, and except for nine migrating blots, had never been seen again. When the wind shifted for a second, the snow fell almost softly; it would have been exhilarating if we hadn't been stranded too high. But at twenty-two thousand feet, everything slows, and winds can kill you that would otherwise just cool. Had we had a rope, Tina and I would have roped together even for the short descent to the wall.

We moved down toward it slowly and dark forms appeared and disappeared through the rents in the snow, while I started to choke on the wind. There was a huge, upright boulder leaning over the rock wall, the boulder beneath which the oxygen was cached, a monstrous thing about ten feet high and dark as obsidian or ice. It was disturbingly like a presence, inclined over the edge but watching us, it almost seemed, with its head turned back on its shoulder. Although we had to peer myopically in front of us to see where the ground itself lay, that boulder seemed so close I felt I could touch it. And somehow I kept veering off to my left, to try and avoid what I thought was a cliff on my right, but Tina kept calling me back to the right with "Temis, Temis, this way."

We searched for the rope for over an hour, while the storm blew all around. Carefully, step by step, we felt our way along the cliff, through a landscape sculpted of snow. In the foreground were valleys filled with snow—snow bulldozed into small mountains, snow dug out into saucers, snow forming cliffs and ledges, snow coating all the rocks. From time to time, color seemed to drift into the grayness and the whiteness, so we dreamed the storm was lifting, but then the pink and gold of daylight faded to gray once more. If there was color, it was color from the sea, a dream born of oxygen starvation, not tangible, not real. I dug in the snow till both my arms ached. But the snow anchor was gone.

So we went back. Practically crawling, we made our way up the slope, and with the last remaining strength in our arms, we dug out the other tent. We fell inside it and fastened the door. There was nowhere else we could go.

▲

The first day was the hardest. I felt guilty about the anchor and about asking Tina to stay there, and she was clearly getting sicker and sicker, though she never once complained. Her lips were cracked, and her throat was sore, and her head hurt all the time, so I went to bring up the oxygen and that did seem to help. We had food and fuel enough to last six days, seven if we stretched it, and the storm couldn't possibly last that long, or so I told us both. But before many hours had passed, there was snow in everything we owned. Snow had become a condition of life, the color of air, an aspect of every thought, an element of the wind. Each gust of wind deposited snow on the tent fly like the sound of gas escaping from a valve. Each pore of my skin had become a receptacle for snow, neatly designed to hold one small grain. My scalp, the part that peeked out from my hat, was covered by snow as if by a net of small pearls, and the inside of every cup and bowl was dusted with snow as with cornstarch. For seven days, while the wind blew and the snow blew, we tried obsessively to fix the tent and slept at night with wool shirts over our heads so the snow wouldn't slap us awake. We woke constantly anyway, and for the time we were awake we ate snow and breathed snow and after a while actually forgot about the snow. We couldn't, though, forget about the wind.

The wind shoved sometimes. Sometimes it roared and shrieked. Sometimes it curled and tangled like nets and sometimes it simply loomed. There was no escaping that wind, which chilled us the way thoughts can chill, which sang even under the sea. After the first day, in an effort to escape the wind, we zipped our sleeping bags up as one bag and wrapped our bodies as one. But though I had dreamed, perhaps, of finding in Tina a love, and sought in her a new Orion, a sibling, a sister, a friend, we slept together just as bodies, still in the heart of the cold. Tina slept more than I did; she did everything more than I did, really, got sicker, worked harder, cared more. I watched her sleep, her shoulders hunched against the cold, her hands always slipping out of the bag. I tucked them back, when I remembered, which got to be less and less often, and I made us water for our raging thirst, so we slowly ran out of fuel. To the extent that I could be obsessed with things, there in that cave in the sea, and to the degree that I dreamed of a world where things were different, a world tilted slightly, like a line of angled stone, I became obsessed with seeing that Tina would survive, and all her fingers too. But on the third day, Tina lost her voice. Not even a whisper emerged.

And so I started to talk. Partly in an effort to keep her entertained, and partly because the world had started to change and fade, I began that day to talk to her, to tell her about my life. If Nicholas never had much faith in words, I somehow through it all preserved mine, and though I started my narration as much to drown the wind as fill up the empty hours, I soon saw that if I ever finished, it would be for another cause. I was beginning, finally, to feel that I would never leave the mountain and I knew then that I couldn't die with so much still untold. So I talked, when I could, and was silent when I couldn't, and sometimes I slept. I slept better before we ran out of oxygen; after that it was hard not to wake myself up with my breath. And though, on the eighth day, Naomi climbed the wall—with slings and ropes and oxygen, with food and Laurie and life—and though, on the ninth day, somehow she got us down, we'd never have lasted that long if not for Tina's great strength. She reminded me that once I'd had a husband. She let me talk, though I could hardly breathe. By the seventh day, I was delirious. Tina was just about dead. But I, at least, was almost happy. After talking, happy even to die.

THE SUMMIT

Nineteen

The day of the avalanche was hot. Orion had arrived unexpectedly the night before, driving up to the front door rather than to the back, so we didn't hear his car pull up. We had finished dinner when he arrived and I was in the kitchen tarring my skis while Nicholas was in the living room trying to get our vast map collection in some kind of rational order. When I saw Ryan's face peering in the window, I felt that utterly unrestrainable joy which is a mixture of amazement and remembrance; I ran my eyes over him like someone licking an ice cream cone. I guess I can't help but believe that whatever you make other people suffer at your hands will be returned to you someday, reversed like a wraparound skirt, and to the best of my knowledge I had never made Ryan suffer, so there seemed then no chance that he would be the vehicle through which my own suffering was carried. Whatever. He was my brother. And he was there.

Maybe it was having Ryan with us again or maybe it was just the weather, but the next morning as we got ready to ski there was nothing but joy in the house. We talked, I remember, about selling the shop or of having Ryan buy in with us, and both suggestions seemed equally appealing and equally susceptible to being brought off. Orion had an idea for a new mechanical belay and Nicholas teased him about it until he explained it, and in explaining, clarified all its problems. When we went about in silence for a moment, it was the silence you share, not the silence that makes you wonder whether you are sharing, and I was suddenly convinced that the only problem Nicholas and I had ever had was that we were, together, only two parts of a three-part person and that it didn't matter if that made us different from the rest of the world; the only error we could possibly make from there on out would be not to admit that Ryan was as much a part of us as we were and that we should all stick together.

You know the way a kitchen smells when it is filled with the odor of cooking, which seems like the smell of home itself, steaming up the windows and leaking around the doorsill? The smell of Thanksgiving dinners and great barrels of apples and toast dripping with butter and honey in earthenware pots. Well, we cooked breakfast together that morning, already dressed for the ski, and the bacon curled and sizzled on the grill like circus acrobats dancing on a trapeze and the eggs landed slap in the frying pan like children diving in a pool. The anticipation of action was on us, and we all filled the confines of our bodies neatly, no wrinkles and no air, knowing that we were going somewhere that day where if we fell we would be hurt, where there would be no walls, as soft as ensolite, around us.

That sense is like a celebration in itself, even before you have left home. You are focused by the knowledge that if you put your hand down and pick up a ball of snow, the ice crystals will sting your palm, and if you jump into the air you will fall hard upon the earth and carry the scrapes and bruises with you for weeks. Nicholas cut great slabs of bread for our sandwiches, as thick as the flesh of a hand, and I wrapped them in tinfoil in some lamplight lying on the counter like a pool of water glistening on a rock. All, all, had been encompassed by the clarity of action, as sharp and geometric as a flight of wild swans. Nicholas grabbed me and flung me over his shoulder and I beat on his back with my fists and called for Orion, but he just tucked his hands in his pockets and drawled, "'Tain't none of my affair, m'am," and walked bowlegged to the door. I hissed in Nicholas's ear, "I'll get you when you're asleep," then tickled him till he dropped me.

When the phone rang we all stared at it, astonished. We had risen in the dark and the first gray of dawn was just now lightening the sky; we had felt ourselves, till then, in sole possession of the world. Nicholas was closest to the phone, so he went to pick it up, but he approached it with the wariness of someone approaching a dangerous animal and he held it to his ear like a man who wanted something proved. Then his face changed and he held the receiver more firmly and mouthed at us, "A rescue. Yes or no?" With one accord, Ryan and I shook our heads. "No, no." Nicholas said he was sorry and hung up the phone with a bang.

Well, Nicholas may have been sorry, but I was even sorrier. Curiosity made me ask what rescue and where and who, and though I didn't really want to know, I learned all the details, an avalanche the day before in the southern Tetons and one man lost and the other in such a state that he had only now managed to get back to the road and call for help, and avalanche warnings had gone out and the Search and Rescue Team was calling for all the help it could get. So of course we all felt guilty right away and told ourselves that there was no hurry to find a body, that it would be different if there was a chance the man was still alive—but we were all remembering other rescues when it turned out by some miracle that the man *was* still alive and we had been there to help him. I almost suggested that we call them back and go, but I knew there was nothing Nicholas hated more than for me to change my mind, so we finished packing the truck and left, mostly in silence; this time, though, the silence that makes you wonder what you are sharing. The silence that makes your voice sound funny when you speak.

The sun was just rising as we parked at Jenny Lake. There is nothing I love more than sunrise in the mountains, when the rays of the sun are divided by the clefts in the hills as neatly as if they'd been cut by a knife and slabs of lightness float in the air like magic carpets, hovering during their flight. But even as the sun came up in that cold, cold dawn, I knew that it would be a hot day and that by noon those slabs of lightness would long have floated away —and I felt uneasy, thinking about the avalanche in the southern Tetons and the body of the man beneath it and the three of us climbing in the sunshine.

I *know* that I thought we should not go on. I know because when I thought it, I was staring at the right front tire of our truck and observing that it was getting stripped and that we should replace it soon or sooner, and that bare tire came back to me again and again in the months that followed that day like boulders, sluggish in the wake of a glacier that has passed on. The tire was all mixed up in my mind with the sunrise and with my own deadly fear not of chaos but of the inexplicable order of life. So that when the sun rose each day with inexorable speed it seemed to me yet another omen of demise, like the tire, bare and still, and the snow it crushed beneath it when it stopped. But then Orion said, "Get your ass in gear now, Wee One," and it had been so long since he called me that that I felt myself a child again, without will-power and without mortality, and I let myself be swept along.

The day was very still. We buckled skins to the bottom of our skis, and climbed and climbed, and the crust of the snow in early morning gave way to the graduated softness of the day and the big firs gave way to smaller spruces until we were finally above the trees. The sun grew so hot that we stripped to our shirts and then to our T-shirts, and there was the silence of heat and the silence of cold as well and once in a while the plopping or swishing of something melting or snow falling down from a branch.

We stopped for an early lunch by a brook that had broken through the snow crust and watched the water bubble up from below and then disappear again into the void. One gurgling bubble or many, and all in the very same place. Some ravens soared above us against the blue and I leaned against my rucksack, my face hot and pink and sweaty, and ate my thick slab sandwiches and was quite, quite still. And there was a line there, a line on one side of which was perfect bliss, the moment when all your mind and body comes together in the stillness, and on the other side of which was sadness, though sadness I wasn't sure about what. Watching the brook bubbling up on the rocks, I suddenly found it odd, somehow, that ravens should fly so fast, so cleverly, on such carefully outstretched wings. The glaciers were pouring down from the mountains, the mountains rising from the sea. We took a long time over lunch and when we took off our skins and fastened on our skis again, the sun was almost at its height.

That stillness and that silence. I seem to feel it yet. We skied on, unroped. Nicholas was breaking trail and I was bringing up the rear. By the time we reached the foot of the glacier we were well spread out and moving fast. I crested the top of the rise and looked out across a vast white bowl, glittering in the sunshine, topped by a steep snow wall, as curvaceous and seductive as the line of a hip thrown down across a sheet, a white place ready for marking. A tiny fir tree stuck up through the snow, but otherwise there was nothing to be seen except the white, with the blue of the shadows that our bodies threw across it as dark as bruises on white flesh. We all felt it, the delight it would be to glide down through that whiteness, bringing to it the smooth curves of our own white hips, caressing and graceful as the wind. But Nicholas stopped at the edge of the bowl, looking down as if in thought, and Ryan stopped too, then turned to me and smiled.

It wasn't that I thought the slope would go. Indeed, to be honest, I hardly thought at all. Orion had a dark-blue sweater looped loosely through his rucksack and he picked up one ski pole and dangled it from his hand. We were idle, gathering ourselves for the moment to come. Nicholas lifted his cap from under his belt and tucked it around his hair. Then without a word he pushed himself off like a racer, and as I saw one elbow bent beside him, one leg braced away from his side, all I thought was how lovely he looked and what a team we made, the three of us, and how lucky we were to be alive. Ryan waited for a moment and then he too pushed forward, and it was only as he glided over the very edge of the bowl that I felt something like panic rise within me and had a sense, not that I should say something—should shout or scream or run—but that I should already have done all those things and that now it was far too late; all that remained was to watch Orion top the bowl and curve down into it, as if into a hand that could close about him, a wave that could snuff him out.

There was just one long moment, in fact, for me to realize that I had been scared all morning, ever since that phone call in the dawn, and that I had fought against it with a stillness to match the stillness of the day because I was tired of being scared, because the fears I had felt so endlessly, the fears like a patchwork quilt that covered me, had drained me just enough to make me stubborn and to want to risk *everything* once again. Then I was moving forward too, following my brother, and I felt something like a victory when I moved into the bowl. The wind of my passage cooled my cheeks and I looked down and down and never up, not even when I heard the fault line crack above me and the roaring of the snow when it started to thunder down. I saw Nicholas look back up and over his shoulder and heard him—faint and far away—scream "Avalanche!" and slant his skis straight downward and toss his poles away, his body bent almost double, a tiny blue dot against the white, moving like a river racing toward the sea. What need was there to look up? In him I saw my own death and the sound was like a thousand windows breaking and it was hot, so hot, and I couldn't hear anything but noise.

I tossed my poles away too and skied as I had never skied before, and the thing that engulfed me before the snow did was something so big that to call it fear is a lie and to call it calm another one. It was a stillness that could stop the earth and I trembled within it like a banner, so that even as I kept my feet I marveled that I had not yet fallen and even as the first wave swept under me and the shock released my bindings I was thinking it was nice that we could all die together, that Orion had been able to come. Then I was riding the wave and staying upright in a flume of whirling white, until the second wave hit and I couldn't breathe and things got blacker and blacker until there was no light at all and I knew that it was done. I forced my arms through the air and snow, shoving them toward me through something dense as water; though I knew it would be worse to live through the landing, then die of suffocation in the end, I cupped my hands in front of my face since that too seemed just then like courage, the one thing I had left to do. Then suddenly there was a little lightness, a tiny glow of sun at the end of a long, thin black, and the light spread and expanded like a puddle of flame and I felt one moment of overwhelming, shouting hope, before the light was all around me and I was sitting on top of the snow, breathing in great ragged gasps.

The slope looked like an earthquake had hit it. Where, a minute or so before, the only shadows that glanced across the sheer white plain had been the shadows of our three bodies, now the slope was rife with shadows, a hundred deep gashes, a thousand black bruises, a million small crevices that pushed away the sun, fostered and protected by the thick, hard snow. Like concrete, truly. Like rock. I stumbled to my feet. My rucksack was still on my back, though one of the straps had torn loose and the extra ski pole that I'd strapped to it that morning hung on by a thread. I was still breathing hard, so hard that my breath in my lungs seemed to shout across the valley and I wanted to shout too, to scream and yell to the others, for mercy, for help. But nothing would come out, no sounds other than that one deadly sound, the sound of a person dying, the sound of a person giving birth. I threw my pack onto the snow and unstrapped the ski pole, watching my fingers trembling as if they belonged to someone else, great lumpy things, cold and white and stubby. I knew that I had no time, less than no time, and yet the moment that I stood in had no real form, no boundaries. When the ski pole came loose, I ripped the basket off it with my hands.

▲

You know, people always said that Orion and I looked very much alike. I never saw the resemblance myself, really, though we both were small and wiry and had blue eyes. But when I dug him out of the snow, he had his arms cupped in front of his mouth and his face was so still; it was exactly like finding myself there. There was snow in his mouth and nostrils and I couldn't find a heartbeat. But he was close to the surface and he was still warm. I don't know how long I worked on him. I forgot about Nicholas as if he had never been. Orion was stiff when I finished. An hour, two? He was stiff. Rigor mortis. Over and over I kissed his lips. My fingers were frostbitten, and I broke one of the bones of my hand. I had cut them, too, in digging. There was blood all over the snow.

The search crew found Nicholas the next day. He was blue and he looked like a stranger, like I had met him once, long years before. He had choked on the snows of Wyoming. But he died in the winds of Nepal.

Twenty

On the eighth day we woke to find the wind had vanished and color was seeping back into the world. First in the east, which the tent was facing, then everywhere around us, a wash of gold and orange and pink and red spread like a pool of bright dye. Tina was lying on her back, and her hands, in the night, had again fallen out of her bag. They lay, still mittened, on the space above her heart; but one of her mittens had almost fallen off. The flesh revealed was stiff and white, and her fingers, when I saw them, were stiff and white as well. She was breathing stertorously, and somehow, in the silence, that hurt more than it had hurt before. The silence was unyielding, so persistent, so demanding, not like the variable days of wind, and when I crawled toward the door of the tent and unzipped it, the world looked so lovely that I ached. There was no wisp of wind, no sound, no trace of motion, but everywhere the cluster of the highest peaks on earth was touched with the movement of light, pouring down the flanks of the mountains to the valleys and the glaciers below. All that had been lost in the storm was now returned to us; it seemed not merely the dawning of a day, but the dawn of the planet itself.

I wiggled back to the head of the tent and struggled out of my bag. Maybe I was delirious, I don't exactly know, but I felt that the time had finally come when I should go for the top. My fingers trembled and I couldn't think just what I had to do. I was dressed, so that was all right, I'd been dressed for days, for weeks, all my life; I was always dressed in the mountains. So my boots came next. But the outers were frozen and the laces hard to undo; they were pictures of boots beneath my fingers, as empty of meaning as plates. My tongue clenched between my teeth, I fought with the boots and fought with them; at last I let them fall. And when I saw them, tipped on their sides like two boats, I started to sob and my sobbing woke Tina, who stretched out one frozen hand. Tina still couldn't speak and I couldn't either; we put our arms around each other and we cried.

▲

I dreamed last night that the wind had died. Had died, you understand, like breathing that finally ends; it lay flat over everything like a transparent veil, sticky and weblike, as troublesome in death as in its life. We put on our crampons and tried to climb past it but it kept getting caught in the teeth of the steel and somehow that seemed like desecration, not to mention how difficult it was to move. And then, as if that weren't enough, I dreamed that we were bearing the wind, you and I, that our bodies had become the vehicles for its passage. By sheer will, we pushed the wind around the mountain, hoping the silence would emerge.

We're so committed, though isn't that a funny way to speak of courting death? Only climbers could come up with anything so crazy—the ultimate of fears, to be committed to something, someone, anything at all. But get into the mountains and here there is no turning back. Perhaps that's why we come here after all, to see the end, to be in the place where there are no choices left, to see at the last that, like it or not, the one thing we're committed to attend is our own funeral and the one place we can never choose to leave is the mountain where we were born.

Remember all the work we did to get here and all of it for nothing? Though so much sweat has set us here, deposited us in this place. Not that it's ever for anything in the end, anything but itself. We didn't come for the summit, after all, to be able to say we had done it; being here, being here now, that's why we all of us came. The ice fog, the dark mornings, the fine white dust that drifts like powdered stone—that's why we came; not the top, but the prayer flags floating like butterflies, the lizards darting like love.

But somehow I still wish that we could climb this mountain; it holds the one of all the summits I really hungered to see. And we're so close below it and the route was so clear above us—even Margaret said that, cautious Margaret, that all the objective dangers were past. I guess, for me, passion has always been an objective danger; and now we have no mode of action, no way of even seeing grace. For where is the path that leads to enlightenment, where the finger pointing to the top?

Remember the women who died in the mountains, the eight who froze to death on Lenin Peak? And at the end the question that they asked was who would take care of the children? Who would see to the babies being born? So we go on, no more or less than women at the last, and I dreamed last night that this was a kind of labor, that you and I together were bearing the wind. So all things come down at the end to what they are and labor is labor and here where all action has been removed from us, where nothing may be done but nothing done, we may not move, we may not climb, but we at least can bear the wind. And if men are strong at battling, we are strong at enduring, and maybe it comes down to being ruled by love, yes, maybe at heart men are always alone and meditate their way to understanding while we must always love our way to truth. I wish, if nothing else, that Nicholas was here, here in the mountains of home.

I still really love those mountains, the thin hard crust of their skin. I've never loved them more than now, although they've taken Nicholas—not because they've taken Nicholas; that, at least, could never be. He was blue when I saw him, I didn't want to see him. He was blue and looked like a stranger I had met once, perhaps, long years before, a face on a subway, a face across a countertop, no more significant, than a sense of déjà vu, but just as significant, I suppose—have I lived before, am I caught forever on the wheel of samsara? A glimpse for a moment into the tunnel of time, a lifting of the veil that blinds the summit, that there are things behind that veil we can scarcely dream of, it's a question that crosses like a cloud for an instant, the question of maybe, again and again, making the same mistakes, seeing the same dim faces, trapped like a river held within its banks, with the illusion of freedom only because we can move.

And Nicholas was such a man. You were such a man, you know, the opposite of velvets and silks, and you wanted to take care of me, and I wanted you to take care of me, only I didn't know it, I was too stupid to see it, too weak to believe that of myself, so I never let you, and that was what went wrong time and time again, that was what weighed us down. Words, words, words, I always filled us up with words, though I had felt it all through my childhood really, the difference that lay between me and my friends like a pool of quicksand, the fact that they seemed to live in a world that was cohesive, that didn't have a split down the middle of it as big as the Mississippi River, so that when they talked it was with the mouth they meant to use and not one they opened specially for the occasion like a bottle of champagne. Oh, Artemis, yes, right, good one, Artemis. But how was I supposed to know?

I never told you that, never told you my real name, did I? I couldn't, then, it was always my secret, though we had read our myths, Orion and I. It was my mother's fault, really; she named us both but she didn't read hard enough or close enough, she just thought two hunters, how wonderful, she loved to hunt and she loved Greek myth, so there we were. But Orion—he was only a man; a giant, but only a man, and he pursued the daughters of a demigod, while I . . . In the name of love, why did my mother name me Artemis? She should have known about hubris. And not just that. But a lifelong virgin, no perfume, no silks, no sweet scent of sweats intermingling on a love-drenched morning. Just moonlight and leather and clear hard muscles and the bow, the drawn bow, the straight clear flight. That was me, Artemis, the virgin huntress of the moon.

But why not something simpler? There was so much contradiction right from the start, how could I help but fail when the moment came? Though the one thing that is clear to anyone who's lived beyond the age of three is that whatever you find, you can be sure it's not the thing you were looking for, and even when you climb a wall direct the summit is never quite where you thought it would be. But when I walked back from school in my new brown loafers, scuffing them on the pavement and dreaming as I walked, Artemis, Artemis, I thought fiercely, and I waited for the time when I could draw my bow. Oh, yes, there's something precious about the ever unfulfilled, the ever possible, but it's not divided up that way, male and female, they're just convenient handles for aspects of the moon. I was never what I was, and if Nicholas thought my sex was something tacked on at the end, a cosmetic touch, perhaps he was not far wrong. Not that I minded. That was me, Artemis, I was always what I was, and if we toned it down for others, became Phillips and Phillips, it wasn't because we doubted ourselves, but because we wanted disguise. Well, we succeeded anyway and if no one remembers our names, still they'll remember our climbing.

Not that I care. Oh, that's just it, it's not that I care; because I would trade it all for Nicholas for one more day and I killed him, I tried to save Orion and so I killed him; becoming a constellation doesn't make up for death. I could have said something then: this slope is going to slide, let's go around, for God's sake, let's be cautious, it doesn't make us less brave. It was hot, so goddamn hot, like Bombay, hot at midnight, like Delhi, hot at dawn, the sun was burning like a furnace, molten steel pouring down the slope, the noise it made was like nothing on earth, a whistling, a screaming, a roaring, a hundred plate-glass windows crashing to the ground, and I was deep within it; it enclosed me like a storm. Ripeness, patience, when have I ever had that—to have been a woman for once in my goddamn life? No, it was the line, we all saw it, the line across the bowl, easily shattered, easily lost, a magic, tantalizing, suicidal line; somewhere up ahead must be an answer. There was something there we had to find. We were pursuing them, the

Pleiades, the snowflakes, the distant stars, and I—why couldn't I have put my hand on his shoulder and said, "Just wait, love. Wait." From the start I was always afraid, afraid to seem like a fool, like a coward. Afraid to seem like a girl. So I let them go and when the slope came down, the fault line was six feet high. And yes, I found Orion first, in that nightmare of ice and snow, but I found just a body, you see, the first body, I could scarcely choose whose it was. You see that, Nicholas, don't you, love? You might even have done the same thing. You were always a breather, I watched you do it, you'd have tried to save Ryan as well. And I didn't forget you, that was always untrue, I believed that you couldn't die. Ryan was weaker, he'd cupped his small fingers, there were bruises around his chin. But you were a whirlwind, not blue like the icefalls, you were brown and as curly as smoke. I shouted, Come help us, Nicholas, help us. *I know you can help us now.*

▲

Together, we managed to get on our boots. Tina couldn't use her hands at all, and her feet were very swollen, so I warmed my hands in her armpits for a while, then managed to cut open her boot heels. We stuffed her feet in, leaning together, and tying the leather on with twine, then afterward tied on her mittens so they wouldn't fall off her hands. Even as we did this, I knew it was all quite pointless. The rope was gone from the top of the cliff; there was no way we could get down. But I didn't want to die inside the tent, not with the world so bright outside it, so we dressed in that landslide of morning and felt bathed by the fall of light. In the sunshine the tent was transformed; it reminded me of the yak herder's hut, where the smoke—rising through the pinpoint holes in the roof like a hundred tiny laser jets of light—had seemed to push not upward but downward toward the ground. As tangible as something you could gather in a cup, they'd been as powerful as rushing streams, and at the end of each stream a penny had lain, glad to bedeck the ground. The tent, light-strewn, was as much a shrine as the chorten I'd found in the gorge, and

I tried to clean it before we left, as if our days were an offering.

Then we crawled out. I'm not sure what we had in mind, but we made our way down the slope and right to the edge of the cliff. There we stopped, two bundles in a brilliant world. And there we sat, not talking, just together at the end. Though I had, I suppose, grown used to loneliness and begun to see it as my fate, fearful perhaps of the desperate intensity that two people such as Nicholas and I could manage to create between us, here there was neither loneliness nor intensity, just the same kind of communion I had felt with the yak herder, or the little girl in Tal. The blue of the sky was cerulean, cobalt, the blue of a monarch's robes. Mist was rising from the glacier below us, pushing up toward the sky, and clouds, like seed pods floating on water, dipped below the hills and disappeared, as if they were being dissolved. A raven landed, or maybe an eagle, amazed at the lilt of his wings. And holding Tina's mittened hand, stranded without a hope of getting either up or down, I felt liberated by the peak there, the snow there, felt as if I had floated clean out of myself and was hovering somewhere freely in the air above my head. I was not sodden now with memory, not damned with it; it had blown away in the wind.

Well, there, in a way, it ended, and there it really began. The sun moved across the sky, and our thirst got truly terrible, and Tina lay down beneath the boulder and didn't move again. And while part of me sat on the edge of the cliff, the other part started to climb, to climb again; it was lovely, the crunch of my boots on the snow. The summit was behind me, not ahead, but there at the last, delirious, half out of my mind, I was in love again, madly in love, not with Tina, not with my life, but with something greater than myself. I had feared it—never again—when Nicholas was blue and I said he was a stranger; but strangers, it seemed, were only people who would not admit their kinship, and you can always tilt the landscape through which you choose to move. And the most wonderful thing of all was that it was not I that was climbing, not anymore, there was someone who had taken over and carried me along. No oxygen, of course, I didn't need the oxygen; the Buddhists know the high thin air is rich enough to breathe. Though there was so much that I couldn't answer, so many questions I'd never seen till then, and in a way, how heavy it all was still, my knees, my hips, my shoulders, my thighs, all the parts moving upward, falling toward the light, still we were doing it, Tina and I, and I knew there was someone else there as well, though I could never see him when I turned to look. I thought it was Orion, first, and called out, "Is that you, Orion? Can children take care of themselves?" There were no footprints this time, no footprints leading to the edge, just the snow and the mountain and the cone of light beyond the mountain, and if there were pages that hadn't been opened, snow that had never been trodden, white places waiting for marking, here they were and there I was, and climbing, like life itself, was something you could never have enough of. I thought, hold my hand, please, then saw that it was Nicholas. He said we'd climbed our mountain. He said I should live my life. Then he changed, became Naomi. Like a dancer, she'd climbed the wall.

▲

So we got down. And before the pain started, and the heat, and the agonizing rawness of my flesh as it fell off, in a time out of time I just dangled in the air, an air where anything might grow. My mind was clear and delirious by turns. There was often great creaking in the ropes. My hands were bandaged and my feet, and my eyes were swathed in gauze against the sun. Tina, I knew, was being lowered beside me, but she couldn't talk and I thought that she had died. "Tina, Tina, are you there?" I'd start to shout, but Naomi told me gently to lie still. Then I sobbed, "Oh, Naomi, let me hug you," and tried to tear the bandage off my eyes.

Then I relaxed. Perhaps I slept. All times became as one. Thoughts rose and fell, swirled and disappeared, and I watched them rise and then again fall as if I were watching a play. Like the landscape as viewed from an airplane, they seemed tiny, in the midst of great space, then huge as they moved up beside me, spoke or were silent, and left. A Brahman came to loom above me, not curious, just saddened, old and still puzzled by the mysterious workings of life. I was visited, too, by my Lyti, and the yak herder, down from his hut. "Look," he said, "look at the yaks groan," in a language I somehow now knew. One little child tried to sell me stamps. "Today is tomorrow," he crooned. Behind him, in the distance, I saw terraces of dried dun earth and golden wheat, and closer in, the purple-flowering ginkgo trees with piles of bright-orange brick around them. In the streets below me, a tiny barefoot old woman carried a battered tin teapot, bending forward at the waist as if she carried great weight. Then she set it down and straightened up, looking out into the hills with a relaxation of the body and the spirit so complete that even her face relaxed, her eyes widened and her fingers dangled, used like all the notes of an instrument. One of her legs was shriveled, useless, but the other leg was still strong. She smiled and told me, "See, you're forgiven. Now go and forgive yourself." I jerked in the stretcher. Naomi held me. She smelled of sweat and sun.